TEEHALT'S PLANET

Spatterlight
Amstelveen 2024

TEEHALT'S PLANET

John Merrill

A novel set in Jack Vance's Demon Princes universe

Published by Spatterlight, Amstelveen 2024

Cover art by Reginald Pollack

ISBN 978-1-61947-498-7

www.spatterlight.nl

TEEHALT'S PLANET

INTRODUCTION

T eehalt's Planet is based on the five-novel 'Demon Princes' series
published by the much-admired author Jack Vance between
1964 and 1981. The series follows its protagonist, Kirth Gersen,
on his quest to track down and destroy the five arch-criminals (so-
called Demon Princes) who, when Gersen was nine years old, raided
his home community, Mount Pleasant, and killed or enslaved all but
Gersen and his grandfather. The context for the series is a future age
during the 1530's — based on a dating system in which the year 2000
has been re-set to zero. Space travel has become widespread due to the
"Intersplit" technology that permits spaceships to span many light-
years in a matter of days. As a consequence, dozens or even hundreds
of potentially habitable planets have been discovered and settled. The
collection of civilized planets becomes the *Oikumene*, or "inhabited
world," and everything else, the Beyond.

According to Vance's narrative, Gersen was born in the year 1490,
the raid on Mount Pleasant took place in 1499; he then spent his matur-
ing years training arduously in physical combat, the use of weapons,
poisons, and espionage. By 1524, as described in the first novel of the
series — *The Star King* — Gersen was able to track down and eliminate
the first Demon Prince, named Attel Malagate the Woe. The dating
of the remaining novels is a bit sketchy, but the best approximation
is that Gersen's quest is completed four years later, at which time
he would have been thirty-eight. In the second book — *The Killing
Machine* — Gersen defrauds a criminal of almost 9 billion SVU, or
Standard Value Units, a staggering sum that makes Gersen one of the
wealthiest men in the Oikumene.

The current work — *Teehalt's Planet* — is conceived as a sequel, and opens when Gersen is sixty years old. Although enjoying a comfortable retirement, he is persuaded to assist the IPCC (Interworld Police Coordination Company) in pursuing a new master criminal, strangely named Malagate, suggesting some connection to the first Demon Prince. The novel unabashedly makes use of many of Vance's concepts and vocabulary, supporting the notion that imitation is the sincerest form of flattery. Nothing, of course, can rival Vance's masterful creative genius or his exuberant use of language, but hopefully Vance aficionados will take pleasure in recognizing some Vance-isms, while new readers will have an opportunity to be introduced to the rich imaginative realm he created.

For readers not familiar with Vance's work, it is useful to note that Vance peppered his main narrative with various supposed excerpts from books, articles, speeches, and the like. Sometimes these provide important adjuncts to the plot — for example, a supposed 'Popular Handbook to the Planets' that supplies information about the geophysical conditions, flora, fauna, and people of a planet where the action is taking place. These little supplements are laced with sardonic humor, and sometimes seem to be inserted out of pure whimsy. Readers of *Teehalt's Planet* should not be surprised to find similar insertions, including an excerpt from *Gerontology Today* that leads Chapter I.

—John Merrill, 2023

CHAPTER I

Excerpt from *Living Well* by Salome Sneed, in *Gerontology Today*, 1548

Humans differ from almost* all other life forms in that they are conscious of their own mortality. Indeed, philosophers through-out the ages have observed that the fear of death is for most humans more unsettling than the fact itself. Alas, however, all the potions, elixirs, prayers, incantations, meditations, seances, sacrificial offerings and other gratuities to imagined gods have been to no avail. In the history of humanity, some hundred bil-lion individuals have lived but not a single soul has escaped the inevitability of their own mortality.

In the modern era, scientists came to acknowledge that their best efforts to achieve immortality had gone for naught. Every living creature had an allotted life span that, while it might vary from one individual to another, was in the final analysis finite. Science therefore focused on making an individual's allotted span as free from premature curtailment as possible.

Thanks to a generous endowment by an anonymous donor, a robust menu of anti-cancer treatments as well as other life-sustaining protocols are now available at modest cost from the new *Living Clinic* at the city of New Wexford, Aloysius. Participation in the clinic's program has, however, so far fallen

---

* The illustrious anthropologist Prof. Podd Hachinsky notes that of the thousands of life forms he has studied, no more than half a dozen merit the adjective 'humanoid.' (*Cosmopolis*, June, 1500). And of these, only a single species, the Star Kings of Ghnarumen, resemble Homo sapiens, albeit with some important differences.

surprisingly short of initial expectations. In an exclusive interview for *Gerontology Today*, the clinic's Executive Director, Dr. Waldo Grote, discussed this shortfall.

"Participants in our program," he explained, "must agree in advance to moderate the body's natural tendency to extremes of calorie intake, ingestion of mood-enhancing substances, as well as both physical and mental lassitude. However, a surprising number of applicants declined to go forward upon learning of these requirements, while others were out-counseled due to noncompliance. Nevertheless, those determined souls who have completed our program may now be assured of living out their allotted lifespan free from interruption."

Kirth Gersen sat in his favorite red leather chair with his feet propped up on the sill of a window that was open to the late afternoon sea-breeze. He had often asked himself where among the vast possibilities of the Oikumene he would settle down once the quest that had been the driving force of his life had been completed. Earth had been an appealing candidate, but exactly what part of Earth was another question. Certainly, there had been an abundance of choices, since the Apocalypse* of 1,200 years earlier had largely stripped the planet of human life. And as Gersen was, arguably, the wealthiest man in the Oikumene, he could take his pick of any number of enticing and largely vacant venues. From the time he saw this spot, a round forty-acre mass of smooth white granite emerging like some primordial leviathan from the blue-green waters of the Atlantic, he knew that this was the place where he could find solitude and peace of mind. Thus, he had acquired the property, known locally as White Island, and

---

* In the year 298 (modern reckoning), the two great military alliances of the day came to irreconcilable loggerheads. Toxic substances were released into the atmosphere and water supplies, by each party against the other. Within two years, virtually the entire human population of earth had been exterminated, leaving a few survivors scrabbling in the dust for subsistence. The event has been dubbed by historians 'The Apocalypse,' a term for total annihilation originating in ancient religious texts.

built a lodge of sturdy native stone on the island's highest point, with sweeping views of the surrounding water. There was enough topsoil for a two-acre vegetable garden, and the leeward side of the island afforded a safe mooring for Gersen's modest fleet of boats. A tiny nuclear power generator and a landing pad for Gersen's Flitterwing rounded out the roster of conveniences. Gersen was not by nature a gregarious person, and the isolation of the place, situated as it was some five miles off the coast of what had once been northeast America, had proven altogether satisfactory. Its one drawback was that it was necessarily a seasonal residence, as winter would bring fierce storms and deep wind-driven drifts of snow. Indeed, the coming winter was fast approaching, but for now Gersen was content to let his mind wander as he gazed at the involute and endlessly variable interplay of breeze and water's surface.

Why, he wondered, was he so fascinated by the sea, not just here on Earth but on each of the many planets he had visited? Was it the vastness, the deep, dark and seemingly boundless realm, a metaphor perhaps of space itself? Or was it the endlessly complex variety of the waves, the randomness and unpredictability, perhaps a metaphor for life? The same body of water at times would present a surface of delicate eddies, like schools of chased minnows darting this way and that for no apparent reason, and at other times a storm far out at sea would send monster rollers crashing in upon the unyielding rocks. Was there some pattern to this, he wondered, some enlightenment to be gained by examination?

Gersen's musing was interrupted by the soft tone of his telescreen. He was annoyed at this invasion of his privacy, but the call must be important as only a handful of acquaintances were privileged to have access to this portal; interlopers who attempted contact were greeted by an ear-splitting screech designed to discourage further unauthorized communication.

Gersen sighed, pulled his attention from the waves, and responded with a quiet "yes" that voice-activated the screen. A cluster of cascading asterisks indicated that security protocols were in force, and then the image of Miles Jaeger, the number three official of the IPCC*,

---

* The Interworld Police Coordination Company.

appeared. Jaeger was about what one would expect of a person who had risen so high in the ranks of an organization whose primary function was tracking down and exterminating violent criminals in the Beyond, the endless expanse of the universe that was outside the legal authority of the civilized worlds. Jaeger had piercing blue eyes, close-cropped iron-gray hair, and a strong jaw with thin unsmiling lips. He wasted no time getting down to business.

"We need your help," he said. "It is a matter of some urgency."

"I'm long out of the weaseling* business," said Gersen shortly.

"I know that. But this is not exactly a weaseling task. And there are some aspects of the matter that may interest you, if you would hear me out."

Gersen nodded noncommittally. "Very well."

"About a year ago," said Jaeger, "a company of slavers raided a community called Willow Grove, on Brandywine in the Beyond. Perhaps you read something about it?"

Gersen felt a knot of tension hardening in his gut. Raids like this were all too common in the Beyond, where the normal laws of civilization did not apply. This was a particularly sensitive subject for Gersen, as such a raid had destroyed his own childhood home, Mount Pleasant, some fifty years earlier, leaving Gersen an orphan with a burning need for revenge. With the help of his grandfather, he had mastered the teachings of physical combat, weaponry, poisoning, and espionage, and upon reaching maturity had set out to find and destroy the ringleaders of the Mount Pleasant massacre — the five so-called Demon Princes. That mission had been accomplished, finally, some twenty years earlier; the experience, however, remained a dismal memory.

"Yes," Gersen admitted, "I did read about it. A tragedy, but such is the temptation of fate by those who choose to live Beyond. Has the IPCC had any success in identifying the perpetrators?"

"Only to a small degree," said Jaeger. "We have a name." Jaeger

---

* 'Weasel' was the term used by criminals in the Beyond to describe suspected IPCC agents. A cooperative criminal organization, the 'De-Weaseling Corp.' specialized in tracking down and exterminating weasels. Unfortunately, from the IPCC's point of view, their methods were soberingly effective.

paused, waiting for Gersen to reply, but Gersen remained silent, so he added, "The name is Mongo Malagate."

Gersen's pulse quickened, "Malagate, you say?"

"Correct."

"What more do you know about this person?"

"Essentially, nothing. Our operative learned only that name; we were fortunate that he was able to file his report before he was eliminated."

Gersen knew well from his own experience that operating in the Beyond was a high-risk undertaking, requiring a level of fierce determination. He found himself imagining the extremes of agony the operative likely suffered before the end, but put aside those thoughts in favor of more urgent questions.

"What relation is this Mongo Malagate to Attel Malagate?" Attel Malagate, known in his time as Malagate the Woe, had been the first of the Demon Princes to have fallen victim to Gersen's quest for justice.

"We can only suppose," replied Jaeger. "He could be a son, a nephew, a clone, or no relation at all. As you know, the procreation functionalities of the Star Kings are obscure. For that matter, this Mongo Malagate may not be a Star King at all. Perhaps he is just borrowing the name of a legendary criminal to enhance his own stature."

"Where is this going?" said Gersen stiffly. "I don't suppose you called me to ponder unknowns."

"Of course not," replied Jaeger evenly. "Let me explain. Some months ago, a gang of thieves managed to break in to the Museum of Musical History in Pontefract, on Aloysius, and to make off with one of the museum's prized pieces, a Broadwood Grand Piano. I have to say, the crime showed daring and imaginative technique as the Museum's security precautions are by no means trivial. Whoever masterminded the theft was no common criminal. The Grand Piano, as you may possibly know, is a musical instrument of unrivalled range and complexity. But its remarkable capabilities remain only in legend, as few survived the Apocalypse, and of these there were only two Broadwoods. What we have today are electrical simulacra. Modern science can imitate, but to the ear of a true musician our contemporary devices fall short of the real thing. It was obviously the rarity and precious nature of the Broadwood that attracted the criminal's interest.

"It is rumored that this Mongo Malagate has a passion for collecting rare things, and what he cannot buy, he steals. You know how our sources work — an idle comment here, a rumor there, a pattern formed by other robberies. Of course, this is only speculation, but putting together what we have, we think there's a good chance that Malagate was responsible for the piano theft. I will share the details with you if you like, but for purposes of this conversation, let's assume that Malagate is our man."

Gersen could not help but find his interest piqued. He was an afficionado of music of many kinds, and indeed had trained himself to play several of the simpler instruments. But he still could not see where Jaeger was taking this conversation.

"Let me get to the point," Jaeger continued. "Several weeks ago, we became aware that an anonymous party was putting out feelers for a piano tuner. But not just any piano tuner. The successful applicant would need skill in tuning the Broadwood Grand. Since there are only two such instruments known to be in existence and one of them remains under tight security here at the Avente Conservatory, it follows that the anonymous party is the criminal who stole the other one. And it is a fair wager that we are dealing with Malagate."

"A reasonable deduction," said Gersen. "But you did not contact me to confirm the quality of your deductive skills. Where do I come in?"

"We want you to be the piano tuner. Apply for the position; when accepted, travel to the anonymous party's home world, discover his identity and location, provide that information to us, and we will take care of the rest."

Gersen allowed himself a facetious smile. "A masterful plan, to be sure, but for one or two small difficulties. One, I am no piano tuner. My lack of qualification would quickly reveal me as an imposter, to my own obvious peril. Two, why not send one of your regular agents, who would undoubtedly be more capable than a man of sixty whose skills have atrophied from disuse?"

"We have considered those points. Taking your second objection first, the tuning of these ancient instruments is very much a lost art, less likely to have been acquired by a younger man. And the very fact of your age makes it an extremely remote possibility that you would be one of our agents. On your first objection, you have not inconsiderable talent in the field of music, and we have someone in mind who can train you sufficiently in the specifics of piano mechanics for you to be credible, especially if, as we strongly suspect, this anonymous party will have no knowledge of the subject whatsoever. Finally, and I don't need to tell you this, if we cannot locate this Malagate or whoever he is, the 5,000 survivors of Willow Grove who are now enslaved will have no hope."

Gersen stared at the screen a long moment. His arm was being twisted, and it annoyed him.

"Let me think about it overnight. I will call you with my answer in the morning."

"Very well," said Jaeger. "I will await your call."

The screen went blank, leaving Gersen alone again with the dark rolling ocean, whose wave crests glinted in the moonlight, as night had fallen during his exchange with Jaeger. Gersen stared into the glowering darkness, and asked himself some troubling questions. This was an impossible mission. Why had he even agreed to "think about it"? He had always relied on his instincts, but what were those instincts telling him now? The fact that they were uncertain was evidence in itself that he was no longer fit for an undertaking of this kind.

He pushed a button on the arm of his chair, and within moments his steward *Ctchm* appeared. Before he spoke, he noticed with satisfaction that *Ctchm* was bearing a tray on which was placed a short, clear crystal tumbler containing Gersen's favorite evening beverage, a measure of *Wild Fowl** just covering a single ice cube. *Ctchm's* ability to anticipate Gersen's wants was remarkable, as were many other of his traits.

"Thank you, Kim. A light supper in half an hour?" Gersen's vocal

---

* *Wild Fowl* was a distilled liquid based on a recipe that Gersen had inherited from his grandfather, Rolf Marr Gersen. It was derived from a blend of old-style grains (not the modern genetically modified ones), 72% corn, 18% wheat, and 10% barley, resulting in unparalleled smoothness and complexity. Gersen had established a small (two employee) distillery to produce the precious fluid. The economic results were less than stellar, since Gersen was the only customer, but he was quite happy to subsidize the operation as long as his quality requirements were met.

apparatus had been unable to adapt to the correct pronunciation of *Ctchm's* name, so he had to make do with 'Kim,' an alternative that *Ctchm* found satisfactory, although somewhat amusing.

"Very good, sir." Kim disappeared as quickly and silently as he had arrived.

Kim was a native of the planet Solitaire, in the Arcturus system, where he had been a member of the *Tzand* race. The *Tzands* were a tough and resourceful breed who, despite their somewhat diminutive stature, had managed to survive on a planet whose other occupants included several types of speedy and voracious, but fortunately for the *Tzand*, weak-sighted and dim-witted carnivores. Kim had been introduced to Gersen by Dwyddion, the Triune, or highest-ranking Fellow of the Institute, in gratitude for Gersen having saved Dwyddion's life.

"I took him into my household after he had been orphaned by an unspeakable disaster," Dwyddion had explained without elaboration. Gersen later learned that the *Tzands* had been attacked by a rival and more numerous clan, the *Tsong*, who sought to impose certain religious conformities to which the *Tzand* objected. The conflict descended into the sort of brutal and relentless war of attrition that so often characterizes religious disputes, with the *Tsong* eventually prevailing, leaving Kim among the few survivors.

"If you treat him with compassion," Dwyddion had advised, "you will be rewarded many times over, as he is both intelligent and capable." If anything, Dwyddion's recommendation had been understated. Although well below average height and slender as an eel, Kim was preternaturally strong and quick as a snake. But perhaps his most important attribute was his unfaltering loyalty to Gersen himself.

Gersen settled back, picked up the glass, a precious antique *Baccarat Harmonie*, and gazed thoughtfully at its amber contents. Then he took a sip, savoring the mild astringency that normally signaled the end the day's routine, and had the effect of settling his mind.

It was madness, he told himself, to even contemplate Jaeger's request. Gersen had everything a person could ask from life — comfort, wealth, respect, a settled and largely untroubled existence. He often had wondered, while his every moment was dominated by the quest to annihilate the Demon Princes, how he would live when that task was accomplished. And indeed, from the very moment when the last of them, Treesong, was dead, Gersen had felt overwhelmed by emptiness. In the years since, though, he had scarcely been idle. He had overseen the resurgence of *Cosmopolis*, which had returned to eminence as the Oikumene's most widely read periodical. Cooney's Bank, in which he held a controlling interest, had made one acquisition after another, changing its name to Universal Trust, and becoming the Oikumene's most powerful financial institution. With the uncanny shrewdness of Jehan Addels, his long-term financial advisor and trusted friend, he had acquired interests in numerous enterprises, mostly in the field of space travel; by far the most notable of these was a minority but influential interest in the tightly controlled Jarnell Corporation, owner of the Jarnell Intersplit technology that had reduced intragalactic travel times from hundreds of light-years to days of Earth time. And by no means less demanding of his time were his charitable endeavors, the most significant of which was the *Living Institute,* which allowed clients to live out their normal lives free of cancer and other life-limiting diseases.

Still, he had to acknowledge that there was a sense of pointlessness to it all. His days were consumed by board meetings, financial reviews, charitable events. Certainly, he lacked for nothing to fill his schedule. In a way, though, he had become a prisoner of his own affluence. Missing was the driving and all-consuming purpose that had held him in its unrelenting grip while even one of the Demon Princes remained alive.

Was he at the age of sixty up to an undertaking of this kind, that would undoubtedly require him to place himself under the control of a savage criminal, while acting the absurd part of a so-called 'piano tuner?' But then, the staff at the *Living Institute,* after a comprehensive battery of poking, prodding, blood sampling, and physical stress tests of various kinds, had pronounced him as having the physique at least as robust as a very fit forty-year-old, along with the reasoning and deductive abilities of a chess master. Moreover, he had kept up with his training in martial techniques and weaponry. If he lacked a bit in speed and agility, he more than made up for that in anticipation and subtlety. No, he told himself, he could not use age as an excuse. If this Malagate was related to his old enemy, Malagate the Woe, he needed to be dealt with. What could that relationship be? he wondered. As Jaeger had explained, the breeding habits of the Star Kings were obscure. Son? Nephew? Clone? There was no way of knowing. But in the criminal world of the Beyond, one could not use the name of a scion of that class indiscriminately without being taken to task. There had to be a kinship of some kind. Then there was the matter of the 5,000 former residents of Willow Grove, or however many survived the assault, who were now enslaved. His own people had suffered the same fate, with most of them perishing before he could take action*. Could he sit idly and allow that to happen again?

Suddenly Gersen felt impatience at his own hesitation. *Enough of this rumination,* he told himself. *Decision time.*

Gersen placed his glass back on the tray, rose from his chair, and walked into the dining room. He observed with satisfaction that Kim had prepared a small salad from their garden, and a piece of freshly caught mackerel, grilled in olive oil with mild spices. Kim was waiting by the door for any further instructions.

"Something has come up, Kim." Gersen said. "I'll be leaving in the morning at first light. Probably won't be back before the end of the season, so I will leave it to you to close things down for the winter."

"Very good, sir." Kim departed into the kitchen, leaving Gersen to his own reflections.

---

* The Mount Pleasant raid occurred in 1499, when Gersen was nine; he did not destroy Malagate until 1524, and required at least four more years to track down the remaining four Demon Princes.

CHAPTER II

Made weak by time and fate, but strong in will
To strive, to seek, to find, and not to yield.
— Alfred Lord Tennyson

Excerpt from *Explaining the Jarnell Miracle* by Otto Z'Beard,
Technology Times (1522)

The Jarnell Corporation is the owner of dozens of closely guarded technologies that underlie a revolution in modern space travel. Edmund Jarnell, the secretive descendent of the company's founder, Delancey Jarnell, rarely speaks in public or to the press. Fortunately, though, this reporter caught Jarnell off guard one evening as he was emerging from what appears to have been a raucous celebration at the exclusive Spacefarers Anonymous Club. I thrust a microphone toward him and asked, "Tell me, sir, what is the secret of the Intersplit?" He looked at me with a crooked grin, and said, "It's really quite simple. As every schoolchild knows, Einstein long ago figured out the relationship between time and matter. The Intersplit simply grabs a piece of forward time and moves the relevant matter into it." Then he staggered off to his waiting transport before I could ask for clarification.

Gersen was up before dawn the next morning. He posted an encrypted message to Jaeger saying that he was on his way, and expected to be in Jaeger's office at Avente, Alphanor, within a week, Earth time. He signed the message 'Lucas,' this being the identity he originally used to pose as a Special Writer for *Cosmopolis*, but which was now how he presented himself for all public occasions and business dealings. Although he had long ago disposed of all five Demon Princes and many of their followers, he had over the years experienced enough near accidents that were more than coincidental to lead him to conclude that Kirth Gersen should drop out of sight. The IPCC had been more than understanding, and arranged to have his identity expunged from all public records. Henceforth, except for a handful of intimate acquaintants, Kirth Gersen no longer existed.

Alphanor was the eighth planet in the 26-planet Rigel system, a distance of 864 light-years from Earth. Normally, the travel time would be several weeks, but Gersen would use his personal spacecraft, *Quicksilver*, which was powered by the latest Jarnell technology, the Intersplit-LF, a model manufactured by the Distis Spaceship Company, but which had not yet been introduced to the public. *Quicksilver* was at the Manhattan spaceport, some 400 miles down the coast, but Gersen could make that trip on the Flitterwing that was tethered behind the lodge, in about 20 minutes. He took several swallows from the cup of tea Kim had set out for him, wolfed down a protein bar, and headed out the door. He set about unclipping the wire cables that secured the Flitterwing, and called a few last minute instructions to Kim who stood watching from the rear entrance.

As he worked on the cables, some well-ingrained instinct prompted a pulse of alarm and caused him to look skyward. There, hovering about fifty feet above the island, barely visible in the pre-dawn gloom, was the shape of a dark gray flying vessel, from which two black clad figures could be seen rappelling down on lines. The pair reached the ground simultaneously and moved with sinister deliberation toward him. As they approached, he could begin to make out their features. The one on the right was a massive, hulking creature with long ape-like arms and a sneering smile that revealed teeth filed into points. The other was a slender, sinewy figure in a skin-tight coverall, with purple skin-tone, a shaved head, and deep-set reptilian eyes. This latter interloper, evidently the senior of the two, addressed Gersen in a voice intending to be soothing, but rather in its feigned silkiness set Gersen's hackles rising.

"Henry Lucas, we will be honored to have you join us on our vessel."

"I think not," replied Gersen, acutely aware that his weapons were already stowed aboard the Flitterwing. "But just for the sake of discussion, where do you propose to take me?"

"Ah, that you will discover when we arrive."

Snake-eyes advanced showing a wry smile, and reached out to grasp Gersen's arm with fingers that gripped like talons. Gersen let himself go slack while at the same time falling backward and pulling his assailant down with him, then simultaneously rolling hard toward the extended arm so that he landed with the full force of his hip on the point of the other's shoulder. He was rewarded by a guttural grunt of pain and an audible snap as the shoulder was dislocated. He flipped himself up to his feet and stood staring down at his erstwhile antagonist.

"Who are you, and who sent you," he demanded. "Tell me before I break the other arm."

But then the ape-man was behind him and had wrapped his torso in a python-like grip. He tried to hack backward with his elbows, but encountered only gristle; he stomped at the other's insteps, but they were protected by footgear of resilient material. The grip was intensifying and Gersen found himself struggling to breathe. He whipped his head backward, but it struck uselessly against the much taller antagonist's chest. Starting to lose consciousness from lack of oxygen, he cursed his carelessness for allowing this ape-thing to get behind him.

Suddenly the constricting arms fell away. He spun to face the threat and discovered that the long arms that had held him fast were now grasping feebly at their owner's head. And there, perched on the monster's shoulders, with legs locked around the neck in an unbreakable figure-four configuration was Kim. And what the creature was vainly trying to dislodge were Kim's fingers that were gouging out its eyes. There was an agonized roar as both eyeballs were snatched from their sockets and flung to the ground. Kim released his legs, dropped off his perch, and danced out of reach as his opponent flailed blindly at the air.

Gersen turned and observed the disabled snake-man limping toward the lines suspended from the aircraft. Gersen bolted after him, but arrived too late; the man was lifted out of reach and into the hovering craft, which silently disappeared into the darkness. Gersen turned back to where Kim stood watching the ape-man stumble across the island, his lanky arms waving this way and that, hoping perhaps to discover the line that would reel him up to safety.

"My thanks, Kim," Gersen said, still breathing hard. "That was a bit of a sticky-wicket."

Kim showed a puzzled look. "Sticky-wicket, sir?"

"An old expression, Kim. It was a tight spot, and you bailed me out. I am grateful. Now let's see if we can catch this monster and find out who sent him."

The two started in the direction of the distant figure, wandering blindly with its arms extended. But it was too late. Their quarry had reached the eastern side of the island, where some ancient cataclysm had sheared off a section of granite, leaving a sheer seventy-foot drop to the pile of broken rocks below. There was a scream of surprise and fear as the ape-man toppled over, then silence.

"We'll get no information from that one," said Gersen. "Let the tide take him away." There was little more to say. Gersen had been assaulted before, for reasons that were sometimes discovered and sometimes not. A frustrated writer turned down by *Cosmopolis*? A bankrupt former borrower from Universal Trust? An anarchist with motives inscrutable? Experience taught that life was full of malcontents with axes to grind, especially against successful persons like Henry Lucas, as hard as he tried to protect his anonymity. Then another thought flashed through his mind, to be banished almost as quickly as it appeared. Could there be a connection between this assault and Jaeger's call? Impossible. Well, perhaps not impossible, but with the multitude of remotely likely connections involved, the probability was vanishingly small — too small to waste time pondering. Whatever the case, there was nothing further to be done. The ship would be untraceable, one of the assailants washed out to sea, and the other escaped.

Gersen shook off the tension of the moment, said goodbye to Kim and boarded the Flitterwing. He completed a quick pre-flight check, entered the coordinates of the spaceport, and lifted off. At a height of 100 feet above the island, he guided the Flitterwing in a slow circle as Sol's early light gradually filled the eastern horizon. He looked down somewhat wistfully at what had been his place of solitude, with its wreath of white-foamed breaking waves along the windward shore, then pulled back on the stick and raced away.

The Flitterwing soared up through the cloud cover, with the low-pitched hum of its ion power units barely audible, then headed roughly west-southwest. Within what seemed like the blink of an eye, the green light on Gersen's Nav display signaled that he was clear to land at the Manhattan spaceport. The spaceport was a central hub for both terrestrial and intragalactic travel, located on a hundred acres at the southern tip of Manhattan Island that had been cleared of derelict office and apartment buildings, long abandoned since the Apocalypse. Gersen smiled to himself at the speedy clearance, one of the benefits of being a premier customer. The Flitterwing descended through the still-dark air, as dawn here was some 30 minutes behind White Island, and settled on to its designated pad. A beige service vehicle with a blue insignia raced out to pick up Gersen as he descended from the cockpit carrying only a small ditty bag. The van took him to the terminal building, where as Henry Lucas he completed the necessary landing protocols. Then he hopped back in the vehicle, which headed out to where *Quicksilver* was waiting, illuminated by floodlights, a five-story silver-gray bullet aiming skyward, fully stocked and serviced, with wisps of evaporation coming from its thrusters.

The valet at the van's controls, a fresh-faced young man in a well-pressed beige uniform embroidered with the terminal's insignia, turned back to look at Gersen as he pulled alongside the spaceship's boarding platform.

"That's quite a rig you've got there, sir."

"It serves its purpose," said Gersen.

"We get a lot of fancy hardware here, but that's the first one of those I've seen."

"Well, that's because this model hasn't been introduced to the public. I guess I'm a sort of test pilot."

"Oh, wow," was all the kid could say.

Gersen handed him a two-SVU* note, and stepped onto the boarding platform.

"Thank you, sir. And have a great trip."

"I'll sure try," said Gersen, and engaged the control that would lift him toward the boarding port.

Once on board, with the hatch secured behind him, Gersen placed his ditty bag on the shelf next to the ship's computer terminal, then settled into the practiced routine of a spaceship pilot. First order of priority was to change into the traditional spacefarer's garb — loose gray trousers and a blue shirt made of *paraflax* fabric that was both comfortable and could withstand the ship's ionic cleaning system. As he did every time he donned these garments, Gersen could not help but recall the days when foul laundry was the bane of the spacefarer's existence. On a multi-week transit, often longer, the space voyager's apparel would absorb stains of all kinds — foodstuffs, perspiration, oil and grease — not to mention their associated odors. The presence of these soiled garments would in due course become intolerable, not only to others but to the wearer him- or herself. Thus, when Gersen, acting in his Henry Lucas persona, had been introduced by Jehan Addels to a physicist with long unruly hair named Klaus Blenkinsop, who had in mind a cure for the problem, he gave the matter his full attention. The idea was an ionic cleaning system, in which free molecules would attach themselves to the molecules of unwanted substances and whisk them away. Early trials proved disappointing, as the ions in their zeal to clean also removed large quantities of the associated fabric. Not to be deterred, Blenkinsop then teamed up with a textile expert, and *paraflax* was born, a fabric that was impervious to the ionic process while at the same time remaining reasonably comfortable and durable. From that point forward, *paraflax* quickly came to dominate the market for spacefarers' garb, earning Blenkinsop much deserved acclaim, and Gersen a handsome return on what had early on been a quite speculative investment.

Gersen proceeded with his pre-flight routine, inspecting fuel and

* The SVU, or Standard Value Unit, was the non-counterfeitable common currency of the Oikumene. It was issued by only three banks, one of which was Gersen's Universal trust, under the strictest of controls.

provisions as well as ancillary equipment such as oxygen generators, gravity simulator, and interior temperature controller. Everything checked out perfectly, and he noted that the interior was spotless — a tribute to the Spaceport's ground crew. He then entered the navigation codes for his trip, strapped himself in to the heavily padded seat that would help offset the urgent pull of gravity during launch, and alerted the control tower that he was ready to go.

"Cleared for take-off, sir," came the response.

Gersen grasped the four harnessed levers that controlled his main thrusters and pushed them forward. The ship gave a slight shudder, something like a person waking up from a deep sleep, as the thrusters whined into full output. *Quicksilver* lifted off, almost imperceptibly at first, and then with astonishing acceleration. Sol appeared for a split second as the ship burst through the clouds, and almost as quickly became a diminishing spot of brilliance in the rear-most view-screen. Once clear of possible space debris within the solar system, Gersen engaged the Intersplit and was on his way to the Rigel Concourse.

Normally, to pass the time during what would otherwise be the tedium of a long flight, Gersen would bring reading or viewing material, sometimes regarding business matters, but more often than not, light comedy or fiction. For this trip, however, he would dispense with light entertainment. Instead, before departing White Island, he had put in a request to the Universal Technical Consultative Service, or UTCS*, for any and all information they could find regarding two subjects: One – Star Kings generally; Two – Malagate the Woe specifically. After a short nap and a light lunch, he withdrew from his ditty bag the data

---

* The UTCS had been formed originally to provide subscribers with quick solutions to comparatively simple electro-mechanical problems. Over time, the Service expanded the nature and scope of questions it was prepared to address, and accumulated an enormous file of published materials on a wide range of subjects — from physics, chemistry, biology, astronomy, medicine, and so forth, then ultimately migrating into the 'softer' sciences such as history, sociology, and economics. Clients could subscribe one request at a time, or if they were charter members like Gersen, they would have unrestricted access to the entire UTCS store of knowledge.

filament containing UTCS's response, and loaded it into the ship's computer. A welcoming message came on the screen thanking him for his patronage, and reminding him that the UTCS expressed no opinion on the matters being addressed, but could only report what was available in public records. He was then asked to acknowledge this limitation of UTCS's liability, and to choose between a written and an audio presentation of the search results. He chose audio. The screen went blank, and a sonorous but distinctly female voice addressed him.

"Hello, Mr. Lucas. My name is Eleanor. Would you like to begin?"

"Yes, let's get started."

"Very well," the voice of Eleanor began. "Subject Number One: the Star Kings.

"We begin our discussion of the Star Kings with certain agreed facts. They are a species unique in the known universe; they are truly *sui generis* — there is nothing else like them. They are understood to inhabit only a single planet, Ghnarumen, the third and only habitable world of the Star Axel 13-274. What little is known about the Star Kings must be inferred from the conditions on this home planet, where they are assessed to have originated and evolved to their present state. Ghnarumen consists largely of ocean and swamp. Apart from the Star Kings, the only life forms on the planet are insects and worms, which make up much of the Star Kings' diet, as well as the diets of one another. The inference is that the Star Kings evolved from something resembling Earth's *lumbricina*, or common earthworm. From that starting point, the evolutionary pathway becomes elusive, particularly because the Star Kings have denied access to their planet to off-world anthropological research teams, while at the same time declining to confirm or deny theories about their origin and evolutionary history. As often happens in academia, when facts are rare, theories abound. One of the most popular of such hypotheses was first propounded by Podd Hachinsky in the June 1500 issue of *Cosmopolis*. Hachinsky opined that the Star Kings were parthenogenic. This notion, however, has been bluntly rejected by various Star King dignitaries, whose angry reactions suggest that the idea was equivalent for them to what humans would view as sexual aberration."

"Mr. Lucas," Eleanor interrupted herself, "are you still with me?"

"By all means," Gersen replied. "I am fascinated. Please go on."

"Oh, thank you. You were being so quiet, I was worried that there might be something wrong with my presentation."

"No, you're doing fine, Eleanor."

The audio made what sounded like a mild throat-clearing sound. Gersen knew he was interacting with an array of several million semi-conductors, pressed into a space no larger than his thumbnail, but the audio function had him imagining a very attractive female, of medium height, with luxurious dark hair, and gentle eyes with alluring lashes, perhaps unsure of herself and seeking reassurance from her listener. A clever device by the creators of the IS, or Intelligence Simulation function, Gersen realized, to make their material more appealing, but effective nevertheless.

Eleanor continued.

"We now turn to the matter of the Star Kings' personal qualities. Those who have observed them — and here it must be emphasized that such observations have been rare — report that the typical Star King is courteous and even-tempered. They are highly competitive, and seek to excel in whatever endeavor they undertake, although they are careful not to extend their efforts in ways that cause harm to others. Despite his apparent error on matters of the Star Kings' procreation activities, Podd Hachinsky remains the acknowledged authority on other aspects of their behavior. Hachinsky observes that on human planets, Star Kings punctiliously model their conduct after the best human examples, although here it must be noted that while several hundred Star Kings are thought to have inserted themselves into human society, only a small fraction have actually been identified, as their semblance to *homo sapiens* is profound. Hachinsky theorizes that since man is the dominant creature in the Oikumene, Star Kings see him as a cynosure, which their competitive nature seeks to emulate and outdo — to beat Man at his own game, so to speak.

"Many observers have been astounded by the remarkable resemblance of Star Kings to men. As one expert mentioned, somewhat facetiously, the Star King is a non-human who nevertheless can speak the human language, walk into a haberdashery and dress himself off the rack, play an excellent game of tennis, or even compete quite successfully in a chess tournament. Nevertheless, they lack human sex organs and consume human food only with great difficulty. Therefore, failing other devices, it is always possible to differentiate Star Kings from humans, although the necessary inspection would be awkward, to say the least.

"That ends Part One of your transcript, Mr. Lucas, do you have any questions?"

Gersen thought for a moment.

"I find one thing puzzling," he said. "Humans have been in contact with Star Kings for something less than a thousand years, since Ghnarumen was first visited. How is it possible that in that short period of time they evolved to almost perfectly resemble us?"

"Unfortunately," replied Eleanor, "the record contains nothing but unproven theories."

"Which of those do you find most convincing?" Gersen asked.

"I am sorry, sir, but as you know, I am not permitted to speculate. It is against Company policy, and would expose us to possible legal liability."

"Ah, the question of liability again. But did I not at the beginning of your presentation release UTCS?"

"You did. But that release covers the Company only for matters summarized by me from the public record, not for additional speculations."

"I see," said Gersen. "In that case, I hereby release you from any responsibility for such speculations. I would still like to know what you think. Will that be sufficient?"

"Well," Eleanor hesitated, "I would normally need clearance from headquarters…"

"Of course, that is infeasible," said Gersen. "We are in hyperspace and hundreds of light-years distant from your headquarters. I suggest you record my release, and let me know your opinion. How were the Star Kings able to evolve so quickly?"

"It is not so much that the Star Kings evolved quickly," said Eleanor, "but rather that humans and other Earthly life-forms evolve with mind-numbing lethargy. Consider their evolutionary process, in which a male and female pair must mate, a zygote is produced with certain attributes; whether or not those attributes are conducive to survival is discovered only during a lifetime, and even then, there is much chance involved. Those lucky enough to survive then mate with others, with results that, by further chance, have some new characteristics that may or may not be suitable for survival, and so on. The whole process is stupefyingly tedious, and indeed it required several billion years for something resembling *lumbricina* to evolve into *homo sapiens*. Now consider the Star King. Each one produces the equivalent of a million gametes, which combine with the million gametes of another, something like the way fish fertilize clusters of eggs, but orders of magnitude more numerous. Then, somehow from the many combinations, the Star Kings are able to detect the ones that move them closer to the target. Then repeat the process, and so forth. And thereby you have earthworm to human in less than a thousand years. Does that make sense?"

It may have just been Gersen's imagination, but he could have sworn he detected a certain prideful breathlessness in Eleanor's conclusion. Gersen smiled to himself. He had encountered various bizarre theories about the Star Kings' seeming evolutionary miracle. Eleanor's explication, he supposed, was as good as any.

"If they can evolve that quickly," said Gersen, "does that not make them a threat to the human race?"

"Not really. You see, what the Star Kings gain in speed of evolutionary change, they lack in creativity. They cannot improve upon themselves — they can only copy."

"I see," said Gersen. "That will be all for today. You have given me a great deal to think about. Thank you."

"My pleasure, Mr. Lucas." The screen went blank, and Gersen switched the control to "external view" and sat pondering what he had heard, while he watched countless stars streaming past, like hordes of fireflies being borne on a dark wind. Could it be, he wondered, that the race of Star Kings posed no threat to humanity? If not, how to account for a malevolent aberration like Malagate the Woe? He would need to pose that problem to Eleanor during the next session. Gersen's features gave a wry smile and he turned the view screen off. After all, the image he was watching was, like the voice of Eleanor, merely a simulation.

In his early days of space travel, he had been in awe of this sight of myriad stars streaming past. But then the Jarnell people in a briefing had explained that because vessels powered by the Intersplit moved in a continuum that was beyond the speed of light, it would be impossible to 'see' the objects being passed. Gersen smiled again at how he had been deceived: sometimes a simulation was better than reality. After a while, he entered the ship's small but serviceable gymnasium, where he put himself through an intense weight-bearing and aerobic routine. Then he threw his clothes into the on-board cleaner, changed into fresh ones, served himself a light supper of fruit-juice and vegetable risotto, and retired to his bunk.

Gersen enjoyed a restful nap, although he could not quite clear his consciousness of what he had learned. The Star Kings were a fascinating species, supposedly non-threatening to humans, but with so little known about them, who could say for sure?

He busied himself with flight routine, checking instruments and marking progress along his chosen route. He was now three days into a nearly seven-day trip, measured by Earth time, and everything seemed to be going according to plan. He brewed a cup of his favorite tea, the dark Araminta* blend that had been discovered by Kim, who had an uncanny ability, among his other surprising skills, for ferreting out and preparing exotic foods and beverages. Then Gersen took his cup and settled himself in front of the computer screen.

"Good morning, Mr. Lucas," came the now familiar voice of Eleanor. An odd expression, thought Gersen, since morning had no meaning here. But he let that thought slide, as Eleanor seemed overly sensitive to implied criticism.

"Good morning, Eleanor. Ready for Part II."

"Part II: Attel Malagate, known as Malagate the Woe," Eleanor began.

---

* *Araminta* was an exclusive blend imported from the plantations of Cadwal, the third and only habitable world of the star Syrene. Cadwal had been settled by a society of conservationists, who needed to export commodities in order to support their oversight activities.

"Attel Malagate is presumed to have originated on Ghnarumen, along with all other Star Kings. On this point, the researcher is immediately struck with a seeming anomaly, for the folk of Ghnarumen are known to be orderly and law-abiding, whereas Attel Malagate was a criminal of exceptional viciousness and cruelty. Moreover, he clearly took pride in his villainy, as the adoption of the cognomen 'the Woe' suggests. What is one to make of this departure from the norm? The few Star Kings who have been consulted on this question declare only that Attel Malagate was a renegade, and then change the subject.

"Attel Malagate's history is little more than a catalogue of his most heinous crimes. He began as an extortionist, demanding payments from settlements in the Beyond, and exacting penalties of varying degrees of brutality for non-compliance. The case of the city Desde, on the planet Caro, is emblematic, and was a startling introduction to the general public of Attel Malagate's criminal career. In the year 1495, the mayor of Desde, one Janous Paragiglia, created a militia and space navy to guard the city, following receipt of Malagate's demands. In response, Malagate kidnapped Paragiglia and tortured him for thirty-nine days, telecasting the entire process not only to the cities on Caro and the other planets in his sector of the Beyond, but also, in one of the most extraordinary acts of bravado, to the entire Rigel Concourse.

"In the year 1499, Malagate was joined by four other criminal kingpins in conducting the notorious raid on Mount Pleasant, a community of some 5,000 persons who had refused to comply with his demands. The junta swept down upon the town, killed any resistors, then captured and enslaved the entire population."

Here Gersen interrupted. "I need no further details on the Mount Pleasant raid, as I am well aware of that event."

"Certainly, Mr. Lucas. Other details of Malagate's career are sparse. He was reported to have maintained a plantation of about 10,000 square miles on a planet named Grabhorne, served by a slave population estimated at 20,000. The enterprise, if one could call it that, produced agricultural products and an assortment of luxury goods, all exported and earning considerable profit. During the period 1523-4, rumors circulated that Malagate had taken on an identity as a member of a prestigious institution in the human world, but none of these were ever confirmed, and thereafter the record ends. Malagate's whereabouts, or even whether he still lives, are unknown. In 1532, the Grabhorne plantation was raided by the IPCC, but was discovered to be deserted. There was no trace of either the slaves or their overseers. That completes my summary of what we have on file."

"One question then," said Gersen. "Do you have any information about Malagate's relatives — sons, nephews, or anything of that kind? Specifically, someone named Mongo Malagate."

"I'm sorry, our files contain nothing on that subject."

"Thank you, then. That will be all for today."

Gersen found himself in a despondent mood. The UTCS report had evoked painful memories, but essentially provided no new information. Indeed, Gersen himself had participated in the Grabhorne raid, hoping to find some remnants of his former family and friends still alive, even after more than thirty years of enslavement. Their disappearance only served to tighten the knot of sorrow.

Gersen forced himself to put these thoughts out of his mind, and resumed his routine activities on the spaceship. In due course, the auto-pilot disengaged the Intersplit, the great blue-white disc of Rigel appeared on his screen, and he vectored toward the eighth planet, Alphanor. He proceeded through a series of identification and clearance protocols, which were conducted expeditiously by the Alphanor authorities, since both he and his ship were pre-registered, and well-known in any event. With the ship's thrusters humming at full power against Alphanor's gravitational pull, he dropped through a layer of scattered clouds, where the coastline of Umbria Province came into view, with its 100-mile-long white sand beach lapped by the waves of the great blue-green Thaumaturge Ocean.

Quicksilver settled gently onto her assigned pad at the Grand Interplanetary Spaceport that served Avente, Alphanor's principal city. A pair of gantry cranes rolled out to meet the ship. One bore a platform that would lower Gersen to ground level; the other attached itself securely to a trammel in *Quicksilver*'s nosecone, by which the ship would be gently lifted and carried to the private hangar operated jointly by the Jarnell and Distis Spaceship corporations. There, skilled technicians would check every detail of the ship's operating systems, and bring her back to as-new condition. Gersen alighted from the platform and breathed deeply of the ocean air as a Spaceport shuttle van sped out to meet him. This was a far cry, he reflected, from the days when arriving passengers had to make their own way on foot to the terminal building and, for that matter, could be accosted by unwanted interlopers such as Malagate's henchmen, Tristano and Suthiro.

"No luggage, sir?" the van operator asked, a young man in the beige uniform of the spaceport, who seemed a near carbon copy of the Manhattan driver.

"No, I'm traveling light," said Gersen. In fact, everything he needed would already be at hand in the suite he owned at Avente's Credenza Hotel.

Gersen checked in at the Concierge desk in the Terminal building, completed the necessary arrival paperwork, then proceeded to the main exit, where a hotel courtesy slidecar was waiting, having been summoned by the Spaceport Concierge while *Quicksilver* was making her final approach. The slidecar operator gave Gersen an understated salute as he held the rear door open; Gersen popped in, and off they went toward downtown Avente.

Alphanor was the administrative center of the 26-planet Rigel Concourse as well, according to its residents, as the cultural center. The Rigel Concourse was generally viewed as the nexus of the Oikumene, or civilized universe, and thus Avente, as Alphanor's principal city, could reasonably claim the status of Hub of the Universe. Indeed, this title was not infrequently found in local press reports. But now, with the slidecar progressing smoothly on its air cushions through downtown streets, it was difficult to distinguish the surroundings from what might be found in dozens of other cosmopolitan locations. Men and women in subdued gray and blue business attire moved briskly and with apparent purpose; street vendors occupied strategic posts on every block; tourists in disheveled travel clothes stood in clusters staring at guidebooks or wide-eyed at tall buildings. In due course, the slidecar arrived at the Hotel Credenza, where a tall, liveried doorman with florid features nodded in recognition and held open the hotel's main door.

"Greetings, Mr. Lucas. Welcome back."

"Thank you, Armand," Gersen replied, and proceeded into the main lobby, thinking that perhaps Armand's get-up, with its purple, yellow-striped trousers, red jacket with brass buttons and tails, and black stove-pipe hat was perhaps a bit overdone, even for the new Credenza.

The Credenza had been completely refurbished a few years earlier, at considerable expense, and the results of that effort were in evidence. The lobby was a twelve-story atrium, with a multi-colored fountain at its center. Subdued musical background tones were barely audible over the gurgling and splashing of the fountain. Six banks of glass-enclosed elevators whisked hotel patrons to the twenty stories of elegantly furnished rooms. As Gersen owned a personal suite, he had no need to check in, so he strode past the reception desk and proceeded to one of the free elevators. At the sixth floor, he exited and walked down the hall to number 615, where his thumbprint permitted access. Gersen tapped the master light switch and noted with satisfaction that the place was spotless. He then conducted a routine arrival protocol, first using his thumbprint to open a heavy metal safe where his cache of personal weapons were secured, then carefully inspecting the entire suite for listening devices. Finding none, he began to feel relaxed and at home. He pulled back the drapes of a large picture window, and looked down at the hotel's outdoor café and swimming pool, with a sweeping view of the Thaumaturge Ocean beyond. Time for a shower and a fresh set of clothes, he told himself. Although *Quicksilver*'s ionic cleaning system had done its job well, there was no substitute after a long flight for an invigorating session under running hot water and a change into something less utilitarian than spaceman's garb.

As he dried himself off after the shower, he contemplated his plans for the evening. After a week's confinement aboard *Quicksilver*, he wanted to be outdoors, and there was no better place in Avente for that purpose than the Esplanade, the grand seaside promenade within easy walking distance of the hotel. From his closet, he selected a pair of tan gabardine slacks, a white and blue striped shirt, and comfortable walking shoes. Before departing, he briefly checked his telescreen and found two messages. The first from Kim reported that the White Island house was secure and that Kim would take the next commercial flight to Avente. The next said simply '8 am?' and was signed 'Jaeger.'

He entered "Yes," equipped himself with a few select items from his weapons safe, and departed.

Gersen walked with long strides toward the boardwalk of the Esplanade, where the press of the crowd forced him to slow down. Here were throngs of gaily attired "Aventists," as the locals called themselves, interspersed with interplanetary visitors — Olphs in brown slouch hats, Krokinole Imps with purple top-knots, moon-faced Sanduskers, crypt-men in black cloaks. Presently Gersen tired of the pullulation, as it only reinforced the sense of his own solitary presence. He selected a table at a decent-looking café, ordered a local ale and a small omelet, and sat gazing out at the expanse of the ocean. He could not help thinking that it was at a place like this on the Esplanade, now more than twenty-five years ago, that he sat with Pallis Atwrode. Poor Pallis! So charming and innocently fresh, but caught up in a web of pure evil due to Gersen's tunnel-visioned obsession. Gersen uttered a choked grunt of annoyance at himself that evoked surreptitious glances from nearby patrons. He was about to embark upon another quest, aimed so it would seem at some re-creation of his old enemy Malagate. Would this become another obsession, possibly ensnaring innocent souls like Pallis? No, he told himself, he was wiser now and would not surrender to passion. He left an ample payment on the table and headed back to the hotel.

CHAPTER III

From *Life*, Volume IV,
by Unspiek, Baron Bodissey:

All humans have basic rights, that principle may be considered universally agreed. It is when the rights of some conflict with the rights of others that the trouble begins.

The dissenters weigh in:

Bah, what is Life? If Bodissey is as all-knowing as he represents himself to be, he would be familiar with the Scroll from the Ninth Dimension which observes (and here we paraphrase) that life is but a viral infection arising spontaneously in an accidental clump of slime. Bodissey should redirect his efforts to something useful such as the theory and practice of hermeneutics.

At a safe interval before the appointed time, Gersen departed the hotel and set out toward IPCC headquarters, a manageable walking distance away. The streets were nearly empty since Alphanor's rotation produced a twenty-nine-hour day, and Aventists chose to spend some of their extra hours at leisure in the morning. The pavement was damp from a brief overnight cloudburst, but now bright blue-white Rigel light filtered through the departing clouds.

Gersen's thoughts turned to the man with whom he was about to meet. He did not know Miles Jaeger well. In fact, he had only met Jaeger physically twice before. The first time was during the deeply disappointing Grabhorne mission. Grabhorne was the planet where Malagate the Woe was reported to have established a 10,000 square-mile plantation, worked by Malagate's enslaved kidnap victims, including Gersen's own former family and friends. Gersen had learned that the IPCC had located the place, which until 1535 had been unknown, and were planning a rescue operation. Through his IPCC contacts, Gersen arranged to join the team. Jaeger, about ten years Gersen's junior, had been a highly regarded officer — straight-backed, clear-eyed, and exuding determination. Alas, though, the mission had been fruitless, one of the bitterest moments in Gersen's memory. The plantation was devoid of human population, the empty bamboo slave barracks a mute testimony to the despairing existence of the inhabitants, the owner's former elegant compound stripped to bare walls and overgrown by vines.

Gersen's second encounter with Miles Jaeger had been at Chancy's Tea House, a popular watering hole for IPCC types, located at an overlook above Sailmaker Beach, to the north of Avente. The occasion had been a modest retirement gathering for Gersen's long-time colleague, Walter Koedelin. At one point during the event, Gersen found himself in a tight conversation group with Koedelin and Jaeger, in which the respect of each for the other was palpable. As the evening was winding down, Koedelin took Gersen aside and confided, "If you ever find yourself doing business again with the IPCC, Jaeger is a man you can trust." Gersen had guarded those words in his memory with care, as trust and the IPCC were not always synonyms.

After all, the IPCC was a bureaucracy, an organization that had grown from green shoots to one of the most powerful, and one of the most respected or feared, depending on one's perspective, in the Oikumene. The genesis of the entity lay in the fact that each planet had its own police force, sometimes several, whose authority did not extend beyond the planet itself. In the era of widespread and economical space travel, when criminals could swoop down, rob, kill, kidnap, destroy, and then disappear into space, either to another planet or into the vastness of the uncivilized Beyond, a planet-based police force was too often rendered impotent. Nor, however, were any planetary officials willing to subordinate themselves to what would have become the over-riding authority of an interplanetary police entity, which would inevitably assume paramilitary and dictatorial control. The IPCC therefore was conceived as a private enterprise, accepting commissions to hunt down criminals on a fee basis. Over time, as a logical extension of its investigative activities, the IPPC naturally migrated into the data collection business, and now managed files on every legal citizen in the Oikumene, in addition to illegals. Reference to the IPCC's database had become a mandatory requirement for any-one seeking to change employment or relocate to a different planet. By virtue of its burgeoning activity, the IPCC had become a bureaucracy, complete with competing fiefdoms, each striving to extend its span of control, with internecine quarrels mollified by a committee of civil-ian Directors. Gersen perhaps could trust Jaeger, but could he trust Jaeger's organization?

Gersen's thoughts shifted to current matters as he arrived at the IPCC building, an unprepossessing affair with an old-style dun-colored granite façade and a tiny, barely legible plaque bearing the IPCC's insignia. The IPCC was obviously not eager to advertise its presence. A young man wearing a junior officer's badge addressed him as he entered.

"Your business, sir?"

"Henry Lucas to see Commander Jaeger."

"Yes, sir, you are expected. Kindly remove any weapons and place them in this container; they will be securely held and returned to you when you leave."

Gersen briskly handed over a small projac and a thin stiletto, while retaining the tiny poison dispenser under the fingernail of his left index finger.

Evidently satisfied with Gersen's contribution to the weapons bin, the officer gestured to the elevator door on his left.

"The elevator will take you to Commander Jaeger's floor; when you exit turn right; his will be the last door down the hall."

After the elevator's door closed, there was barely a hint of motion. How high up was Jaeger's floor? It was impossible to tell. But when the doors opened, Gersen followed the instructions and found himself in an ante-room staffed by another junior officer, this one a female with close cropped hair and sharp, angular features.

"Mr. Lucas, one moment please." She picked up a phone set, "Your 8 o'clock appointment is here, sir. Very good, sir." Then she looked up at Gersen, and motioned him toward the half-open door behind her.

As Gersen entered, Jaeger rose from behind his desk. He was a figure in late middle-age, of average height, with athletic shoulders and erect posture. The office was utilitarian: several filing cabinets, and a shelf on the wall behind the desk that contained mementos of various kinds. Jaeger gestured to several chairs grouped around a conference table. Gersen's attention, though, was immediately drawn to a large window above the table, that looked out upon a spectacular view of the Thaumaturge Ocean. For a moment Gersen was bemused. The vista he was seeing appeared to be from a height of at least twenty stories, with a sweeping image of the long white-sand beach that ran to the north of the city. Gersen could almost identify the spot on the Esplanade where he had sat musing the previous evening. And yet the elevator had given no sense of traveling to that height.

Jaeger's features exhibited a slight smile. "Remarkable sight, isn't it," he observed.

Gersen nodded his assent.

"All the more so because we are four stories underground," said Jaeger with the tone of a performer delivering a punch-line. "What looks like a window is actually a view-screen. But not an ordinary one. This is an MVS VistaVision 6000, a very ancient piece of technology actually. Created by a company called Maxwell Vision Systems, named after the physicist in the nineteenth century (old reckoning) who first gave mathematical expression to the idea of visualized beauty. These screens were quite popular during the pre-Apocalyptic era when crowding was intense — over sixty billion inhabitants on Earth alone. Space was scarce and panoramic vistas even more so. The difference between the VistaVision and ordinary screens is the remarkable sense of depth, as you can see. Can't tell the difference between this and the real thing. The MVS screens have gone out of style now, though. With hundreds of planets to choose from, and the population thinned out, so to speak, by the Apocalypse, who needs artificial when they can have actuality? In any event, the Directors insisted for security reasons that my office be underground, and the expense of procuring the

VistaVision was a concession to make this dungeon tolerable. It also serves as a reminder that the balance between illusion and reality is elusive and the ability to distinguish one from another is a useful skill."

Gersen nodded in acquiescence. There was an element of pedantry in Jaeger's pronouncement, but the substance, he had to admit, was valid.

Jaeger pressed a button on a handset and the screen went grey.

"On to business," he said. "While you were travelling, there was a development."

Gersen became alert.

"Does the name Rundle Detteras mean anything to you?"

Gersen thought for a moment. "Yes. Detteras was a high-ranking official at Sea Province University. I had some dealings with him…it must have been at least twenty-five years ago. Haven't heard from him since."

"Well," said Jaeger, "he apparently remembers you. While you were travelling, he contacted our information bureau asking what we had in our files on Kirth Gersen. Of course, the specialist who took the call told him that our files had no information on such a person. Detteras became quite indignant. Tried to throw his weight around, announcing that he was a senior person at Sea Province University, and that in fact he already had in his own files information about Kirth Gersen that had formerly been provided by the IPCC, so we were evidently withholding, perhaps illegally. Does any of that make sense?"

Gersen pondered. "Not completely, but I can fill in some details. I had become convinced that Attel Malagate was impersonating a Sea Province official, who had commissioned a certain Lugo Teehalt to act as a locater on the University's behalf. The problem was that Malagate could have been one of three such officials and I didn't know which, so I contrived to interview all three. Detteras was on my list of possibilities. Prior to my meeting with him, Detteras had used the influence of his position to extract what information about me the IPCC had on file at that time. Quite pleased with himself for having done so, as I recall. What did he find? That I was born in 1490, place of birth unknown. Arrived on Earth at age 10. A few inconsequential school records. Enrolled as a catechumen at the Institute, reaching the 11th Phase by age twenty-four, then withdrew. Thereafter the record was empty."

"Your memory is intact," observed Jaeger. "That was the information that would have been provided to a qualifying person at that time. Of course, even those sketchy details are no longer publicly available. Impressive accomplishment, by the way, making Phase 11 by age twenty-four. I take it, though, that Detteras did not turn out to be Malagate."

"Correct, Detteras, for all his pomposity, was not Malagate. That role fell to Gyle Warweave, who was an Honorary Provost, or something of that sort. In any event, Warweave/Malagate perished on the planet that Lugo Teehalt had discovered, and that was the end of my connection to Sea Province University."

"The question we must ask, then, is why is Detteras making this inquiry after all these years?"

"I have no idea," said Gersen.

"Perhaps we should inquire," said Jaeger, with a lilt in his voice somewhat akin to his punch-line about the MVS view-screen. "The mention of Kirth Gersen triggered an alert in our security system. The call was reported to me promptly, and I took the liberty of inviting Detteras in for an interview. In fact, he should be arriving just about now."

Jaeger pressed a button on his hand-held control and the screen opened to reveal a small room with two chairs and a table in between. In one chair was seated a prim young woman with close-cropped russet hair and wearing a light green tunic, evidently an IPCC representative. She was glancing through a sheaf of papers on the table in front of her, but then looked up as a figure of ponderous bulk entered the room. This was unmistakably Detteras, Gersen instantly recognized — the over-sized frame, the coarse features, the confrontational posture, all had become, if anything, even more stark with the passage of some twenty-five years. Detteras was a man whose unappetizing appearance was exceeded only by his truculence. Indeed, one could imagine that he cultivated these physical characteristics as a way of signaling his disdain for the opinions of others. Gersen noted with amusement that Detteras was attired in the same quasi-military uniform with which he had decked himself out at their first meeting — that of a Baron of The Order of Archangels, complete with black boots, loose scarlet breeches and gold epaulettes.

"Good morning, Mr. Detteras," the young woman said.

"Kindly address me as Director Detteras," he muttered.

"Excuse me, sir. Our records show that you retired from your Directorship at Sea Province University three years ago."

"That is correct, but I retain the title Director Emeritus."

"Very well, Director Emeritus Detteras, thank you for coming in."

"I was told that I must subject myself to the inconvenience of this interview in order to secure the information I seek. I certainly hope that will be the case, as my time is very valuable."

"We will do the best we can, sir. But please understand that the files you are asking for are restricted. They are only available to authorized persons."

Detteras leaned forward and laughed, a heavy booming sound in the small room. "Bah! That is the same obfuscation your representative used to put me off when I called. But, if you have a record of that call, which I am sure you do, you will know that I already have more information about the subject matter — one Kirth Gersen — than you say is absent from your files. And further, that information came from the IPCC itself! What do you say to that?"

Satisfied with this pronouncement, Detteras lowered his bulk into the empty chair on his side of the table and scowled at his interlocutor.

The IPCC interrogator was unperturbed by Detteras's remonstrations. "Before I can respond to that, Director Emeritus Detteras, I need to clarify a few points. First, what is the nature of your interest in this Kirth Gersen?"

"I don't see the relevance of that," said Detteras stiffly. "I am a private citizen and this is a private matter."

"I must point out, sir, that you made the inquiry as a Sea Province University official, not as a private citizen."

"What difference does that make?" objected Detteras.

"Misrepresenting yourself as a public official when the matter is private is a violation of Code B14-327. Depending on the circumstances, this can be a serious offense."

Detteras' mouth drooped, and he made no response.

"I would need to know the nature of this personal business. If it was as innocent as you imply, we can perhaps put aside the code violation."

"If you must know, then, the request came from someone else. I was merely acting as an intermediary."

The young official raised an eyebrow. "I see. But I am forced to point out, Director Emeritus, that we are getting into deeper water here. Requesting information from the IPCC on behalf of an undisclosed third party is a violation of Code D16-432, and the penalties are trebled if the information is in a restricted file, as is the case here. Perhaps you had best tell me the whole story."

Detteras' shoulders had slumped and he seemed to have shrunk within his somewhat threadbare Archangels' uniform. Gersen, meanwhile, had been observing from Jaeger's office with close attention. He turned to Jaeger and nodded.

"Your interviewer is comporting herself well."

"She is Ensign Lori Tyng," said Jaeger. "Top of her cadet class, and one of the first to make officer." Of course, that sidebar conversation was not audible in the interview room.

Detteras took a deep breath. "I was approached by a stranger," he began. "He was a sinister figure — a hawk-faced man with red hair cut to bristles down the center of his scalp, and exhibiting the tattoos of a Brinktown* enforcer. He demanded that I provide him with the coordinates of Teehalt's planet. I must say, I was taken aback. There were only four people, apart from myself, who knew about Teehalt's planet. Three of them were dead — Teehalt himself, Malagate, and my dear colleague, the late Clagge Kelle. The fourth is the mystery man Kirth Gersen, status unknown. I told him that Kelle and I after we returned from Teehalt's planet, had agreed to destroy the filament that contained its location coordinates. The planet was pristine, and should be left that way. He questioned me closely on this, but I stood firm because it was the truth.

"The stranger adopted a threatening tone. He demanded to know the whereabouts of Kirth Gersen. I told him I had not seen hide nor hair of Gersen in twenty-five years, and would be just as happy if I never saw him again. Gersen was a man of dark secrets and brooding

---

* Brinktown: an establishment on the edge of the Beyond, inhabited and used as a rendezvous by criminal elements.

obsessions. The stranger then claimed to have information about irregularities in the budget of my former department. Of course, I am completely innocent of any wrong-doing. But an investigation would be both tedious and embarrassing and, if I may speak plainly, certain members of the University Ethics Committee would not be unhappy to see me taken down a notch or two. Not to mention that my pension could be at risk. So I gave him the information about Gersen that I had in my possession and, upon his further insistence, agreed to make the inquiry to the IPCC."

"Perhaps," said Ensign Tyng, "we can identify this mysterious stranger. Let me know if you recognize any of the faces I'm going to show you." She pressed a key on a handset, and a screen on the wall blossomed into a series of whirling colors. Then she keyed in some additional codes, and an image appeared of a round-faced man with orange skin tone and a scornful look.

"What about this one?"

"No, that doesn't look like him at all."

Next appeared a pale face, a conspicuously broken nose, and deep staring eyes.

"No."

Third was a hawk-faced man with red bristles running along the center of his scalp.

"That's him!" Detteras blurted out. "It gives me tremors just to look at that face!"

"You have identified Sligo Patch, known in Brinktown circles as 'Dirk.' Your assessment of his tattoo was observant, because he is known in our file as a Brinktown enforcer. A dangerous man."

"Well," said Detteras, "I was a Professor of Symbology, after all. A trained observer, you might say." Detteras showed a bleak smile, like a reprimanded child seeking reassurance.

Ensign Tyng briefly examined the sheaf of papers on the table in front of her, then she looked up, fixing Detteras with a sympathetic gaze.

"I can see, Director Emeritus Detteras, that you have undergone a trying experience. Your inquiry to the IPCC, while perhaps irregular, was made under considerable duress. The inhabitants of Brinktown are known to exact harsh remedies against those who frustrate their wishes."

"You have perceived my predicament precisely," pleaded Detteras, in the most ingratiating tone a person of his customary bluster could summon, "I am truly at a loss as to how to satisfy this stranger's demands."

"Perhaps I can help," said Ensign Tyng. "I have made the decision to share with you certain information, strictly in confidence and off the record, you understand."

Detteras brightened considerably, and he leaned forward. "Of course, I understand completely."

"I have in front of me the complete IPCC file," Ensign Tyng continued. "I am prepared to release it to you, subject to two conditions. First, you are to share the information with no one other than this stranger. Second, you are to return the file to me intact, along with the information you earlier secured from the IPCC. Are we agreed?"

"Of course," replied Detteras eagerly.

"By the way, when did this stranger say he would return to determine the success of your inquiry?"

"Within a week. That was three days ago."

"Very well, I will expect you back here with the file within four days." Ensign Tyng passed the file across the table. Detteras opened it and looked through the contents.

"Why, there is nothing here but a re-hash of the information I already have, plus some personal data — height, weight, that sort of thing. This will make the stranger — Sligo or Dirk or whatever his name is — very fretful, or worse."

"Not necessarily. This personal data could be found nowhere else. It could only be obtained from the IPCC. It will show that you have completed your assignment in good faith. And a resourceful criminal could make good use of this; it is more important than you think. Besides, that is the entire IPCC file on this Kirth Gersen. As far as we are concerned, he ceased to exist after 1524."

"This...this is most unsatisfactory," Detteras spluttered.

"Of course, if you are dissatisfied, you may appeal to my superiors. But then the question of Codes B14-327 and D16-432 would come into play..."

"I suppose I must make do with what you are offering."

"You have come to the only feasible conclusion, Director Emeritus Detteras."

Detteras scooped up the file and prepared to leave, but as he reached the doorway, he turned. "Just to be sure, are we agreed that the question of accounting irregularities is nuncupatory?"

If Ensign Tyng recognized Detteras' malapropism, she did not let on. "Have no fear on that account, sir. The IPCC takes small interest in the peculations of University officials. The matter is already forgotten."

Deterras departed and the door closed behind him. Ensign Tyng then turned to the hidden camera in the corner of the room, "Did the interview meet with your approval, Commander Jaeger?"

"Indeed it did. Fine work. Now what we need to do is establish surveillance at Detteras' residence, and wait for this mysterious stranger to appear."

"Yes, sir. With your permission, I would like to volunteer for that assignment."

"You shall have it then. Tell scheduling that I have agreed, and have the Quartermaster issue any special equipment you might need. Good luck."

"Thank you, sir."

Jaeger closed the screen and turned to Gersen. "A good day's work, I would say."

"Perhaps," said Gersen, "but I'm not too happy to have my personal data circulating among the Brinktown crowd."

Jaeger showed a sly smile. "Have no fear on that account," he said. "Here is a copy of the personal data we provided."

Jaeger handed Gersen a single sheet, which he quickly scanned, then reproduced Jaeger's smile. The height for Kirth Gersen was shown as 5' 10"; his was 6'; the weight was 195, he was 180; the eyes were brown, his were grey-blue; blood type was B-negative, his was A, and best of all was the gencode, the singular genetic typing that was unique to every individual and could not be counterfeited. On the page was a 12-digit code that bore no resemblance to his own.

"I take it that you are satisfied that we did not betray you?" said Jaeger.

"Yes, indeed."

Jaeger's smile faded; he looked down at the table-top as if in thought, then looked up and fixed Gersen with a steely gaze.

"It would seem that the stakes of the game have changed," he said. "When you arrived this morning, we were expecting to begin the hunt for a criminal named Mongo Malagate. But if I were to interpret what we just heard, I would say that some person — as yet unknown — has also launched a hunt for you. This Sligo Patch low-life is obviously not a principal, but is acting on instructions from someone higher up. And there seems to be a connection to the earlier Malagate, that is, Attel Malagate the Woe. Perhaps you could explain. And where does this planet — Teehalt's planet — come in?"

"Lugo Teehalt was a locater," Gersen began, "He was down on his luck and desperate for employment. Malagate the Woe, in the person of one Gyle Warweave, had made a substantial grant to Sea Province University, through which he was accorded the title of Honorary Provost, and given considerable influence over the University's exploration program. In that capacity, Warweave/Malagate hired Teehalt to search for undiscovered and habitable planets."

Here Jaeger raised a palm to interrupt. "Why would Malagate do that?"

Gersen smiled. "You have hit on the salient point. Malagate confessed to me before he died that he had planned to be the father of a new race of Star Kings, superior to both men and to the inhabitants of the Star Kings' native planet, Ghnarumen. And this new master race would make its home on a planet superior to Earth. Finding such a planet was the unrevealed objective of Teehalt's commission and, of course, Teehalt had no idea that his patron was the notorious Malagate the Woe."

Jaeger gave a nod of understanding, encouraging Gersen to continue.

"The job of locater is, if I may be permitted to use an archaic term, a godforsaken one. One is confined to a one-person spacecraft, usually in those days the old Model 9B. Minimal provisions, cramped quarters, unmentionable sanitary conditions for Earth months on end. Travelling ever farther into as yet unplumbed reaches of space, an emptiness where no man has gone before nor in all likelihood will venture again in a lifetime. All in the hope of finding a planet sufficiently salubrious to support human population, from which some economic benefit might be derived. Of course, adding to the locater's sense of futility, the standard locater contract awards most of such benefits to the financial sponsor.

"In sum, there are few pursuits more lonely, more forlorn, more subject to wracking disappointment than that of locater. Imagine. One is hurtling through mind-numbing blackness for days on end; then at last, out of the void, a star gleams in the distance. As you approach, you see a circlet of planets. You ask yourself: will this be the one? However, time after time, you find nothing but cold pumice and dust, or smoke and ammonia, monoxide winds, acid rain — in short, desolation.

"Nevertheless, Teehalt persisted. Perhaps there is a resolve that hardens with isolation. I don't know. Such things are described in literature. At times I have experienced that feeling myself. But then after months on end of nothing but rock and mud and sulfur, he came upon a planet too beautiful to describe. There were mountains washed by rain, clouds as soft and bright as snow floating over green valleys. The sky was sapphire blue, the air sweet and cool. I could go on, but you get the point. Teehalt was not over-stating the magnificence of the place: I have seen it myself.

"Teehalt was so entranced by his discovery that he resolved to keep it pristine, unviolated by human presence. However, many a man's resolve has been undermined by companionship and drink and that regrettably is especially the case for spacemen. On his return from the Beyond, Teehalt put in at Brinktown. He chanced to pass the evening at Sin-Sin's Tavern, where he entertained a group of rapt listeners with the tale of his discovery, as well as his determination to keep the planet's location secret.

"Alas for Teehalt, among his audience was Hildemar Dasce, one of Malagate's henchmen. Dasce revealed to Teehalt that the true identity of his sponsor was Malagate the Woe, and ordered Teehalt to Smade's Tavern on Smade's Planet for a rendezvous with Malagate. It was a summons Teehalt could not refuse."

Here, Gersen paused, as if reflecting on the extraordinary role that fate can have in the affairs of men. Then he took a deep breath, and continued. "By chance, I myself had checked into Smade's to recuperate from a grueling adventure of my own. To make the story short, Teehalt was murdered; Malagate and Dasce hurried away in both their ship and my own Model 9B, thinking that it was Teehalt's and that its navigation monitor would contain the location of Teehalt's discovery. In fact, Teehalt had surreptitiously landed his 9B in a nearby valley. I departed in that ship before Malagate could discover his error, and thus came into possession of the monitor.

"I returned to Alphanor and tracked the ownership of Teehalt's 9B to Sea Province University. There were only three officials at the University with the authority to commission Teehalt's expedition; one of them had to be Malagate. After much wrangling, it was agreed that the three — Warweave, Kelle, and Detteras — would accompany me on a University vessel to the planet. In the course of that venture, I hoped to expose and put an end to Malagate, which I was able to do.

"Thus, Malagate's ambition to found a new race came to an end. And the spectacular planet discovered by Teehalt, which was to have been the private world from which this new race was to dominate the civilized universe, instead became Malagate's lonely grave."

There followed a silence in Jaeger's office, while both men pondered the significance of Gersen's story.

"It seems clear from this history," said Jaeger after a moment, "that what we suspected is in fact true — namely the connection between Attel Malagate and Mongo Malagate. Only an intimate of Attel Malagate would have known about both the existence of Teehalt's Planet and the involvement of Kirth Gersen. I will wager that if we play our cards deftly, this Sligo Patch, who is undoubtedly just an underling, will lead us to Mongo Malagate. As a first step in that direction, we should wait to determine the results of Ensign Tyng's surveillance. In the meanwhile, I suggest that we temporarily suspend 'Operation Broadwood,' as we designate the piano tuner gambit internally. There is no point starting down that rather labyrinthine path, if Sligo Patch can lead us to our quarry by a simpler route. I will contact you if there are new developments."

Gersen could see nothing to add to Jaeger's plan. He nodded his acquiescence, rose, and left the office.

CHAPTER IV

From Introduction to *A Brief History of the Institute* by Clagget Grebe:

> An organization maintaining strict admission requirements, as well as a rigid hierarchical structure requiring both determination and effort for advancement, is bound to attract individuals of ability and ambition. Overlay that with a culture of studied detachment, which must intensify as one moves up through the ranks, and there you have the Institute. It would not be unreasonable to conclude that the Institute's most senior Fellows are borderline schizophrenic.

Excerpt from *A Commentary on Technology and the Human Condition* by Ambrose Rucker, Fellow of the Institute, Phase 67:

> Of all the technical developments we have examined, virtual reality must be deemed the most insidious. Half of the stimuli purport to make their subjects happy and entertained, while irrevocably addicting them; the other half promote anger and fear, which are the precursors to enslavement. If the Institute had its way, the purveyors of these perversions would be summarily executed and their remains shot off into space.

Gersen returned to the hotel Credenza in an unsettled frame of mind. Jaeger's observation about the connection between Mongo Malagate and Attel Malagate was likely correct. How else could this Patch character have known about Teehalt's Planet, not to mention the involvement of Kirth Gersen? To test this premise, Gersen forced himself to review other possible sources of that information. Pallis Atwrode? No, the poor creature had been long dead, by suicide at least 10 years earlier, as Gersen had learned when the monthly stipends he had arranged to send her were returned unspent. The brutally demanding lechery of Hildemar Dasce had been too much for her simple-hearted psyche to bear. What then of Dasce himself, who had been Malagate's lieutenant? Impossible, Dasce had been left on Teehalt's Planet and was ultimately captured by his erstwhile victim, Robin Rampold. Even if Dasce had managed to escape, he was still isolated on the planet, with no means to communicate much less depart. The last remaining party to the saga of Teehalt's Planet had been Malagate's other henchman, Suthiro, the cobra-eyed Sarkoy venefice, who had died by Gersen's own hand. The elimination of these possibilities left only one feasible way for Mongo Malagate — assuming he was Patch's employer — to know about the existence of Teehalt's Planet and Gersen's connection to it: somehow that information had been communicated by Warweave/Malagate before his death. There was nothing further Gersen could do to pursue this matter but wait, as Jaeger had advised, for the outcome of Ensign Tyng's surveillance. Gersen was not by nature a patient person, but on occasion, when stalking a quarry, patience was the prudent course. Not to mention when the quarry was apparently stalking you.

Putting aside consideration of the Malagate matter opened the way for reflection on another nettlesome question — the intrusion at White Island. The attempt to capture Henry Lucas had to have been, upon examination, more than the act of some random malcontent. Discovering Lucas' remote and private location, hiring two thugs, as well as the vessel and its crew, was an undertaking requiring significant resources and planning. Certainly, this would have been within the means of Mongo Malagate. But to connect Henry Lucas to Kirth Gersen? That seemed impossible or, if possible, there had to have been a serious breach of Gersen's carefully contrived security arrangements. That prospect, however remote, was troubling. If Gersen had been able to detain one or both of the intruders, he would have extracted the name of their sponsor. But he had failed to do so, and that seemed to bring the matter to a dead end.

Perhaps not, however. Gersen had been impressed by the precision with which Ensign Tyng had been able to identify Sligo Patch based on Detteras' description. The White Island duo also had distinctive features. He would minute himself to enlist the IPCC's help, once the surveillance of Sligo Patch was concluded.

Further brooding on these matters seemed unproductive. Gersen walked over to the window of his living-room and looked out. It was early evening, and Rigel's glare was shimmering off the waves; the café on the deck below was beginning to fill with patrons. Gersen found himself of a mind to join them. He threw on a loose blue linen shirt, white cotton trousers, and rope sandals, and departed his quarters.

Arriving at the café, Gersen selected a table at the ocean side of the terrace, where a crisply clad waiter offered to be of service. Gersen had no need to consult the menu, as he knew it well, and ordered a salad of local greens and a soup of blended Thaumaturge mollusks and curry. He was pleased to see that Quiritavo, a light and fresh wine imported from Cadwal, was among the café's recent offerings, and added a glass of that to his order. While waiting for the refreshments to arrive, Gersen relaxed and gazed out at the expanse of the Thaumaturge, an activity of which he never seemed to tire. He observed with interest that a sailboat race was underway — eight 30-metre foil boats with 50-meter masts and micron-thin, multi-colored sails. These vessels, which rose up on their foils so as to cause minimum frictional resistance, could hurtle across the waves at speeds of 60 knots or better. Although it was difficult to tell for sure from this distance, the competition looked intense. First magenta was in the lead, then yellow, then the fleet rounded a buoy and bright green broke out ahead. Gersen himself was a life-long sailor; he had tried his hand at racing these swift high-technology rigs, but ultimately decided that the sport was 90 percent money and 10 percent talent. Anyone with a large enough bank account could hire a top designer, commission a hull constructed from the most expensive ultra lightweight materials, hire the necessary 23-man professional crew, and thus become a winner. The cost of the campaign was roughly ten million times the value of the silver trophy. Gersen of course could easily afford to compete in this league, but the whole undertaking had soon enough become tedious, so he had given it up. More to his liking was single-handed sailing on his old-style monohull. Not nearly so fast, of course, but there was no need to cater to the whims of prima donna crew, and there was still the challenge of teasing out the greatest speed of which the hull was capable.

Presently Gersen's order arrived. He took a sip of the wine, which was delicate and delicious as expected. He contemplated his present situation, and had a thought that brought a smile to his lips. He was about to embark on an undertaking that was both challenging and dangerous. It was not unlike taking his sailboat far offshore on a day when mariners were being warned of high winds. Was this not how he had spent most of his early life? And was it not likely to be an energizing change from the tedium of reading financial reports and minutes of meetings? He took another sip of wine, then replaced his still half full glass on the table. He had scheduled an early morning session with Lex, his combat trainer; Lex would work him hard, as always, and he needed to be rested and ready. Gersen signaled the waiter, signed his check, and departed for his quarters.

Gersen returned the next day stiff and sore, but on the whole pleased with his performance. As expected, Lex had pressed him to the limit, but he had held up well. A few more sessions like this, and he would be back to peak performance. As he entered his suite, the amber message light was glowing, indicating a communication from an important caller. He walked over to the control unit, tapped a key, and the image of Jehan Addels appeared on the screen. Addels had a narrow face and somewhat weak jaw, with icy pale blue eyes. His wispy hair had thinned during the twenty-five years that Gersen had known him, exposing a prominent forehead that seemed in a permanent state of wrinkled concentration.

"Sorry to trouble you," said Addels' message, "but a matter has come to my attention that I think you will find of interest. Please call me at the New Wexford office when convenient."

The screen went grey. Addels served as Gersen's financial manager, lawyer, and all-purpose factotum. He had built Gersen's fortune from the incredibly large starting point of 9 billion SVU to the even more incredibly large current value of 25 billion SVU, all the while keeping Henry Lucas, the notional principal, discreetly out of the picture. He had proven himself unfailingly loyal and perspicacious. Although the relationship between Gersen and Addels was professional, it had also over time evolved into one of mutual respect, admiration, and even fondness. When Addels said he had a matter of interest to convey, Gersen wasted no time to respond. He tapped in the code that would connect him directly to Addels, who appeared once more, this time live, on the screen.

"The financial world is like a quiet pond," said Addels, "whose denizens are hyper-sensitive to any perturbation. Cast a pebble into its midst and multiple observers become instantly alert."

"And today's pebble is?" queried Gersen, allowing Addels to relish his aphorism.

"A forty-five percent interest in Jarnell Corporation is soon to be offered for sale."

Gersen rarely found himself non-plussed by any news, but this was a development of staggering implications. Jarnell Corporation owned the entire suite of technologies that underlay the Jarnell Intersplit propulsion system that, in turn, was responsible for modern space travel. In the centuries since its introduction, the Jarnell Intersplit had facilitated the location and eventual settlement of innumerable habitable planets, and now supported a growing network of interplanetary travel and trade. Jarnell was arguably the most profitable and powerful corporation in the Oikumene. But most important from Gersen's point of view, entities controlled by Henry Lucas currently owned twenty percent of Jarnell's shares, one of Addels' early deft financial maneuvers. The acquisition of a further forty-five percent would give him a controlling interest.

"Are we positioning ourselves to be a buyer?"

"Of course," said Addels. "I assumed that would be your wish."

"The purchase price will not be trivial. Will it be within our capacity?"

"Again, yes. Or rather, probably is a more accurate answer. It is too early to know for sure who the other bidders will be, and what are their resources. Fortunately, our liquid assets at the moment are substantial and put us in a strong competitive position. As this plays out, I suspect that you will be happy that I dissuaded you from some of your more frivolous undertakings."

Gersen smiled to himself. At times over the years, Addels' conservative financial leanings had made him feel like a child asking for an increase in its allowance. But he could not dispute the soundness of Addels' advice, that on more than one occasion had talked Gersen out of certain of his more fanciful investment schemes.

"Who is the seller? This seems to be an exceptionally large bloc."

"Your instinct is correct. Actually, there are three sellers — three half-siblings each with 15 percent. However, they are determined to act as a unit, thinking that this approach will garner the highest price. My understanding is that they have bound themselves legally together for this purpose, and awarded an irrevocable commission to Glyphon and Blum to handle the transaction on their behalf."

"I see. Glyphon and Blum are a reputable firm, are they not?"

"Yes. Although when the stakes are this high, reputable can become a relative term. As the referees in ancient pugilistic contests used to advise: 'protect yourself at all times.'" *Addels is in rare form today,* thought Gersen. *He relishes a financial challenge like this.*

"What about prospective buyers?" Gersen asked.

"Of course, the number of buyers would be limited by the size of the transaction. But in this case, there may be only two."

"Only two?"

"Yes. Braemar Holdings, which is us. And Galactic Enterprises."

"Galactic Enterprises? Are they related to Galactic Freight?"

"Exactly. Enterprises is the holding company that owns Galactic Freight among its other properties."

Gersen experienced a sensation that would have been his hackles rising, if he had hackles to rise. Galatic Freight owned a fleet of cargo ships that purported to be in the interplanetary contract freight business. But in fact, the operation was a front for all manner of unsavory activity — hijacking, black marketeering, customs running, receiving stolen goods, and so forth. Galactic had also enriched itself by selling anti-hijacking insurance, so they were profiting in two ways from their criminal activities. If he and Addels were going to compete with this group for the Jarnell interest, it would be a bare-knuckled contest for sure.

"Not the competitor I would choose, if I had a choice," he said. "But how can you be so sure that they will the other bidder, and for that matter, that there will likely be only two of us?"

Addels paused for a moment, as if working himself into a prepared dissertation. "First, the Jarnell by-laws require that any transfer of company shares must be approved by two-thirds of the shareholders. Of course, the sellers will vote their 45% to whomever they choose to sell. So a further 22% is needed to approve the transaction. Second, the last remaining Jarnell descendant, Fauntleroy Jarnell IV, has made it known that he wishes no further shares to leave the family, and he will vote against any transaction. That leaves Braemar Holdings, which is us, with 20% and Galactic with the other 20%.

"Now I need to share with you some history. Galactic has owned its 20% for quite some time. How they secured the required two-thirds approval, I do not know. However, when the 20% piece came on the market that we eventually acquired, they should have been a competitor. But for some reason they dropped out. Rumor has it that they had suffered a massive financial setback due to the bankruptcy of Interchange, in which they were principal owners. In any event, their absence cleared the way for our acquisition of the 20% interest; this was one of the first transactions I completed on your behalf, not long after you hired me and funded my activities with that extraordinary amount of money. So it was rather serendipitous that just as we had the funds to consummate what seemed like a once-in-a-lifetime opportunity, our principal competitor failed to make an offer. I have wondered from time to time whether there was a connection between those two events, but have elected not to dwell overmuch on the matter."

Addels paused as if to take a breath. Gersen suspected that he knew, or could guess, more than he was letting on. In fact, Gersen had managed to fleece 9 billion SVU from Interchange, and that was the source of the funds he had turned over to Addels. No law had been broken as the event had occurred in the Beyond, where no law applied, and Interchange itself was a criminal operation.

Addels concluded: "Nevertheless, here we are — only two plausible bidders for what would become a 65% stake, a controlling interest — but neither can move forward without the other."

"What about the Institute?" said Gersen, "I have heard rumors from time to time that the Institute wished to accumulate a position in Jarnell."

"Ah, the mysterious Institute," said Addels. "As you might imagine, I have heard the same rumors. Although most of those rumors are propagated by people who know little about Jarnell and less about the Institute. The Institute does a masterful job keeping their plans and goals opaque to the outside world, so one never knows for sure. However, in all the years we have owned our stake in Jarnell, there has never been the slightest whisper of interest from them. Therefore, while nothing is ever certain on transactions of this magnitude, my working assumption is that this will be between Braemar and Galactic."

"Who is the principal of Galactic?" Gersen asked.

"It is a well-kept secret, shrouded by layers of holding companies and trusts, in very much the same way that Henry Lucas is not identified as the principal of Braemar. But the name that is whispered about is Bruno Bolfo."

This was not a name Gersen recognized. "Would it serve any purpose to discuss this matter with Bolfo?" he asked.

"Not at this point," said Addels. "Besides I would sooner sit down to tea with a crocodile."

"What are the next steps, then?"

"In matters of this type," replied Addels, "patience is of paramount importance. We must not betray our interest too quickly, nor appear too eager. The sellers' representatives surely know who we are and will come to us when the time is appropriate. Once the intent to sell is official, so to speak, it would be appropriate for us to communicate with Fauntleroy Jarnell, to ascertain the firmness of his opposition to the transaction. But in the meanwhile, patience must be the watchword of the day."

Gersen considered ruefully that this was the second time this week that he had been admonished to be patient. Nevertheless, Addels knew best on such matters, and Gersen would be guided by his advice.

"Very well, I assume you will keep me informed."

"Indeed, I will," said Addels, and disconnected.

Two days later, Gersen found himself once again in Miles Jaeger's office at IPCC headquarters, this time joined by Ensign Lori Tyng. The left sleeve of Tyng's tunic had been cut away, and her upper arm bandaged to protect what appeared to be a substantial wound. Jaeger's assistant had set out a pot of tea and three cups, from which Gersen inferred that this was going to be more than a perfunctory meeting.

After the briefest exchange of bromides, Gersen gestured toward Tyng's bandaged arm and asked, "Did that result from your surveillance of Patch?"

"Yes," she replied, "but it's not as bad as it looks. The IPCC med team has a tendency to overdo things."

"As well they should," interjected Jaeger. "Good officers are hard to come by. If you don't mind, Ensign, would you repeat for Mr. Lucas' benefit what you've already told me, about what happened yesterday evening."

"Very well, sir. I had taken a concealed position behind some shrubs at the side of Detteras' residence. Just after nightfall, a slidecar pulled up and a figure — unmistakably Patch — exited the vehicle and proceeded to the front entrance. He was granted admission and nothing more happened for about fifteen minutes. Then I heard a sharp cry followed by a muffled gurgling. Not possible to know what caused it, but the sound was unsettling. The front door flew open and Patch emerged, hastening toward his vehicle.

"I had to make a fast decision. I had planned to follow Patch, in the hope that he would lead me a step closer to whomever he was working for. But the commotion from inside the house suggested foul play, so I accosted Patch before he could enter his vehicle. He brandished a knife — a nasty little stiletto actually — but I was able to disarm and handcuff him.

"I then called the Avente Constables, who dispatched a team within minutes. Upon investigation, we found that Detteras was dead; his throat had been slashed from ear to ear. Not a pretty sight. Lots of blood from a wound like that. Patch has been taken into custody, where he will await the normal judicial proceeding. If I had to guess, this will lead to him being charged with murder. I feel badly for Detteras, though. He was a bit of a blowhard, but he didn't deserve to die."

"Thank you, Ensign, you performed well," said Jaeger. Then he turned to Gersen. "Any questions?"

"Just one. What happened to the packet of information you gave to Detteras?"

"Patch had it tucked in his jacket. I retrieved it, and secured it in my vehicle before the constables arrived."

"Good thinking," said Gersen, "but too bad that the fake information didn't make it to Patch's higher-up."

"Actually," said Tyng, "I'm fairly sure that it did. I discovered that Patch had scanned the file into his mobile device. In all likelihood, he immediately transmitted the contents to his home base. In any event, I secured the device as well, and our tech people will be able to confirm that."

"Another good move," said Jaeger. "Just as well that the Avente authorities don't have either the file or the device. We have good relations with local police, of course, but those items could have prompted some awkward questions. Speaking of local authorities, I have asked that we be able to participate in the interrogation of Patch. They should be expecting us just about now."

Jaeger turned off the panoramic view on his screen, keyed in some codes, and an officer wearing the grey and maroon uniform of the Avente Constabulary appeared.

"Good morning, Commander Jaeger. If you are ready, I'll have Patch brought to the interview room. In the meanwhile, I'll place on the screen the file we have assembled on him."

Not surprisingly, Patch was quite an unsavory character — wanted for murder on two planets and sundry crimes on two others. No reported connection to Mongo Malagate, though, Gersen noted.

Patch arrived and was cuffed to a chair facing the screen. His skin tone had been washed away, leaving his face marmoreal white, which only served to accentuate the vivid purple bruise on his left cheek bone. His right arm was in a cast from wrist to shoulder. The red bristles running down the center of his otherwise bare scalp were exactly as Detteras had described.

Commander Jaeger introduced himself and said he had some questions.

"Save your breath," growled Patch. "I have nothing to say. And if that she-wolverine is with you, you can tell her I'll be filing charges for assault."

"You are facing serious charges yourself," said Jaeger. "You can help your cause by cooperating."

"Serious charges? For what, a simple accident? I had my little letter opener out, and the old man tripped and fell on it."

"Who sent you to Detteras?"

"A fellow I met in a bar. Can't recall his name."

"Was it Mongo Malagate?"

"Never heard of him."

"Last chance, Patch. You'll be doing yourself a favor if you help us."

"Don't do myself no favors telling stories about Malagate."

"That's all from us. Thank you, constable."

Jaeger pressed a button and the glorious view of the Thaumaturge reappeared.

"Well, he didn't tell us much, but it's obvious he knows who Malagate is. That's better than nothing. That's about all we can do today."

"There is one thing more, sir," said Tyng, and produced a small rectangular piece of plastic. "I found this on Patch. It's a parking permit for the lot at the Spaceport, and it includes the identification code of the permit-holder's ship. I thought I would wander over to the Spaceport and see what I can learn."

"Should that not have been done right away?" asked Gersen. "The ship could be gone by now."

"Unfortunately, it was already gone. As soon as I finished with the constables, I called the Spaceport. The ship had left. My guess is that when Patch failed to return promptly, those were their orders. However, there still may be some things I can pick up from the Spaceport ground personnel. There's usually all kinds of chatter between spacemen and ground people. You never know what might have been said."

On the next afternoon, Gersen found himself back in Jaeger's office, where Ensign Tyng had an interesting piece of news.

"It cost me a beer at the Spaceport Canteen, but I was able to interview the ground crew member who was the last aboard Patch's ship before it left. By coincidence, he happened to notice that the Nav screen was set for Sector B-127. To have that reading logged in so close to launch makes it a fair bet that was the direction they were heading."

Gersen was momentarily encouraged, but the sense that they were making progress vanished almost as quickly as it arrived. There were 100 billion stars in the Galaxy, which for navigational purposes had been divided into 10,000 sectors, B-127 being one. This still left 10 million stars, on average, in that sector. A smaller haystack, perhaps, but still hiding a very tiny needle. As if anticipating this thought process, Ensign Tyng continued:

"I took the liberty of requesting UTCS to compile a list of all the potentially habitable solar systems in B-127. This reduced the search field to 1,424 candidate systems."

There seemed to be no alternative but to laboriously plow through this reduced, but still formidable inventory of possibilities, so Gersen, Jaeger, and Tyng set to work, bringing them up one at a time on the screen in Jaeger's office.

Gamble's Gamble, second planet of Bellerophon 14-61, first surveyed by locater Slack Gamble in 1492. Hot and dry with soil unsuitable for agriculture. Possible mining opportunity in rare earths.

Braxton's Folly, sixth planet of Kalliope 17-C21, locater Struther Braxton reports surface area 90% ocean, with land mass filled with active volcanoes. Possible seafood export business.

Gaia's Glen, sole planet of Gaia 76, gravity 1.26 Earth standard, atmosphere in need of oxygen supplement. Reportedly settled by a small colony of Third Morning Adventists, but a tramp freighter found no sign of survivors as of 1512.

And so forth…

✳

After two hours, the trio had isolated thirty-two possible targets, having screened some 200 candidates, or less than 20% of the UTCS list. Gersen was beginning to feel bleary-eyed, and sensed that the others shared his mental fatigue.

Jaeger emitted a choked groan of frustration, shut down the screen, stood up, and began to pace around his office.

"There must be a better way than this," he said. "Let me think."

He sat down behind his desk, with his head in his hands, and remained that way for perhaps a minute, then looked up.

"I've figured out what's been bothering me. The Grabhorne mission. When was that? 1535, I think. I was the Nav officer for that project. And I believe Grabhorne was in Sector B-127."

Jaeger strode back to the screen, and tapped some codes into his monitor. Sure enough, Grabhorne appeared on the UTCS list of Sector B-127 possibilities.

"This was Attel Malagate's plantation," said Jaeger. "If Patch was one of Mongo Malagate's hirelings, and his ship was heading to B-127, I'll give you heavy odds that Mongo has set up shop on Attel Malagate's old base. This means we change our plans. The original idea was to send Henry Lucas to wherever Malagate would convey the piano tuner, and his purpose was to find out where that would be. That no longer seems necessary. What we need to do instead is to dispatch a survey team. If they detect activity on Grabhorne, then we've found Malagate."

Gersen nodded his acquiescence. But he felt mixed relief and disappointment. Relief because the piano tuner gambit had always seemed bizarre, but disappointment because his role in bringing Malagate to justice now appeared obviated.

"I suppose then that I am relieved of duty," he said.

"At least for the time it takes to dispatch a survey team and get their report," Jaeger replied. "We seem to be on the right track, but if you don't mind standing by, that would be appreciated."

"How long are we talking about?" asked Gersen.

"I would think two weeks — three at the most, depending on what the survey team finds."

Gersen smiled. "I suppose I can manage that. I have no pressing plans."

"Well, as I said, that would be appreciated."

"Perhaps you could do me a favor in return."

"As long as it's legal and inexpensive."

"There are two unsavory characters I would like to track down. Perhaps I could give their descriptions to Ensign Tyng and see what she can come up with."

"No problem," said Jaeger. "If the two of you would confer in the outer office, I have some calls I need to return."

Gersen and Ensign Tyng adjourned to the outer office, where Gersen related to her as much as he could remember about the two White Island assailants. She promised to send him a report via coded transmission by the close of business the next day. They entered the elevator together and as they glided silently toward ground level, Gersen found that he was quite taken by the young lady. She was mentally sharp and physically competent, two qualities that he admired. Her skin tone and close-cropped hair seemed a bit severe, perhaps an intentional aim at plainness, that matched the utilitarian aspect of her IPCC attire. He could see, though, that with only modest alteration in her dress and appearance, she would be quite fetching. Gersen briefly toyed with the idea of asking her to join him for the evening, but then restrained himself. Better to stick to business — at least for now. They parted company at the front entrance, and moved off in separate directions.

Darkness found Gersen in his quarters at the Credenza, staring out to sea as the majestic starlight of the Rigel system cast a luminescent pattern on the waves. Why, he asked himself, had he declined to invite Lori Tyng to join him that evening? Was it shyness? Certainly not. She would have accepted, he was sure. Instead, it was his ever-present reservation about mixing business with pleasure. This, for him, was not some puritanical aphorism, but a hesitancy learned from bitter experience. His obsessions left no room for romantic attachments, and his was a history of failed relationships. Alusz Iphigenia, the lovely Thamberite princess whom he had rescued from the Demon Prince, Kokor Hekkus, surely would have settled down with him. But there still remained three Demon Princes alive, and as she saw him, the pursuit of their destruction had left him spiritually starved. With sadness, she had returned to Thamber. Pallis Atwrode, charming and innocent, had been the first woman to have found him interesting, but had been caught in the evil web of his quest to destroy the first Malagate.

Then his thoughts turned to Drusilla Wayles, perhaps the most painful memory of all. She had been created by the third Demon Prince, Viole Falushe, to serve for his exclusive pleasure. Gersen had rescued Drusilla and sent Falushe plunging 10,000 feet to a watery death; but when Drusilla had begged him to take her with him, he demurred. His fascination was too intense to bear the thought of losing her as he had lost Alusz Iphigenia, and there were still two Demon Princes at large. So he had sent her back to Earth in the care of the erratic but compassionate Navarth, along with her identical four-year-old twin, another of Falushe's creations who he thought of as Drusilla IV. He had promised himself that he would visit, but he never had; Drusilla would have been a prize for any man and he doubtless would have found her comfortably settled. He could barely tolerate such a speculation, much less the reality.

Now he was embarked on yet another quest, and he had no wish to repeat the pain of loss.

CHAPTER V

Life is like a wind that blows where it wills; we hear the sound
but cannot divine from whence it comes or whither it goes.
— Navarth the Mad Poet

—⁓—

E arly the next morning, Gersen was on his way out of Suite 615
when he noticed a fresh communication on his screen. He
wished to avoid being late for his session with Lex, who treated
time with the same meticulous care that he applied to his instructions,
so he gave the transmission's salutation only a cursory glance. It said
'Good Luck' and was initialed 'ELT.' He smiled to himself as he strode
down the hall to the elevator. Ensign Tyng must have worked very late
last night or risen very early this morning to complete her report by
this hour. A determined young lady, he elevated her another notch in
his already high estimation.

He returned from the workout with Lex feeling pleased that he
was approaching top form, and proceeded directly to the screen to
see what Tyng had discovered for him. First was a police photograph
of the long-armed thug with a placard identifying him as Igor Zhufsa.
The occasion of the photograph was a conviction for robbery and
assault on the planet Kallirhoe, with a notation that he had escaped
from a work gang three years earlier. Current whereabouts unknown.
There was no further information about his place of origin or past
employment. Well, Gersen thought to himself, we don't need to worry
about Zhufsa's whereabouts or employment — he's feeding crabs in the
waters off White Island.

Next on the screen was what appeared to be a surveillance

photograph — a distant shot enhanced by technicians to produce a granular but nevertheless closer view. It was almost certainly the snake-eyed intruder with purple-tinted skin whose shoulder Gersen had dislocated in the White Island scuffle. The subject of the photograph was identified as Lom Kutz, last known domicile Hobson's Hole, on the world Ouranos, in the Kronos system. He had served five years for attempted kidnapping, and had been released several years ago. There were no further convictions, but the entry added that he was currently suspected of hijacking and trafficking in stolen goods. The surveillance photograph had the notation 'IPCC Trooper S. Kingsley MPD.' The letters MPD, Gersen knew from unfortunate experience, signified 'Missing Presumed Deceased.' One final entry caused Gersen's brow to furrow: 'Last known employer: Galactic Freight.'

Gersen felt his thoughts being locked into the sort of mental intensity that always seemed to portend an important decision. He seated himself in front of the screen, typed out a brief "Thank You" to Ensign Tyng, then opened up the *Handbook to the Planets* and tapped in the codes for Ouranos:

> *Ouranos was discovered by locater Wilder Hobson in the year 1312. It is the third orbital planet of Kronos, a Sol-sized green-white star. Its diameter is approximately 7,100 miles and it has a mass of .92 Earth standard. The terrain is mostly volcanic rock, with a single modest-sized ocean at the equator. The only vegetation is algae, and there are no indigenous fauna.*
>
> *In his survey of the planet, Hobson found only one item of possible commercial interest — a large deposit of high-quality marble. As his discovery was made during the heyday of interplanetary exploration, with opportunities being revealed in abundance, and fortunes being made across the Oikumene, Hobson was able to persuade an investment group to provide the funds necessary to establish a quarry, and to found the small village of Hobson's Hole that would support its workers. The quarry initially secured a modest export market, but since there were no domestic sources of goods or food of any kind, the cost of imports soon exceeded the export earnings and, as the best veins of marble were eventually exhausted, the project was*

abandoned after three decades. The population of Hobson's Hole shrank to a handful of diehards, including Hobson himself.

Proving once again that it is better to be lucky than good, Hobson's Hole secured a new lease on life as a trans-shipping port, due to its felicitous location with respect to sixty-two other planets, at a time when the boom in interplanetary trade was just getting off the ground…

Here Gersen's concentration was interrupted by a wry laugh, as he imagined the writers of the *Handbook to the Planets*, who had the mind-numbing task of creating and editing several hundred thousand entries of this type and must occasionally subject themselves to linguistic foolishness.

Ouranos was positioned within convenient Intersplit distance of this collection of sixty-two planets, thus becoming a popular hub for 3,782 trade pairs, for which trans-shipment was economically superior to direct service.

The original village of Hobson's Hole expanded to become a modest city of some 50,000 inhabitants, mostly involved in stevedoring, warehousing, and the servicing of visiting space-freighters. Hobson, having bought out his original backers for centimes on the SVU, retained ground leases on all properties and became quite prosperous until his death in 1378.

In recent years, a modest hostelry trade has been established to serve interplanetary passengers seeking to exploit the efficiencies of Ouranos' hub-and-spoke capability. Length of stays of these itinerants, however, is rarely more than two or three days, and preferably fewer, as Ouranos is devoid of tourist attractions.

As he read the information about Ouranos in the *Handbook to the Planets*, a plan was forming in Gersen's mind. When he completed the report, he entered the codes for his private account at UTCS, and was amused to be greeted by the voice of Eleanor. Evidently, UTCS had decided that henceforth Eleanor would be his designated representative.

"Good morning, Mr. Lucas. How may I help you?"

"Good morning, Eleanor. I'd like you to calculate the round-trip travel time between the Rigel and Kronos systems."

"Using what mode of transport, sir?"

"A ship powered by the Jarnell LF."

"I'm sorry, sir, but Jarnell lists that technology as experimental. They have not released performance data."

"Then take the speed of a standard Model 9B, and increase it by a factor of one-point-seven."

"My goodness, Mr. Lucas. That seems highly speculative."

"Please do it anyway, Eleanor."

"UTCS does not want to be held responsible for any losses resulting from actual travel times being less than projected."

"I will take that responsibility. You may record that I am releasing your employer from liability with respect to your calculation of travel times."

There was a brief pause while Eleanor ran the numbers. Then she reported:

"Assuming departure and arrival at the median position of each solar system, round trip flight time for the hypothesized speeds specified by the client, for which UTCS disclaims responsibility, is 12 days, 4 hours, and 6 minutes."

"Thank you, Eleanor, that was very helpful. But please do not save those speeds in your data-base as estimates of the Jarnell LF's performance. Jarnell considers that information proprietary."

"Of course, sir."

Gersen knew full well that the information would in fact go into the UTCS data-base, as they saved everything. But he was not concerned. In fact, the actual performance of his *Quicksilver* was closer to 2.6 times that of a standard Model 9B, so he had not betrayed any confidential Jarnell information. He could adjust Eleanor's data with a simple calculation on an antique vernier.

"That will be all, then, Eleanor."

"Very good, sir." There was a brief hesitation, in which time the screen would normally close, but Eleanor apparently had an additional thought.

"If you don't mind my saying so, sir, Ouranos has only one settled community; it has no tourist attractions whatsoever, and the population is reported to include criminal elements."

"I am aware of that, but thank you for pointing it out. I will be sure to exercise caution."

"That's good to hear, sir. The welfare of our clients is of paramount importance."

The screen went blank. Perhaps, Gersen mused, UTCS was overdoing its SI function a bit. But then his attention turned to other matters. He could easily make the trip to Ouranos, spend two or three days tracking down this Lom Kutz character, and return, well within the two-week window that Jaeger had said the scouting mission to Grabhorne would require. First, he called the Spaceport and told them to ready *Quicksilver* for a morning departure. Then a note to Lex cancelling his appointments for the next two weeks. A note to Jaeger saying he would be out of communication for a few days, but would return within the two-week window. A lengthier note to Kim, who would be arriving from Earth while he was gone, advising where he was going and why. In the event of unexpected difficulties, Kim would know what to do. He debated advising Addels of his plan, but decided not to. Addels would only fret, and probably advise him not to go. There was nothing else he needed to prepare for the trip as *Quicksilver* was already equipped with whatever weapons and personal effects he would need.

With his mind clear, as it always was when all preparations were in place, he would spend a relaxed evening and be ready to depart at early light.

Four days later found Gersen guiding *Quicksilver* into a gentle equatorial orbit ten miles above Ouranos, on an easterly route into the pale greenish light of Kronos. The *Handbook to the Planets* had not understated the planet's barrenness. Its surface was coated with an endless expanse of reddish-brown algae, interrupted only by polar ice and the snow-capped peaks of several mountain ranges. A small ocean thrust a finger-like bay toward the single identifiable settlement, a cluster of whitish structures that must have comprised Hobson's Hole.

Gersen allowed *Quicksilver* to descend for a closer look, and was able to discern a small spaceport on the outskirts of the town, with some dozen vessels of various shapes and sizes parked in a disorderly array. There being no landing protocol specified in the *Handbook to the Planets*, Gersen picked an empty spot and set *Quicksilver* down amidst a swirl of disturbed algae dust. A subdued hissing sound confirmed that the vessel was automatically fine-tuning her atmosphere to match local conditions, which were reported to be close to Earth normal.

Gersen exchanged his space garb for a pearl grey business suit, consistent with the identity he planned to assume of a prosperous commercial traveler. If the population of Hobson's Hole was, as cautioned by Eleanor, suffused with criminal elements, there was likely to be an active de-weaseling unit, and Gersen had no desire to share the apparent fate of IPCC trooper S. Kingsley. He supposed that no one would mistake *Quicksilver* for an IPCC vessel, nor a well-dressed gentleman for a weasel. He conducted a final check of his weapons and, there being no de-boarding gantry in sight, lowered himself to the spaceport deck on *Quicksilver*'s auxiliary disembarkation unit. Once on solid ground, he sent the unit back to the cockpit, where it would automatically lock the ship down and could be recalled with a thumb-print-activated touch-pad.

Looking around, he saw a dilapidated, open-top slidecar heading his way from what looked like a shabby, marble-fronted terminal building. The driver was a big-bellied, ruddy-faced man wearing a khaki sleeveless shirt that displayed tan and well-muscled forearms.

"Discharging or picking up?" he called out as he approached.

"Neither one," said Gersen. "I'm here on business."

The man uttered a low-pitched grunt of disbelief. "Business, eh? What brings a slick dandy like you in a ship like that to 'The Hole'?"

"Well," Gersen replied genially. "I'm looking for a man."

"And who might that be?"

"Lom Kutz. Do you know him?"

"Can't say that I do. But if he's here, you'll find him easy enough — it's a small town. How long do you plan to stay?"

"Only as long as it takes. Maybe a day or two. As you say, it's a small town."

The driver tugged at his chin doubtfully. "Still don't make sense —

flying that rig all this way just to find a man. What do you want him for?"

"My company wants to hire him. And this is a company boat, not mine."

"Is that so. What company?"

"Braemar."

"Don't know them. What do they want to hire this man for?"

"I don't know. I'm just a messenger. How much do I owe you?"

"We charge by the day — 50 SVU."

Relieved that the conversation was getting down to money, and away from the purpose of his visit, Gersen reached into a pocket and produced some notes. "Can't imagine I will be more than three days. Here's 150 SVU in advance. If I finish early, keep the difference. Then we will both be lucky. By the way, I'm Henry Lucas."

"Marlo Thong — Terminal Manager," the man said. His expression brightened and he took the notes. "Hop in and I'll give you a ride to the terminal."

Gersen jumped aboard and the slidecar started off. "What do you do about security here," he asked.

"No problem on that account," said his new friend Marlo. "We're all in the shipping business at The Hole. What folks do off-planet is up to them, but at this facility, nobody messes with anybody else's boat. Any trouble and I can have a dozen enforcers here in five minutes."

"That's good to know," said Gersen, thinking that was true in more ways than one. If he was discovered to be an undesirable, the response would be quick and numerically awkward.

"What about transport into town?" was Gersen's next question.

"Most people walk. It's about thirty-five minutes, if you have a long stride and don't mind the rain."

Just as Marlo spoke, Gersen felt himself pelted by a few large raindrops that presaged a cloudburst from the ominous black cloud formation that had moved in off the ocean. He jumped into the shelter of the terminal and brushed the water off his shoulders.

"Is there no other way?"

"Well, there's Tush Tuttle, if he's awake. Want me to call him?"

"Please do."

Five minutes later another slidecar rolled up to the front entrance, this one even more battered than the one operated by Marlo, but at least it was a hard-top version. Tuttle was a scrawny antique of a man with a white beard and rheumy eyes.

"What's the fare, here to town?" Gersen asked.

Tuttle tugged at his chin and looked Gersen up and down, as if gauging what the market would bear, "Five SVU."

"I'll give you twenty SVU to take me to town and back, and stay with me for the day. Ten now, and ten when we return."

"Fair enough," said Tuttle, and pushed the passenger door open.

The slidecar proceeded toward town on a track that was no more than disturbed algae, the dust from which at least had settled down due to the rain. Gersen noted ironically that the vehicle rolled and rattled on faltering air cushions, moving scarcely faster than Marlo's image of a long-strided walk. The shower had passed, leaving behind a heavy mist. The car entered what seemed to be the town's main street, flanked on either side by low buildings constructed entirely of marble. It would have been an impressive sight, thought Gersen, except that these blocks were cracked, stained, chipped, and otherwise disfigured — evidently rejects from the former quarry's quality control inspectors. Pedestrian traffic was sparse, slow-moving figures in dark capes or ponchos, hunched against the heavy mist, wearing broad-brimmed slouch hats pulled low over their features. What little signage there was to be seen referred to warehouses, freight forwarders, or dealers in unclaimed goods. Then Gersen saw some letters scratched crudely into the façade of one of the buildings:

HOBSON'S HAVEN
FOOD AND DRINK

"Pull up here," he told Tuttle, "and wait for me."

Tuttle did as he was told, Gersen climbed out and entered the building. He paused in the entryway as his eyes adjusted to the low light provided by several small marble braziers burning something that he guessed were clumps of algae. The room was a low-ceilinged affair, in which half a dozen table-size marble blocks were distributed

haphazardly, each surrounded by smaller blocks that provided seating. Clusters of patrons sat at several of the tables, hunched over what
looked like mugs carved out of marble.

"What will it be?" came a booming voice from behind another row
of blocks that evidently served as a bar. Gersen glanced toward the
sound, and observed the bartender, a massive brute, distinguished by
his roan-colored skin, and slick hairless pate.

"I'm looking for someone. Perhaps you can help me," said Gersen.

"I don't make conversation with *iskish* who aren't customers,"
snorted the bartender, who Gersen now recognized without a doubt to
be Darsh, a native of the planet Dar Sai where Gersen had experienced
some memorable times many years earlier. The Darsh, like this one,
were a swaggering, flamboyant tribe, but not necessarily mean-spirited
unless provoked. *Iskish* was their term for non-Darsh.

"What's on offer, then?"

"Beer."

"What kind?"

"Only one kind, brewed from the finest local algae. No match for
Dar Sai beer, but drinkers can't be choosers."

"I'll have beer, then," said Gersen, in the most accommodating
tone he could muster. He remembered the Darsh beer, also distilled
from local algae. It was repulsive stuff, but he guessed the local version couldn't be worse. The bartender plunked a marble mug in front
of Gersen, and scooped up the five SVU note that Gersen had laid on
the counter. Gersen took a careful sip — he was wrong, this was worse.

"Now that I am a customer in good standing," he said, "perhaps you
can help me. I'm looking for a man called Kutz — Lom Kutz."

"What do you want with him?"

"My company wants to hire him."

The Darsh uttered a disgusted expletive. "Half the men in this room
can do whatever you want this Kutz *iskish* for. Why don't you try one
of them?"

"Not possible," said Gersen, "I have my orders."

"Errand boy, eh? Well, I can't help you. I don't know this Kutz person."

"Thanks anyway," said Gersen and turned to leave.

"You didn't finish your beer," the bartender called after him.

"Sorry, short on time," Gersen called back from the entrance. "Keep the change." The latter comment being superfluous, as the bartender had already pocketed the 5 SVU note.

Gersen hoisted himself back into Tuttle's vehicle, and asked, "Are there any more taverns like this in town?"

"Just one," replied Tuttle, "but it's not so nice as this one. Not recommended, I should advise you."

"Take me there, anyway."

Tuttle shrugged his shoulders, but withheld comment. He proceeded a distance that Gersen estimated to be two standard city blocks, stopped outside an alleyway, and gestured with a head movement. "In there," he said, "if you're still of a mind to go."

Gersen exited the vehicle and sauntered to the entryway at the end of the alley, where he paused and looked inside. The place was smaller and even gloomier than Hobson's Haven, with no more than half a dozen occupants, slouched over marble mugs in what seemed to be the standard leisure-time position of the town's denizens. But there, in the corner to Gersen's right, was a solitary figure whose right arm was in a sling, and who was unmistakably Lom Kutz. Gersen walked over and stood looking down, while Kutz stared fixedly at his mug.

"Hello, Lom," Gersen said, "how have you been?"

"Do I know you?"

"I think you do. Henry Lucas."

Kutz looked up, transferring the fixed stare from his mug to Gersen. He had the same narrow features, purple-tinted skin, and bare scalp that Gersen remembered from their White Island encounter. He examined Gersen with a dead-eyed look that prompted Gersen to half-expect a forked tongue to emerge flickering out from between his closed lips.

"That was a dirty move you made on me. Won't be so lucky next time."

Gersen ignored the comment and took a seat adjacent to Kutz. "I have two simple questions for you. Who sent you, and where were you going to take me?"

Instead of replying, Kutz's left hand darted toward his waist, but

Gersen moved faster, locked onto his wrist and twisted hard, forcing him to drop a small projac.

"I have nothing to say to you," said Kutz, while he rubbed his wrist.

Gersen picked up the projac and sat quietly gazing at Kutz. After a few moments, he asked: "Do you feel that tingling on your wrist? I administered cluthe. Do you know what that is?"

"Cluthe? That is a Sarkoy poison. You are not Sarkoy."

"No, but I learned the art of poison on Sarkovy, from Guild Master Litsas."

When he heard the name of a legendary venefice, Kutz's features became distorted with what could have been anger, fear, or both.

"Do you doubt me?" asked Gersen. "Then wait and see. The tingling on your wrist grows worse. I should administer the antidote within seven minutes, five to be safe. After that, cluthe will have spread through your body. There will be nothing I can do, and you will die the most painful of deaths. Have you ever seen a man die from cluthe? It is not a pleasant sight."

Kutz hissed air out between his teeth, "Give me the antidote."

"First, answer my questions. Who sent you, where were you going to take me, and for what purpose?"

"I don't know where we were going. My job was to get you on the ship."

We're making progress, Gersen thought. Once the subject starts talking, the going becomes easier. "For what purpose?"

"That I also do not know. I was told only that there was a business matter to discuss, and you would be more favorably disposed to bargain after enjoying my employer's hospitality."

"And who was the employer?"

Kutz took on a desperate look. "I must not say the name."

"Your choice," said Gersen. "Take your time. Is the sensation getting worse? I would say you had two minutes left, possibly a few seconds more if you want to press your luck."

Kutz rubbed his wrist on his pantleg. "It burns," he groaned.

"Almost there," said Gersen.

Kutz let out an anguished sigh. "Bolfo," he whispered.

"Very good," said Gersen. "Now, a bonus question for good measure.

What did Mr. Bolfo say when you returned without me?"

"He was not a happy man. I was fired, of course."

"You did not explain that I had played a dirty trick?"

"Of course not. Do you think I would admit that Zhufsa and I were defeated by an old man and a midget? If he had known the truth, he'd have fed me to one of his pet bunters. I told him that the rappelling line slipped and dropped me on my shoulder, and that Zhufsa wandered over a cliff in the dark and fell into the sea."

Gersen allowed himself a sardonic smile, "That would be half true."

"The antidote!" cried Kutz.

Gersen rose from his seat, displaying the projac casually, and backed toward the entrance.

"The antidote!" came Kutz's anguished cry again, but Gersen was gone.

Gersen moved briskly to the end of the alley, where he discovered Tuttle snoozing soundly in his waiting vehicle. Gersen jumped in and shook Tuttle awake. "Back to the spaceport, Tuttle. Make your best speed."

Tuttle maneuvered the car 180 degrees, and headed back the way they had come. As they passed the alley, Gersen could make out several figures emerging from the entrance of the tavern.

"Faster!" he admonished Tuttle, although he could see that Tuttle had the speed lever hard over.

Tuttle's slidecar rocked along on wheezing air cushions at agonizingly slow speed. Gersen took a backward look and could see a band of at least half a dozen figures in pursuit and gaining. At the terminal entrance, Gersen handed Tuttle the 10 SVU he was due, and strode into the building. Marlo the Terminal Manager was nowhere in sight, so Gersen headed out onto the landing field and trotted briskly toward *Quicksilver*. On his way, he passed four figures in space attire heading in the opposite direction, from a ship with yellow and green stripes and 'Galactic Freight' emblazoned on its hull. The four stopped to stare briefly at the spectacle of a suavely dressed businessman jogging toward a luxurious boat, while Gersen threw them a jaunty salute as he passed. He reached *Quicksilver*, called down the boarding platform, and was soon in the cockpit pressing buttons and turning dials in preparation for takeoff. As *Quicksilver* whined to full power and lifted off in a reddish froth of algae dust, Gersen chuckled to himself at the sight of a pack of angry pursuers, led by Kutz, bursting out of the terminal. By now, he thought, Kutz had discovered that the burning on his wrist was a preparation the Sarkoy called 'false cluthe,' and he was not going to die. Within several minutes, Kronos was a fading light green speck; Gersen engaged the Intersplit and was gone.

Gersen's flight back to Alphanor was uneventful. On arrival, he was pleased to find that Kim had returned to Avente from closing the lodge at White Island, and had settled into his own quarters adjoining those of Gersen on the sixth floor of the Credenza. Gersen's first order of business, after messaging Jaeger that he was back and awaiting news from the Grabhorne surveillance mission, was to brief Jehan Addels on what he had learned. He included Kim on the call, and the conversation was one that the three would remember for years to come.

Gersen began by relating for Addels' benefit the attempted kidnapping of Gersen (as Henry Lucas) on White Island, emphasizing Kim's role in thwarting it. Then, how through the good offices of the IPCC, he had learned the identity and location of Lom Kutz, one of the assailants, and had traveled to Hobson's Hole on Ouranos to confront Kutz.

"Hobson's Hole was a dismal place," Geresen reported. "I will be glad to never return there. One can see, however, that it is an important logistical hub for the interplanetary space trade, including especially an operation like Galactic Freight, at least one of whose ships I saw parked there. To make the story short, Kutz confessed that he had been sent to White Island by none other than Bruno Bolfo, and the purpose of abducting me was to make me amenable to some sort of business transaction. In view of what you told me earlier, Jehan, about ripples in the quiet pond of the financial world, we must conclude that if we were aware of a pending sale of Jarnell shares, so was Bolfo. Further, if we could guess that Bolfo would be our main competitor, so could Bolfo guess that Henry Lucas would be his. And his goal in the White Island abduction was to neutralize that competition.

"We must be especially vigilant now, because if Bolfo tried once to use abduction as a means to achieve his goals, he may well try again.

And you, Jehan, could also be a target. After all, you have complete discretion in the disposition of holdings that are legally in my name. You should arrange for around-the-clock protection by the most competent security service in New Wexford. In addition, I am going to dispatch Kim to support this effort."

There was a moment of silence on the line, as Addels came to grips with the prospect that he could be at risk of a violent attack. Addels was a man of iron will in financial matters, but not one of physical courage. In that sense, he and Gersen were perfect complements, Gersen being physically fearless, but a will-o-the-wisp where money was concerned. Addels would welcome Kim's presence, though, as he and Kim had developed a mutually respectful relationship.

After that pause, Addels replied, "Yes, I suppose it is only prudent to do what you say. But what about your own security?"

"I have a reliable system here in Avente, but will take steps to reinforce it. In the meanwhile, I have been thinking about possible ways to locate Bolfo. This could be a case where a good offense is the best defense."

"I will put my mind to work on that as well," Addels said. "For the moment, however, if there is nothing further, I am going to see to the security arrangements."

"There is one more thing," said Gersen. "Kutz said something whose meaning escaped me. He said that if Bolfo knew the truth of his failure, he would feed Kutz to his bunters. I have no idea what he was talking about, but possibly it was significant."

"I can help with that," interjected Kim. "The bunter is a large, six-legged animal that can be tamed to be ridden, although they are vicious and the sport is dangerous. There are two species — one originating on Cadwal, and the other on my home world Solitaire. When interbred, they produce a beast of exceptional speed and endurance. These specially bred bunters are used for racing, although because of the strain from Solitaire, they are also carnivorous. My guess is that the remark about feeding Kutz to Bolfo's bunters tells us that Bolfo has a stable of highly bred racers."

Although Gersen had learned to never be surprised by the insights that came from Kim, he could not restrain his astonishment at this one. "How do you know so much about these bunters?" he asked.

"Simple, my cousin Kwan is a professional jockey. He learned the art on Solitaire, and is one of the best riders on the racing circuit, which is now located on yet a third planet — Rosalia. This is a sport not well known to the public, however. The cost of breeding and keeping racing bunters limits participation to the extremely wealthy — not more than perhaps two dozen stables. Among each other, it is a competition for bragging rights, and it is intense. They try to avoid publicity, though, because the fatality rate among riders, trainers, and stable hands would shock the public and produce demands for regulation."

"Perhaps your cousin would have some ideas about where to locate Bolfo, if Bolfo is one of these competitors."

"I will inquire," said Kim, and the call ended.

Several days passed, and then a call came in from Jaeger. His features were a mask of tension, his jaw locked, his eyes narrowed to slits.

"The Grabhorne surveillance mission accomplished its goal," he reported. "Grabhorne is clearly Malagate's base. The slave quarters have been rebuilt, and slaves could be observed at work."

"Good news," said Gersen. "No need for a piano tuner, then."

"I'm afraid that's not the case. The goal of discovering Malagate's location is no longer necessary. But a new objective has arisen."

"How so?"

"Malagate has a Thribolt cannon. It must be located and neutralized before we can launch a rescue mission."

"A Thribolt cannon? How do you know?" Gersen asked, although he feared he knew the answer as soon as he uttered the question.

"The Thribolt cannon destroyed our surveillance craft."

Gersen's focus was shaken by this news. The results of a direct hit on a spacecraft by a Thribolt cannon would be the vessel's utter disintegration, along with all its crew. Nothing would remain but scattered molecules dissipated in space.

"The crew was lost?" Again, he knew the question to be redundant before it left his lips.

"All four," said Jaeger. "Including Ensign Tyng."

Chapter VI

Excerpt from *Modern Weaponry* by E. Mortimer Snerd:

Chapter 7
The Thribolt Cannon

The invention of the Jarnell Intersplit, as has been well documented, enabled humanity to explore for, discover, and inhabit countless planets throughout what came to be known as *The Oikumene*, or civilized universe. Unfortunately, the same Jarnell technology also facilitated a rapid rise in interplanetary piracy. Raiders could base themselves out of the reach of civil authorities — that is, in the Beyond — then enter the Oikumene at will to raid, pillage, and enslave inhabited worlds. The pirate vessels, powered by the Intersplit, could achieve speeds that made them invulnerable to conventional weapons, thus rendering the victimized populations essentially helpless. A new defense mechanism was needed, and needed urgently. Jarnell came to the rescue with a cannon named the Thribolt. This was only fitting, since it was Jarnell technology that had enabled the pirates in the first place.

The underlying mechanism of the Thribolt is, of course, a closely guarded secret. The layman's version, however, is that the cannon launches an Intersplit-powered projectile that explodes on contact. The velocity of the impact, as much as the force of the explosion, serves to utterly destroy the target. Within ranges that spacecraft need to shut down their own Intersplit propulsion units to avoid collision with the intended victim planet — say a million miles or so — the Thribolt's missile reaches its target virtually instantaneously, such that the target has no chance of taking evasive action.

———ɯ———

Two days later, Gersen found himself in the hotel courtesy car, driven by Bane, a highly trained and trusted bodyguard, heading south from downtown Avente toward the IPCC technology center in Remo, adjacent to Sea Province University. The proximity to SPU dredged up old memories — of Detteras, Kelle, and Warweave — and of the fateful journey to Teehalt's Planet. However, all that was long in the past, and this morning Gersen could not stop himself from replaying in his mind his angry exchange with Jaeger two days earlier. Why, he had challenged Jaeger, had Ensign Tyng been allowed to join the surveillance team? How could I deny her? Jaeger had shot back. She had requested the assignment and had earned the right to participate. After all, it was largely due to her initiative that we were able to identify Grabhorne as Malagate's likely base.

Still not satisfied, Gersen had demanded to know why Jaeger had not considered the danger. All missions have their risks, Jaeger had declared, and this one, which was only surveillance after all, had seemed routine. Was Gersen suggesting that he should limit Tyng to clerical duties in the records department?

To that question, Gersen had no answer. He was forced to admit to himself that his anger was due to the sorrow of losing Tyng, for whom he had felt a growing affection even though he scarcely knew her. In the end, he acknowledged that Jaeger was right.

The conversation then turned to the altered nature of 'Operation Broadwood,' as the IPCC had labelled it. The original plan, Jaeger reminded Gersen, was to have Gersen gain access to Malagate's location, simply to find out where it was. Now, of course, they knew where it was — on Grabhorne. However, as long as Malagate's base was defended by a Thribolt cannon, any attempt to rescue the kidnap victims on Grabhorne would be suicidal. Therefore, the new mission, if Gersen was still willing to undertake it, was to gain access to Malagate's base, locate the Thribolt cannon, and render it ineffective. That, of course, would be immeasurably more difficult, not to mention more dangerous, than simply finding out where Malagate was located. Jaeger had then asked the central question:

"The help wanted requests for a piano tuner are still appearing in various publications. With the new objective of posing as the piano tuner to gain access to Grabhorne and render the Thribolt cannon inoperative, are you still willing?"

Gersen did not have to consider long. His anger at Lori Tyng's loss was transferred against the one truly responsible: Malagate.

"Yes," he had replied.

A few minutes ahead of the appointed schedule, Bane pulled up at the front entrance of the IPCC Technical Center. Quite unlike IPCC's downtown headquarters, the technical center was a structure of understated elegance. The façade was constructed of polished granite columns interspersed by plates of glass refined from spent solar slag — transparent as normal glass, but resistant to even the most powerful hand weapon. As Gersen entered the lobby, he noted that it was floored with marble tile, and amused himself with the thought that this material had possibly been quarried on Ouranos.

A young officer at the desk greeted him, "Mr. Darby? Dr. Stingley is expecting you."

Gersen was impressed that the IPCC was already identifying him by the name he would assume — Edgar Darby — in his piano tuner role. Dr. Stingley, of course, was the IPCC Technical Director, a high-ranking position, perhaps at the same level as Commander Jaeger, although Gersen had only rudimentary knowledge of the IPCC pecking order.

A whisper-quiet lift carried Gersen swiftly to the twenty-second floor, where he was guided down a brightly lit and spotlessly clean hallway to Stingley's office. As he always did when entering an office for the first time, Gersen cast a very quick glance around, and noticed that apart from the conspicuous orderliness of the room, its dominant feature was a window that provided a commanding view of the Thaumaturge, this time the real thing, Gersen supposed. Stingley himself was a man of below average stature, but with an air of energy and precision about him. He greeted Gersen with a warm smile and extended his hand.

"Mr. Darby, welcome to the Technical Center. I am Dr. Herbert Stingley—most of my colleagues call me Bert. Commander Jaeger has briefed me thoroughly on the operation you are about to undertake. Let me say on behalf of IPCC Tech that we are most mindful of the risks involved, and will commit our full resources to reducing these to a minimum."

Gersen could not help but be struck by the sincerity of Stingley's welcome, but he could not, as well, avoid a certain feeling of discomfort. His life had been spent confronting and overcoming risks on his own, and putting himself in the hands of others, no matter how well intentioned or competent, was a new and somewhat unsettling experience.

The rest of the day, with only a couple of brief breaks, was spent going through the most elaborate physical examination of Gersen's experience, including at the hands of the Living Clinic. All manner of technicians pushed, pulled, prodded and otherwise tested or measured everything it was possible to test or measure. At the end of it all, Gersen sat down with the Tech Center's Medical Director, Dr. Harriet Shansky, a severe-looking middle-aged woman in a white lab coat, with prematurely gray hair done in a tight bun.

"Well, Mr. Darby, I am pleased to report that you are in superb physical condition for a person of your age. Indeed, if you were twenty years younger, I would still give you that rating. I am therefore able to certify, with no qualms whatsoever, that you are fit for the planned mission. Do you have any questions?"

"Yes," said Gersen, "I spent the better part of an hour hooked up to something that looked like a plasma bag, as if I was getting a blood transfusion. What was that all about?"

"Indeed," replied Dr. Shansky, "that's exactly what it was. We have altered your blood type from A to O. Type O is what the IPCC files will show as the blood type for Edgar Darby, and of course is different from the blood types of any other person—I won't mention names, but you know who I mean—an investigator might suspect you of being. The alteration will last for at least 90 days, after which you will revert to type A."

Gersen found himself impressed by this level of thoroughness.

The information that had been given to Sligo Patch, that was presumably now in Malagate's hands, gave Kirth Gersen's blood type as B-. Moreover, if by chance Malagate had found some other way to gain access to IPCC's files, they would not show anything different for Kirth Gersen, but would show type A for Henry Lucas. It appeared that all the possibilities by which his disguise could be penetrated had been covered. He nodded his appreciation, then asked,

"What were they doing to the palms of my hands with that laser-like device?"

"Look closely at your palms," instructed Dr. Shansky.

Gersen did as he was told.

"Do you see those fine white lines, running from the base of your index and ring fingers to the lower part of each palm? Those are artificial scars. This is exactly what would appear on your hands if you had undergone surgery for something called 'DePuytrens Contracture.' In ancient times, this was quite a common disease; today, not so much, as there are techniques for treating it before it advances too far. Nevertheless, it does occur occasionally, causing the fingers to contract in such a way that they become unable to manage many simple tasks. In those cases, surgery is necessary. The fingers are thus liberated, so to speak, but nevertheless, the fingers remain permanently compromised with respect to certain delicate motions —"

Here Dr. Shansky paused, as if for effect, then smiled knowingly.

"— such as playing the piano."

Gersen smiled back, as he continued to study his palms. "I see," he said.

"It occurred to us," Dr. Shansky continued, "that in your role as a piano tuner, you would be expected at some point to play. Now, simply show the scars, and explain why that is infeasible. By the way, these scars, like your altered blood type, will disappear within several months, well beyond the completion of the mission."

"I've wondered how I would handle such a request," said Gersen. "Glad to have that issue out of the way. Thank you."

"Now, if you have no further questions," said Dr. Shansky, "the medical team would like to make a small contribution to your already impressive collection of skills."

Here, Dr. Shansky reached into the pocket of her lab coat and produced a small vial, with the flair of a magician conducting a card trick.

"We noticed during our investigation," she continued, "that you have an extremely acute olfactory system — that is, sense of smell. Your ability to detect odors is really quite remarkable, such that we conclude this is not naturally occurring but instead must result from some form of conditioning, because your abilities are beyond what would be found in 99.9% of normal humans. Can you explain?"

"Certainly," said Gersen. "I was trained on Sarkovy by a master venefice. The heightened sense of smell is most useful in detecting the presence of poisons, or even soporifics — for example, things that can be added surreptitiously to one's food or beverage."

"I see," said Dr. Shansky. "That does explain what we observed. But I have something here that could enhance those capabilities even further. This little vial contains a fluid that, when inhaled, will temporarily stimulate the olfactory sensors in your nasal passage. This could have many uses. The most obvious one is detecting Star Kings who, as you know, are for practical purposes impossible to distinguish from humans. They do, however, have a very subtle but nevertheless quite distinct odor which this olfactory-enhancing fluid will permit you to recognize. Another useful application is the ability to distinguish between humans who are lying and those who are telling the truth; when they are lying, their perspiration glands give off a certain scent which can be detected by an enhanced olfactory system."

"Very interesting," said Gersen. "I can think of any number of instances where this detection ability would be useful."

"A word of caution, though," said Dr. Shansky. "Use this fluid sparingly. Over-use will cause your olfactory system to pick up dozens or even hundreds of unfamiliar scents. Your brain will quickly become over-loaded and unable to process all this unfamiliar information, with potentially damaging consequences. We learned this much to our chagrin during the early trials, when one of our technicians over-used the fluid and had to be placed in a sanitarium for an extended period. A word to the wise, then."

"Understood," said Gersen, taking the vial. "I will be careful."

✳

The next morning, Gersen boarded an IPCC Flitterwing piloted by Bert Stingley. Their destination was the Jarnell Research Compound, some hundred miles inland. As the Flitterwing accelerated to cruising speed, the terrain below changed dramatically. Gone were the gleaming towers of Avente, and the long white beach extending both north and south of the city. Gone was the city's suburban residential belt. Then they were soaring over grasslands where occasional herds of ruminants could be seen. Soon enough, Stingley brought the aircraft into a gliding descent toward a group of low, stolid-looking iron-gray buildings, nestled in the foothills of a distant mountain range. Adjacent to the buildings, a substantial landing field had been carved out of the rolling hills, on which some two dozen spacecraft of various shapes and sizes could be seen. From personal experience, Gersen knew that this was where the Distis Spaceship Corporation brought their vessels for the final stage of the production process — to be equipped with the Jarnell Intersplit*. Indeed, he had last been here himself to witness the final outfitting of his own *Quicksilver*.

Stingley guided the Flitterwing to a small landing pad, not part of the main field, that was adjacent to one of the buildings. Here, there was an inconspicuous side-entrance flanked by two heavily armed guards in dark blue uniforms with gold 'J's emblazoned on the breast pockets. The guards had evidently been prepared for Gersen and Stingley's arrival, as they required no identification and instead tapped in a code that caused the door to slide open. The two visitors entered a small chamber at the opposite end of which an elevator door opened and a tall man, slender as a bean-pole, strode out with a welcoming grin.

"Good to see you, Bert," he saluted Stingley. Then, addressing Gersen, "Welcome to Jarnell Research, Mr. Darby."

This was Jarnell's Research Director, Rolf Woodward, and no introductions were necessary as he and Stingley obviously knew each other well. As for Gersen, Woodward of course knew him as Henry

---

* The fully manufactured spaceships would be flown in from Distis' own production facility, powered by conventional ion thrusters. Distis had long urged Jarnell to license the Intersplit technology so that Distis could perform its own installation. However, Jarnell had thus far declined, arguing that the technology was far too sensitive to be trusted to a non-Jarnell installer.

Lucas, both as the owner of Jarnell's most advanced spacecraft, and as a person linked in some important albeit undefined way to Braemar Investments, a 20% shareholder. By addressing Gersen as 'Darby,' he signaled that he had been briefed on the Grabhorne mission.

"We appreciate your cooperation on this project, Rolf," said Stingley.

Woodward's smile faded and his lips pursed. "We can scarcely do otherwise," he said. "We are deeply embarrassed that one of our weapons has fallen into criminal hands, and even more so that it has apparently been used to destroy an IPCC ship. This should never have happened, as we thought all of our weapons were secure."

"Let's start by talking about those security arrangements," said Stingley.

"Of course," said Woodward, and nodded toward the elevator. "I suggest we remove to my office and I will explain everything."

Once the three were settled around a small conference table in Woodward's office, he began his account of how a Thribolt cannon had been stolen.

"As you know," he said, "Thribolt cannons have been made available to civilized societies on planets in the Oikumene. The very nature of these weapons, as you will soon learn during your visit today, makes them unsuitable for anything other than planetary defense. Of particular importance, the Thribolts require a highly skilled operator, such skills being acquired only through training that Jarnell provides. Here, I must confess that it never occurred to us that in addition to stealing a cannon, a criminal organization could also secure the services of an operator. This, however, is what happened.

"A Thribolt was supplied to Larson's World, in the Hyperion system. Larson's World was thoroughly vetted by our punctilious approval process. We trained five operators, all of good character. One of these was a certain Alistair Sand. The weapon was installed, and all five trainees passed competency tests. Everything seemed to be in order. About a year ago, however, a freighter landed at the local spaceport, having passed routine clearance protocols. That evening, the vessel discharged a heavy-duty vehicle operated by four armed bandits. They proceeded to the Thribolt installation, overpowered the single guard, detached the Thribolt from its base, loaded it onto their vehicle, then hurried back to the spaceport and departed. Two days later, when Sand did not appear for his regular shift, he was nowhere to be found. The unavoidable conclusion was that he had departed with the thieves.

"Local authorities were mystified, as Sand was well known as a responsible and trustworthy person, not one to be swayed by monetary or other inducements. However, investigators discovered that Sand's eight-year-old daughter Kara was also missing, and had not been seen by her teachers or schoolmates since nearly a week before the theft. Again, the unavoidable conclusion was that Kara had been kidnapped prior to the theft, and that Sand had been compelled to cooperate with the thieves under threat of injury to his daughter. And that, gentlemen, is how the Thribolt cannon came to be on Grabhorne. And how, it sorrows me to say, that weapon has been used with deadly results."

The mood in the room was somber. Woodward paused, as if waiting for questions; there being none, however, he continued.

"Before we move on with our planned agenda, I wish to tell you what Jarnell has done to assure that such a disaster can never be repeated. When we learned what had happened on Larson's World, we developed a device that would render the sights inoperative if the weapon was removed from its base. Work has proceeded with urgency to retrofit all Thribolts. As of today, thirty-seven installations have been upgraded, and the remaining two will be completed by the end of this month."

Woodward placed his palms on the table with an air of closure. There being no further remarks from Gersen or Stingley, he offered the following concluding comments:

"You will next be meeting with two of our ablest technicians. The Thribolt is their baby and they have worked on its development almost since inception. Of course, they know about the loss of the Larson's World Thribolt, but they are unaware that it was taken to Grabhorne, or that it has been used against an IPCC vessel. That, of course, is a closely guarded secret, known only to the most senior managers. They know nothing about the pending mission, and have been told only that the two of you are important potential customers. Feel free to ask questions about disabling the weapon, but frame them in the context of providing security."

Then Woodward guided them out of his office to take up the main part of their agenda.

The trio proceeded down a long corridor and into a spacious vaulted chamber. The ceiling had been rolled back, and bright Rigel light flooded the space. In the center, on a raised platform, stood a Thribolt cannon. Gersen was impressed. The device was both larger and smaller than he might have imagined — smaller because its massive destructive power might have suggested an equally massive weapon, but larger in the sense that it was nevertheless an imposing piece of machinery. The barrel was a thick, eight-foot cylinder pointing upward at a forty-five degree angle. Above the barrel was clamped a tubular object, much narrower than the barrel and about half its length. This, Gersen supposed, was a sighting device of some kind. The body of the cannon was a thick, sturdy-looking metallic structure, with protruding shapes of various sizes and configurations, and unknown function. At the rear portion were metal buttresses supporting a seat and a viewscreen, obviously an operator's station. Swathed in natural light, the cannon seemed to glow with a metallic sheen. Placed as it was on its elevated platform in the middle of this vaulted hall, Gersen imagined that a primitive people would have worshipped it as a deity.

Standing to the side, like acolytes, were two technicians who Woodward introduced as Tibo Gatz and Hans Snell. Gatz, who was pink-faced and plump, and had a mop of unkempt blond hair, was the ballistics expert; Snell, who had a fragile, bookish look about him, was in charge of sighting. Neither of the two, Gersen judged, was more than thirty years of age. Gatz was invited to lead off. He began to speak with the air of one who had sat through countless lectures to arrive at his present position, and relished the opportunity to be the instructor.

"The basic principle of ballistics," he began, "is that the force of impact is a square function of the velocity of a projectile, times its mass. In other words, the faster a projectile travels, the smaller mass is needed for the same impact, other factors being equal. The Thribolt cannon that you see in front of you deploys an Intersplit-powered projectile whose speed can only be roughly approximated, but for calculation purposes is close to infinite. To summarize, the Thribolt missile is so fast that even with its very small mass, it — if I may be permitted a non-technical term — blows its target to smithereens."

Here Gatz smiled and lovingly patted the bulging barrel of the cannon, while waiting for his witticism to take effect. Gersen for his part managed a glum smile, mindful that the young technician was unaware of the fate of the IPCC craft. Then Gatz continued:

"An Intersplit-powered projectile also travels vast distances in the blink of an eye, so there is no opportunity for the target to take evasive action. However, the direction of travel once Intersplit is activated is a straight line. Unlike some other missiles, it cannot seek out or home in on its target. The sighting, therefore must be flawless; the slightest deviation and the missile simply speeds right past the target and onward into space. This of course presents the danger that, even though space is vast, a projectile that misses its target could keep on going until it strikes an unintended object. To avoid such unwanted occurrences, the Intersplit power unit on each missile is programmed to deactivate if the target is not contacted within a prescribed period of time. Any questions?"

"Yes," said Gersen. Although he thought he knew the answer, he wanted to reward the young technician for his clear explanation. "How long before deactivation occurs."

"Of course, that depends on the distance of the target, as my colleague will explain in more detail. But in general, between two one-hundredths and four one-hundredths of a second."

Gatz then nodded to Snell, "That is a good segue into your part of the presentation, Hans."

Snell stepped forward, and spoke with a surprisingly deep voice for such a fragile-looking figure. "All Jarnell-powered spaceships disengage their Intersplit within at least a million miles of their planetary destination. Any closer at Intersplit speeds would risk a disastrous collision. It is at approximately this distance, then, that the Thribolt operator would focus on an invading ship. If he could just point and shoot, there would be no sighting problem because, as Tibo described, the Intersplit-powered projectile would travel in a straight line and hit its target almost instantaneously — even at a distance of a million miles. Unfortunately, however, that is not the case. As you gentlemen undoubtedly know from your own experience, Intersplit cannot be operated within a planet's atmosphere. This is because the explosive force created at Intersplit speed would collide with the molecules in the atmosphere. The results would be catastrophic — a painful lesson we learned in the early days of developing Jarnell technology. Just as no spaceship would attempt to activate their Intersplit drive within a planet's atmosphere, the same is true for the Thribolt's Intersplit-powered projectile.

"Therefore, the Thribolt has been designed as a three-stage missile. Stage One ejects the missile from the cannon barrel; stage two powers the missile out of the atmosphere using conventional ion drive; stage three engages the Intersplit. Of course, every planet's atmosphere has its own thickness, but if we assume a median case of twelve miles, and a speed under ion power of 20,000 miles per hour, the time required to escape the atmosphere is a bit over two seconds. Now, however, consider the target vessel — decelerating from Intersplit speed, and travelling with no air resistance or gravity to overcome, say 100,000 miles per hour. In the two seconds required to engage the projectile's Intersplit, the target will have moved approximately fifty-five miles from the point at which it was sighted. Therefore, the operator must lead the target by that amount, adjusted of course by the angle at which the target is travelling away from a straight line. The calculation to make this adjustment involves elementary trigonometry, and the Thribolt of course contains software to accomplish that. However, the operator must locate the target, and enter the necessary parameters, all within a space that feels like a heartbeat, or the target will have moved out of range. That, in a nutshell, is why skilled operators are so important."

There followed an energetic discussion in which Gersen and Stingley probed aggressively to discover means by which an interloper could disable a Thribolt cannon. Gatz and Snell defended their creation with vigor. Everything sensitive was encased in hardened metal alloy; the device had its own internal power supply; the control panel was sealed inside a locked compartment whose combination was known only to the operator. And so forth. At the end, Gersen and Stingley congratulated the young technicians enthusiastically, disguising their own discouragement that the Thribolt security seemed impenetrable.

They shared a brief meal with Woodward in the Research Center cafeteria and then were on their way. In the privacy of the Flitterwing, Stingley glanced despondently at Gersen as he prepared for takeoff.

"I'm afraid we failed to accomplish what we came here for. There seems to be no practical way that the Thribolt can be made inoperable. Does this mean we call the mission off?"

"Not necessarily," said Gersen. "If I can't disable the cannon, I will have to incapacitate the operator."

When he arrived back at the Credenza Hotel, Gersen was handed an envelope at the concierge desk. On the way up in the elevator, he opened it. Inside was a brass key with a plastic tag that read:

UNIT 406

LOOKOUT LEDGE APARTMENTS

SAILMAKER BEACH

There was also a note saying: *Call when convenient — Jaeger.*

Once inside his suite, Gersen tapped the code for Jaeger into the communication console, and the latter's features promptly appeared on the viewscreen.

"I understand from Stingley that your visit to Jarnell was productive," Jaeger began.

"That would be a reasonable conclusion," said Gersen. "The Thribolt cannon is well protected, but there is more than one way to pluck a goose, as the saying goes."

"Indeed," said Jaeger. "On the strength of Stingley's report, I have activated 'Operation Broadwood.' The full resources of the IPCC will be deployed as necessary. As a first step, we will reply on behalf of Edgar Darby to the help wanted advertisement. Obviously, we can't use your suite at the Credenza as a return address, so we have installed Edgar Darby in a leased apartment at Sailmaker Beach, the key to which is in the envelope we sent you. It is perhaps not up to the standards of the Credenza, but I think you will find it satisfactory. It is quite secure and free of snooping devices. Of that I can assure you because it is an IPCC safe-house. The superintendent, by the way, is one of ours. The leasing company records will show that Darby has been in residence for two years. In addition, an IPCC data file has been created for Edgar Darby, a person with your exact physical details, but with a sketchy employment history as might be expected from a part-time piano tuner. The record will suggest a modest inheritance early in your life. We have also opened a bank account in the name of Edgar Darby, with a balance of 432 SVU."

"What bank?" queried Gersen.

"Universal. But don't worry about the account details. You will find more than enough cash for your needs in the apartment. Hopefully, you can move in as early as tomorrow, because we don't want to send the help wanted reply until you are there. It would be rather embarrassing if the advertiser came to call and found the place empty. You need not worry about clothing, as we have stocked the closet at the apartment with a wardrobe appropriate to a somewhat down on his luck piano tuner. And by the way, do not bring to the apartment any clothes you care about, as what you arrive in should be consigned to the trash chute, for thorough incineration. Do you suppose you could make the move as early as tomorrow?"

"No problem," said Gersen, while smiling to himself. He knew the Sailmaker Beach residential area quite well, and was already thinking about a number of former haunts — restaurants and taverns — that he might now have an opportunity to revisit.

"Once you are settled in," Jaeger continued, "it will be time to acquaint you with an actual Broadwood piano. For that purpose, we have spoken to the Managing Director of the Avente Conservatory. The Conservatory has custody of the only other Broadwood known to exist, apart from the one that was stolen from the museum in Pontefract. The Director, whose name is Augustus Grindstone, expressed a willingness to cooperate, although we provided him the bare minimum of details about our plan. He knows only that this is an IPCC undertaking, and one of its objectives is to return the stolen artifact. The curator of the music section at the Conservatory is a woman named Gabrielle Richet, and as luck would have it, she is something of a Broadwood expert. Can I tell the museum people to expect you, shall we say, the morning of day after tomorrow?"

"I will be there," said Gersen.

"Very well," said Jaeger. "There is a hot line in your Sailmaker Beach apartment that connects directly to me, and we will stay in communication as appropriate. In the meanwhile, Operation Broadwood is officially underway."

As was his frequent habit, Gersen rose before dawn on the next day. He quickly dressed in denim trousers and a faded green singlet, along with a worn-out pair of boat shoes. He glanced out the window as he left his suite, to glimpse an early sheen of Rigel light filtering into the far horizon. He rode the elevator down to an empty lobby, seemingly unnoticed by the drowsy night clerk at the front desk. Gersen strode briskly to the main dining room and from there into the empty hotel kitchen. A door at the rear of the kitchen gave forth into an alley at the side of the hotel, from which Gersen proceeded unobserved in the pre-dawn gloom along empty city streets until he came to the Esplanade. From here, it would be a two-mile walk to Sailmaker Beach, with no company but the murmuring surf on his left, and the rising sun above shuttered places of entertainment on his right.

Gersen found himself in a buoyant mood. In making good his surreptitious departure from the Credenza, he had effectively shed his Henry Lucas identity. The feeling was liberating. In retrospect, there had been a comfortable aimlessness about being Henry Lucas that he now found tiresome. What then would life as Edgar Darby be? That would only be discovered as events played out. Nevertheless, one thing was clear. Darby would have a singular goal and would summon the determination to achieve it: to find and destroy Malagate.

The blue-white early light of Rigel had barely topped the horizon when Gersen arrived at the district of Sailmaker Beach. This area, Gersen reflected, was in distinct contrast to the neighboring city of Avente. The latter was a typical interplanetary metropolis with glistening, soaring structures. Here, by contrast, the buildings were mostly one and two-story affairs, constructed of color-washed coquina-concrete whose pastels of lavender, blue, and white blazed intensely when Rigel was at its height. The neighborhood was inhabited by citizens from dozens of worlds, whose very diversity made anonymity possible for any single resident.

Soon enough, Gersen identified the Lookout Ledge apartment building, a white two-story affair extending laterally along an elevated outcropping above the main neighborhood. Gersen located the entrance, climbed a set of stairs as there was no elevator, and found unit 406 half way down the hall on the second level. The key that Jaeger had provided gave him access. The place was orderly and freshly cleaned, and Gersen was pleased to find a balcony overlooking the random collection of rooftops below, then beyond to the Thaumaturge Ocean. As a first order of business, he stripped off the clothes in which he had arrived, and stuffed them down the disposal chute. Then he went to the closet and selected a set of aggressively plain and evidently well-worn alternatives. So this, he thought, is how someone at the IPCC thought a piano tuner should look. On the kitchen counter, he discovered a pamphlet entitled:

The Broadwood Piano: its History and Distinctive Features

With nothing that morning demanding his attention, he strolled out to the terrace, seated himself, and began to read.

John Broadwood & Sons, Gersen learned, was a noted piano manufacturer in London, England, for some 300 years during the pre-Apocalyptic era. Approximately 2,500 pianos were produced, of which only two are known to have survived — one at the Avente Conservatory on Alphanor, and the other at the Museum of Music History at Pontefract, Aloysius. The Broadwood name reached its height of fame in the 1820's (old reckoning) when the company gave a specially made edition to the famous composer Ludwig van Beethoven. The piano's thicker soundboard, longer hammers with stouter leather, as well as smaller dampers made it especially suitable for Beethoven's robust musical scores.

There followed a detailed discussion of tuning issues, including the thickness, length, and material of strings, pin placement and tightening methods, the smoothness of hammer faces, uniformity of hammer heights, and so forth. After two hours of concentrated reading, Gersen put the pamphlet aside. The concepts were not completely foreign to him as he had taught himself many years earlier to play certain primitive stringed instruments. He would by no means pass for an expert on piano mechanics, but he guessed that he could give a convincing account of himself to Malagate, who presumably knew nothing of the subject. Moreover, thanks to the IPCC medical team, he could demur convincingly if asked to play.

After that period of uninterrupted work, Gersen decided to reward himself with a stroll around the old Sailmaker Beach neighborhood. He was soon wandering through a rabbit warren of narrow streets and alleyways, trying without much success to locate familiar places from the past. He found himself musing about the old saying that the more things change, the more they remain the same; but now, he was discovering that the obverse is also true: the buildings and streets appeared the same, but their names and functions had all changed. What he remembered as a vegetable store was now a haberdashery; what used to be an outlet for greeting cards, was now a travel agency. And so forth. After a while, he began to doubt the reliability of his memory. Then, near the foot of Ard Street was one establishment that was impossible to forget — the Sandusker Victualling Emporium, as the place grandiosely identified itself. It was actually a rather small and undistinguished shop, where the smells were evil and the taste of its offerings worse. Gersen held his breath as he walked past, thankful that he had not tried Dr. Shansky's olfactory-enhancing potion at this moment. At the corner of Ocean Avenue, he came to a tavern — The Plough and Stars. This he remembered as a comfortable watering hole that used to serve the finest beer and ale. He tried the door, but as it was still early in Rigel's 29-hour day, they were not yet open for business. He resolved to return when time permitted.

Gersen sauntered on, and at the intersection of two streets he came upon a kiosk with an extensive inventory of printed offerings — maps, street directories, travel brochures, restaurant guides, newspapers, and periodicals of all kinds. The stall was attended by a massive dark-robed Darsh woman sporting a fulsome black handlebar mustache. She was squatting on a low stool, deep in concentration, studying one of her printed offerings. This one heralded *Best Bungle Boys* in vivid blue lettering on the cover, and featured three frolicking dwarfs clad in nothing but pink G-strings. As the attendant seemed absorbed in her own perusal, and could be heard issuing occasional contented murmurings, Gersen proceeded to explore the various rows of publications. He was pleased to discover that the current issue of *Cosmopolis* was on display; he picked up a copy and flipped through its contents, noting with satisfaction that his former assistant, Maxel Rackrose, was now a senior editor.

Then another brightly colored periodical caught his eye. This one was *Spread Betters Advantage,* whose cover promised unimaginable winnings to readers who followed the betting tips inside. Gersen had never ceased being bemused by the astonishing range of subjects upon which humans could be induced to wager, and for the most part lose, their hard-earned wages. He started to replace the magazine on the rack, when he noticed in the lower right-hand corner the following item: *Just released! Latest odds in Bunter semis. See Page 32.*

As he thumbed toward the referenced article, his attention was interrupted by a hoarse scold from the Darsh attendant, who had pulled herself up from the stool and was glaring at him with her hands on her voluminous hips.

"Are you going to stand there all day like a hypnotized fish? If it's free reading you want, there's a public library in Avente!"

Gersen smiled diffidently, glanced at the price, and plunked 50 centimes on the counter.

The woman gave a derisive snort, and muttered something about *iskish*, along with an expletive unprintable except perhaps in the raunchiest of her offerings.

Gersen rolled up his purchase, stuffed it in his pocket, and walked briskly back to Lookout Ledge. In the quiet of unit 406, Gersen settled into a chair and opened the betting guide to page 32. Dominating the article was a red-lettered headline advising readers that 'Pari Mutuel Betting for Bunter Racing Now Available.' Accompanying the article was a photograph of an exceptionally hideous beast, which appeared to be about six feet high and twelve feet long, on six splay legs — much as Kim had described the breed of bunters in their earlier conversation. The animal in the photograph had a serrated dorsal ridge which terminated in a hump over its hind quarters, to which a saddle was attached. From its head protruded a pair of optic stalks which were covered by leather caps. The jaws were crocodilian, and were partially open to reveal a set of razor-like teeth. The skin was mostly black, with occasional purple splotches, and hung in flaps and folds. Alongside the bunter, sporting multi-colored silks and a jaunty cap, stood a diminutive human figure who by his pointed ears and protuberant mouth Gersen supposed to be a Highland Imp from the planet Krokinole. The caption described bunter and rider as 'Black Hole of Galactic Stables and Jockey Myron Jolt, winners of the preliminary series and favorites in the semis.'

The body of the article informed readers that bunter racing until this year had been a closed sport, with wagers being possible only between the thirty-two member stables of the Intergalactic Bunter Consortium. Now for the first time, under the sponsorship of Galactic Insurance, pari-mutuel betting would be available to the general public. In-person attendance at the races, to be held on Rosalia, was limited to Consortium members; however, closed circuit viewing would be available to the betting public. As a special service to readers, *Spread Betters Advantage* had retained the exclusive services of noted handicapper, Boxford Grebe, who would be posting advisory columns in each of the next six weekly issues in the run-up to the semi-final event. The size of the betting pool was expected to be enormous, and well-advised betters could profit commensurately.

Gersen put the journal down, sat quietly for a few minutes, then reached over to the communication console and tapped in the code that would give him exclusive access to Jehan Addels' mansion in Ballyholt Woods, outside Pontefract on Aloysius. The call found Addels, along with Kim, in the comfortable elegance of Addels' 'smoking room,' as he liked to call it in memory of the pre-Apocalyptic practice of inhaling combusted tobacco products for after-dinner digestive assistance. Gersen was not surprised to find Addels in this room, it was after dinner hour in the Pontefract time zone of Aloysius.

After a brief exchange of pleasantries, Gersen got to the point.

"I've just been reading that the Bunter semi-finals are to be held on Rosalia in about six weeks' time. A beast named 'Black Hole' that is likely to be one of the favorites, is apparently owned by Galactic Stables, which I am guessing means Bruno Bolfo. My idea is that if we could attend that event, it would be an opportunity to sort out Jarnell matters with Bolfo."

"Not sure I like the sound of that," Addels replied. "Bolfo is not likely to handle negotiations in a civilized way."

"You are probably correct, Jehan, but here is my thinking. The way things stand now, we are at an impasse. Neither party can increase its stake without the consent of the other. If we cannot reach some accommodation, the opportunity is lost to both. I understand, of course, that Bolfo is not to be trusted to negotiate in a gentlemanly fashion. For this reason, we would never consent to meet with him on his home ground. Nor, I suspect, could he be persuaded to a venue that we control. Rosalia, however, is neutral territory. I've done some checking, and their local police — The Rosalia Constabulary — has a reputation for integrity. Also, they are an IPCC affiliate, and the IPCC is considerably in my debt at the moment. So, if we are ever going to find some way through with Bolfo, Rosalia is the place to do it. I understand that one must be a member of the Bunter Consortium to attend the event. How can we make that happen?"

"Possibly my cousin Kwan can help," injected Kim. "He is currently riding a beast called 'Moonbeam' for the Lyonnesse Stable. Kwan tells me that the stable is short of funds and would welcome a new partner. Under consortium rules, each stable is permitted up to fifty partners, so there is room."

"How much money is involved?" asked Addels, ever the sharp-eyed accountant.

"However much," said Gersen, "it is small change compared to the Jarnell stakes. Besides, it would be great sport to watch Kwan ride. Jehan, I am going to be out of contact for a few weeks, so I will leave matters in your hands."

"I will see to it," said Addels. "But should I be concerned that there is a connection between your few-week absence and the favor the IPCC owes you?"

"Ah, my good friend, you worry too much," said Gersen, and broke the connection.

CHAPTER VII

Tell me where, in which country
Is Flora the beautiful Roman;
Archipiada, or Thais
Who was her first cousin;
Echo, speaking when one makes noise
Over river or on pond,
Who had a beauty too much more than human?
Oh, where are the ladies of bygone times?
    — François Villon (1533, old reckoning)
    — translated by Navarth the Mad Poet

Excerpt from *Notable Literary Figures of the Modern Age,*
E.P Snodgras, ed. Entry #17 'Navarth':

Navarth, who styled himself 'The Mad Poet,' burst onto the literary scene in the year 1477, with the publication of his collection
of erotic verses, *Pullulations*. Acclaimed as a prodigy thought to
be in his early twenties (his exact date of birth is unknown), he
was especially popular among the youth of his generation. Soon
after the publication of *Pullulations*, he was named 'Outstanding
Young Poet of the Year' by the Byron Society, and was scheduled to receive his award at a ceremony during which he would
read selected verses to the audience. At the appointed hour, with
some 3,000 attendees rapt and waiting, Navarth failed to appear.
A frantic search by the event sponsors discovered him backstage,
lying comatose beside an empty jug of 'Old Sidewinder.' This

episode was prescient of how Navarth's career would evolve. One further volume, *Happenings*, was celebrated by young enthusiasts, but deemed excessively vulgar by more mature critics. Thereafter, Navarth dropped out of public view. He was reported to be living on a houseboat in the precinct of Ambeules, a suburb of Rolingshaven, in the Netherlands on Old Earth. There, he entertained a small cadre of devoted followers, organizing them into periodic bacchanalian festivals. According to rumor, Navarth perished some time in the early 1530's when he fell off his houseboat and drowned.

—ᘰ—

The Avente Conservatory was situated on a 20-acre compound in the eastern outskirts of the city. Its main building was a monumental structure of pre-Apocalyptic architecture, consisting of four stories, with an exterior of hardened alabaster and a translucent central dome. It had been built during the heyday of space exploration, discovery, and financial exploitation, when vast fortunes were being made, and their recipients vied with one another to donate to charitable causes and have their names recognized commensurately with the size of their contributions. The main building was flanked by a one-story utilitarian office, to the entrance of which Gersen's taxi pulled up, punctiliously early for his morning appointment with Augustus Grindstone, the Conservatory's Managing Director.

Gersen, dressed in the unprepossessing grayish-brown outfit that someone in the IPCC's Quartermaster office thought was appropriate for a piano tuner of modest means, exited the vehicle, paid the fare along with an intentionally parsimonious gratuity, and strode into the administrative center's lobby. He gave his name, Edgar Darby, and purpose of his visit to the receptionist, and sat patiently until some ten minutes after the appointed time. Then a tall woman with militaristic bearing entered the reception area and stood looking down at him.

"Mr. Darby? Mr. Grindstone will see you now."

Gersen nodded diffidently, rose to his feet, and followed her as she marched with a nearly perceptible cadence to the entrance of Grindstone's office, then stood to one side and signaled Gersen onward with a nod. Grindstone was a plump man of late middle age, whose balding pate left him with a pale gray tonsure. He gave Gersen a brief appraisal, apparently from the practice of quickly determining whether a visitor was buying or selling. Evidently, his scrutiny of Gersen was inconclusive, because his features took on a quizzical expression.

"Mr. Darby, Commander Jaeger did not reveal the exact nature of your business. I suppose it's a case of what we don't know won't hurt us, eh? Nevertheless, two of our most active Directors are also on the IPCC Board, so we are always glad to be of assistance. Provided of course that we stay within the law…ha ha."

Gersen nodded politely and said, "I want to learn everything I can about the Broadwood piano. I understand that the Conservatory's music curator — Ms. Richet, I believe is her name — is something of an expert."

"Ah yes, the Broadwood," said Grindstone. "I suppose this has something to do with that scandalous theft from the museum in Pontefract. Needless to say, we beefed up our own security as soon as we heard the news."

Gersen withheld comment to the effect that now that Malagate had one Broadwood, he scarcely needed two. The Conservatory's Broadwood was probably safer than the stone statue of a dead dog. Instead, he said, "A prudent course of action, I am sure. What would be most helpful would be an introduction to Ms. Richet."

"Yes, of course. She has been told to expect you. I just felt it would be best if you came from my office."

"Very sensible," said Gersen.

Grindstone spoke into his desk intercom, "Gertrude, would you please escort Mr. Darby to Gabrielle Richet's office." Then he turned to Gersen, "I'll have Miss Bottomley show you the way. From here to the main building is a bit of a labyrinth."

Gersen followed Miss Bottomley through a maze of corridors, needing to match her stride for stride in order to keep up and feeling somewhat like a new trooper at boot camp. Eventually, they came to an office whose door was open. Miss Bottomley entered and said, "Good morning, Gabrielle. I have Mr. Darby here to see you."

Having completed her task, Miss Bottomley executed a crisp

about-face and marched off the way she had come. Gersen then stood in the entrance as he and Gabrielle briefly appraised one another.

Gabrielle Richet stood perhaps a sliver below average height; she was slender and carried herself with an athletic posture. Her hair was black and adorned her head in well-trimmed glossy curls. Her features were regular, but seemed to lack animation, giving the impression perhaps of someone who had suffered sorrow in her life. Her eyes, though, blazed with a blue intensity that belied her otherwise placid expression. There was something strikingly familiar about her that Gersen could not quite place, but he quickly put that thought aside to avoid staring.

"Good morning, Mr. Darby. How can I help you?"

Her demeanor was polite, thought Gersen, but without warmth.

"I want to learn as much as I can about the Broadwood piano," he said. "I understand that you are the expert."

"One might say that," she replied, "but since, as you undoubtedly know, there are only two Broadwoods known to be in existence, there is not a great deal of competition to become an expert. However, I will do what I can to help you. I suggest that we start by visiting the instrument itself. The Conservatory is not open to the public for another two hours, so we will have the Broadwood to ourselves."

She led Gersen silently through another series of corridors, while he struggled to begin a conversation but found whatever came into his head to be inane. Eventually, they arrived at a large vaulted chamber, which Gersen could see was illuminated by the natural light flooding in from the building's translucent dome. At the center of this monumental space, on an intricate floor of Zacaranda rosewood parquet, stood the Broadwood Grand Piano.

"Here it is," said Gabrielle. "This is what you came to see."

Gersen had to admit the setting was monumental. And the piano itself, with its gracefully curved housing and polished mahogany surfaces was equally elegant. Nevertheless, it struck him as an antique curiosity, lacking the metallic bulk and massive destructive power of the Thribolt cannon that he had witnessed in a similar setting only days earlier. He withheld comment to that effect, of course, and instead said, "Most impressive. Tell me about its history."

Gabrielle began a speech that Gersen imagined she had given to countless groups of gaping tourists, few of whom understood, or much cared about, most of what they were hearing. She told of the John Broadwood and Sons company, producing these hand-crafted masterpieces in the pre-Apocalyptic era, and of their use by celebrated composers of the day. Gersen, of course, had learned all this from the briefing paper the IPCC had furnished him. But he listened attentively and kept asking questions, to which he mostly knew the answers, just to hear the sound of her voice.

After about an hour, he could see that Gabrielle was tiring, and he risked wearing out his welcome, if he had not already done so.

"Thank you for a most informative session," he said. "The public will be arriving soon, so I suggest we take a break, and resume early tomorrow, when I would like to take up the question of actual tuning."

Gabrielle nodded her acquiescence, without much enthusiasm, it seemed to Gersen. She gave him directions for accessing this space the next day without the need for Gertrude Bottomley's good offices. They said a perfunctory goodbye, and he was out the door and into a taxi heading back to Sailmaker Beach.

As the taxi, a self-driving slidecar, moved silently on air-cushions toward its destination, Gersen was in a despondent frame of mind. He could not escape the thought that he found this woman fascinating. And yet the more he tried to be polite, even to the point of ingratiation, the more he felt as though he was being received with studied indifference. As the taxi pulled up at the entrance to his building, he shook his head in frustration and resolved to stop brooding on the matter. This was scarcely the first time, and probably would not be the last, that he would be plagued with woman troubles. He had other matters more pressing that demanded his attention.

Despite this resolution, the subject came up again that evening. He had wandered into the Sailmaker Beach neighborhood, and found himself in the Plough and Stars tavern — a venue perfectly suited, so it seemed to him, for brooding on unsolvable dilemmas. The establishment was a low-ceilinged affair with walls and flooring of tan-colored sandstone blocks, illuminated by simulated whale-oil wall sconces. The bar extended along an entire length of the room and was made of darkened wood mottled by generations of circular stains. The bartender was a stubby man with orange skin-tone and russet hair, who seemed to enjoy making conversation with his patrons. As Gersen was at the moment one of only two standing at the bar, he soon enough received the bartender's attention.

"Hoy, my good man," the bartender saluted him, as he served Gersen a second stein of dark ale, "and what, if I may be so bold to ask, is your profession?"

"Piano Tuner," said Gersen, without looking up from the beverage at which he had been staring.

The bartender uttered a hearty guffaw, "Hah! I've heard many fancy stories in this tavern, it's a pantheon of tall tales, you might say. But Piano Tuner — that is a new one. Strong first place finisher with a client who once claimed he was an earthworm farmer. But what is truth, after all, but a commodity as cheap as the air."

Gersen took another swallow of ale, which seemed to put him in a more convivial mood. "I have a question for you," he said to the bartender, "since you seem to be a purveyor of wisdom in addition to fine ale."

"Ask away," said the bartender, "and I'll do what I can to enlighten you."

"What makes a woman displeased with a man?" said Gersen.

"Ah ha, so that is the cause of your somber mood. What a woman wants is what we just discussed — that is the truth. Are you hiding something? If so, she'll detect it instantly, and it will be a source of vexation. Trust me, my friend, a woman can see through a deception even if it be as well-hidden as a flea in a sandstorm."

Gersen lurched himself upright; this conversation was going beyond what he had intended. He placed a generous payment on the bar, thanked the bartender for his advice, and departed the tavern, leaving behind his half-finished ale.

"Come back soon," the bartender called after him, "my name's Mike by the way." Then Mike the bartender stood gazing after him, reminding himself that there was no end to odd occurrences in an establishment like this.

＊

Another self-driving taxi ride brought Gersen the next morning to a side entrance of the main Conservatory building, where Gabrielle's instructions from the previous day guided him to her office. He knocked lightly on the door frame to signal his presence; she looked up from something she had been studying with an expression that, if anything, was even more distant than the day before. But he had resolved to maintain a positive attitude, so he suggested that they proceed with some actual tuning mechanics.

They moved to another part of the building where there was an ordinary piano that Gabrielle said that they could use for demonstration purposes without disturbing the more delicate Broadwood. After nearly an hour of tightening and untightening strings, replacing pins, smoothing hammer faces, and so forth, Gersen finally could no longer tolerate Gabrielle's apparent coldness.

"You seem put out about something," he said. "Have I done anything to offend you?"

She put down the tightening wrench she had been working with, and looked at him with an expression that, while scarcely warm, at least showed some animation.

"I think I have a right to know what's going on," she said.

"What do you mean?"

"Do you take me for a fool? I know very well that the Broadwood was stolen from Pontefract. In fact, it was less than a year ago that they brought me in to tune it. And do you think I have not seen the ads for a 'piano tuner' with Broadwood experience? Those ads have obviously been placed by the criminal.

"Then you show up wanting me to train you to be a piano tuner — which by the way is a hopeless assignment unless you are prepared to devote at least a year of your life. And I know from Gus Grindstone that the IPCC is involved. It took more than an ordinary burglar to make off with the Pontefract Broadwood, and if the IPCC intends to pursue him, it is for reasons more important than recovering an antique piano — as precious as that instrument might be to some of us in the music world.

"So I ask you again, what is going on?"

Gersen was trapped, and he knew it. He could not say that 'nothing' was going on — Gabrielle's logic was too unshakable for that. He could not say something like, 'it's a confidential matter,' as that would not only insult her but — and here he had to admit where his real interest lay — would spoil any chance he had of getting to know her better. It came to him with a certain grim irony that Mike the bartender's words the previous evening had been prophetic: don't try to deceive a woman you care about. He therefore came to a decision.

"All right," he said, "let's take a break and go somewhere we can talk."

Gabrielle guided Gersen to the Conservatory cafeteria which was mostly empty as it was still mid-morning. They took a table in the corner, and Gersen explained the nature of his mission, trying to be truthful but still providing as few details as possible. She had been correct, he said, in her judgment that the piano thief was no ordinary burglar; instead, he was a master criminal named Malagate. The same Malagate had been responsible for a raid on a community called Willow Grove whose residents had been massacred or enslaved. The survivors had been taken to a planet called Grabhorne, which was protected by a Thribolt cannon. The IPCC planned a rescue mission, but that would be suicidal unless the cannon could be disabled. Gersen's mission was to respond to the advertisement posing as a piano tuner, travel to Grabhorne, and find a way to disarm the cannon.

Gabrielle listened attentively, not interrupting, while her expression changed from one of cold indifference to one of intense focus, with her blue eyes blazing with inner energy. When he was finished, there was a pause, and then she said, "I should go with you."

Gersen was taken aback. This was not at all what he was expecting.

"You want to go? Do you not understand how dangerous this is? Malagate and his henchmen are cold-blooded killers. How could you even suggest such an idea?"

"My family was at Willow Grove. If any of them survived, they are now enslaved at this planet — Grabhorne. If there is to be a rescue mission, I must help."

"Your family? How is that possible?"

"The Richets are my adoptive family. On Earth, they raised me from the age of five, and cared for me as if I was their own. When I was twenty, they decided to join the Willow Grove community, to find a new life in a new world. I elected to come to Alphanor to pursue my music studies, which would not have been possible in the pioneer world of Willow Grove. But they are still my parents, and my step sister, her husband and their son went with them. If there is to be a rescue mission, I must join."

Gersen could see that she was determined. But this was completely impractical.

"Impossible," he said. "How do I persuade the advertiser to hire two people when they are only looking for one? But even if I could persuade them, it is far too dangerous. And I would be worried about protecting you instead of dealing with the cannon."

"You had better find a way to persuade them," she replied. "Your piano skills are pathetic, and if they know anything about music, you will be discovered as a fraud. And as far as protecting me, I can take care of myself."

"There's more to something like this than you understand," said Gersen. "Just as I know nothing about piano tuning, you know nothing about violence."

Here Gersen was bemused to see the hint of a smile, a subtle pout of Gabrielle's lower lip as if she was hiding a mischievous secret.

"I actually know more about self-defense than you will ever know about piano tuning," she said.

Gersen did not want to argue this point, or to insult her by pointing out that in the real world of physical threats, he imagined she would be as hopeless as he was at piano tuning. Instead, he thought of a different way to resolve this.

"Do you know where Lex Larson's studio is?" he said.

"I think I can find it."

"Very well. Meet me there at 8 am tomorrow, and we'll put your self-defense skills to the test."

Gersen returned to the lookout ledge apartment well satisfied with the day's proceedings. He had warmed the chill with Gabrielle, who he continued to find fascinating. They could now speak candidly even if there were points of disagreement. He felt confident that he had found a workable solution to resolve the principal difference between them — that is, her impulsive desire to join the Grabhorne mission. The session the next morning would convince her that she was ill-prepared for the dangers involved. It would then be her decision, not his, to give up the idea of participating.

He was preparing to wander down to the Sailmaker Beach neighborhood to locate an inviting spot for an evening meal, when the buzzer sounded in the apartment signaling a visitor downstairs. He depressed a button and his viewscreen revealed a male figure of indeterminate age dressed in medium blue business attire.

"Mr. Darby?" the man addressed him, "I am Jasper Kranz, a senior associate with All-World Recruiters. I'm here about the piano tuner position."

"Come on up, then," said Gersen and pushed the button to open the front entrance.

After a moment, there was a rap on his door and Gersen opened it. Kranz had a smile that looked as though it had been painted on; he was slightly red-faced and out of breath from the single flight of stairs to the second level. What appeared to be a light brown hairpiece was slightly askew.

"Jasper Kranz," he repeated, and handed Gersen a business card. "You are, I take it, the Edgar Darby who responded to our ad?"

"The same," said Gersen.

"Excellent. I am pleased to report that on the strength of our research, our client is very interested in employing you. There are other candidates, of course, but you are near the top of the list."

"What research is that?" said Gersen.

"Well, we have checked your references, of course."

The only reference, Gersen knew, was Augustus Grindstone, who had been well briefed by Jaeger to confirm that Edgar Darby had been an employee in good standing for two years.

"On that subject," said Kranz, "you only gave us two years of employment history. Our standard procedure is to ask for at least five."

"You will have to make do with those two," said Gersen. "Before that, I was attempting to write a music score, and living on a small inheritance. When that ran out, I applied to the Conservatory."

"Yes, I see. Well, I suppose we could make an exception, assuming that everything else checks out."

"What else are you referring to?"

"Well, I need you to sign this authorization, which permits us to access your IPCC identity records."

Gersen, of course, was prepared for this, and there was a convincing file on Edgar Darby at the IPCC. But this gave him the opening he wanted. He did not want to appear too eager.

"You seem to be asking a great deal about me, when I know nothing about your client. Who is he? Where is he? How long does he propose to employ me? What compensation is involved?"

Kranz began to fidget nervously with the authorization form in his hand. "The client wishes to remain confidential at this time. But I can tell you that he is off-world."

"What about transportation costs and lodging, then?"

"The client will provide transport on his own craft, and first-class accommodations are available at the site. As for the length of employment, you would know better than I. How long does it take to tune a piano?"

"That depends on its condition. Has this one been damaged?"

"I don't believe so."

"Then two weeks should be sufficient, four at the most. What about compensation?"

"My client is prepared to offer five hundred SVU per week."

"I was thinking a thousand per week."

"I'm sorry, but I'm not authorized to offer more."

"In that case, I will settle for five hundred per week, including travel time, and with a minimum guarantee of two thousand for the job. Your client should understand that, after all, he is asking me to leave my regular employment and travel to an unknown place for an uncertain period of time."

"I will consult with the client and let you know. Meanwhile, I need your signature on the authorization form."

Gersen signed. Kranz took the form, wiped his sleeve across his forehead, and departed. Gersen was pleased with the exchange. He had not wanted to appear too eager, and had no doubt but that Malagate would accept those terms.

*

Lex Larson's studio was a repurposed warehouse in an industrial district of Avente, where it stood inconspicuously among similar utilitarian structures. The interior space had high ceilings, with lighting provided by hanging luminescent bulbs, and could be divided into subsections by the arrangement of heavy-duty, sound-proof curtains. Gersen arrived comfortably in advance of the appointed meeting with Gabrielle, in order to brief Lex on what he hoped to achieve in the upcoming session. Lex greeted Gersen in the front lobby with the cordiality of a colleague of long association. Lex, who was some ten years Gersen's junior, was a block of a man, deep-chested and square-shouldered. He had come up through the ranks of the IPCC, where his early history was shrouded in secrecy, but was rumored to have involved a unit colloquially named the 'death squad,' thought to be assigned only the most difficult and dangerous missions. Lex had retired honorably, and now managed this studio which trained clients in combat skills.

Gersen informed Lex about his assumed name, Edgar Darby, and his assumed identity as a piano tuner — the latter evoking a wry chuckle from the combat trainer. The purpose of this morning's session, Gersen then explained, was to disabuse young Gabrielle Richet of the notion that she was fit for hazardous duty. Lex nodded his understanding, but withheld comment. Then the two of them set about arranging hanging curtains to create a space where the exercise could occur in private. Just as they finished that task to their satisfaction, Gabrielle arrived. She was dressed in loose-fitting white trousers and a sleeveless shirt. She addressed Lex warmly and he said, "Good morning, Gabrielle." They obviously knew one another, and Gersen found himself annoyed that Lex had not mentioned this, but even more so that she had smiled at Lex with a warmth she had never shown to him. Lex led them to the enclosure that he and Gersen had cordoned off, then explained the rules. No injury-causing moves were to be allowed, and best three of five throws wins.

Gabrielle stood facing him, her weight slightly forward and her knees slightly flexed — good defensive posture. Her eyes were locked on his, her face a mask of concentration. He launched a sudden strike that would have landed on the soft spot where neck meets shoulder with the knife-edge of his hand, but she caught his arm, twisted and used his momentum to throw him over her hip. He somersaulted in the air and landed on his feet, but it was a point for her. Out of the corner of his eye, he saw Lex looking on, his arms folded across his chest and wearing a knowing smile. Gersen had underestimated Gabrielle. The next one won't be so easy, he told himself. He began the same attack, but held back as she countered, locked on to her arm and twisted it behind her back. His point, all even.

He could see that Gabrielle was well trained and knew what she was doing. But he had to find a way to prove to her that there was a difference — a life-and-death difference — between these practice moves and the real thing. He moved laterally left, to her right, and she adjusted her stance to keep facing him. As she did, he threw himself cross-wise with one shin at her ankles and the other behind her knees, then rolled, a hard twisting move that toppled her. Two points, one more and the game was over.

This time he would use the same chopping attack, but with his left arm and hand. When she countered, he would hold back and catch her arm behind her as before. But instead of falling back, she stepped forward, put her leg behind him, and tripped him backwards. Again, he somersaulted away, but the point was hers.

Lex stepped into the conflict area, softly clapping his hands. "Well done, both of you," he said. "I suggest we call it a draw before someone gets hurt."

Gersen considered briefly. He had only been operating at three-quarters force; to win the bout would require more, and injuring Gabrielle just to prove his point was not something he cared to risk.

"I agree," he said.

"Then I can join the mission?" said Gabrielle. She looked flushed and happy.

Gersen was caught in his own gambit. He could not refuse. Besides, what she had asserted earlier, she had proved. She could obviously take care of herself. He needed time to think.

"Let's find a place to talk," he said.

"You can use my office," Lex offered. "There's coffee there, and water if you want it."

Gersen turned to Lex, half smiling, half serious, "You might have told me she was one of your clients." Almost as soon as he uttered that thought, he knew how Lex would reply.

"You ignored the first rule," said Lex. "Never underestimate an opponent."

A few minutes later Gersen and Gabrielle were seated in Lex's office, in chairs in front of Lex's desk, facing one another at angles. Gersen regarded her with a studied look. "You are not what you appear to be," he said.

Her face broke into a mischievous grin and she laughed. "Is this the pot calling the kettle black? You are scarcely what you appear to be, either."

Gersen experienced a sensation that ancient authors would have described as one's heart skipping a beat — a quick surge of pleasure that he had said something that amused her. Nevertheless, Edgar Darby, formerly Henry Lucas, formerly Kirth Gersen could hardly dispute her point.

"Touché," he said, "and I accept your offer to join the mission. However, I still have to convince the client."

"I have already thought of that," said Gabrielle. "Do you play the piano?"

"No, but I have an excuse, these scars show that surgery has made me incapable."

"Well, the client is going to expect to hear the instrument played once it has been tuned, don't you think? That will be my role. Now I have another question — what is your plan?"

"I don't have one," said Gersen. "We can expect Malagate to have tight security, and as I have already told you, his hirelings are cold-blooded killers. First, we must convince them that we are harmless piano tuners and hope that will give us some freedom of action. Then we exploit opportunities as they arise."

"Isn't that rather risky?"

"It is, but there is no other way."

Three days later, in the early evening, Gersen was at Chancy's Tea House, where he planned to meet Miles Jaeger for a farewell libation.

He selected a table discreetly in the corner of the open-air terrace, and sat enjoying the serenity of the evening as Rigel dropped below the horizon. Soft lighting was now provided by a widely spaced ring of hanging lanterns, with individual candle globes at each table. Chancy assured his clients that the space was free of eavesdropping devices, one of the features that made it popular with the IPCC, and an added source of comfortable privacy.

While waiting for Jaeger to arrive, Gersen reviewed the events of the past week. Jasper Kranz, the headhunter, had vigorously protested Edgar Darby's proposal that he be accompanied by an assistant, but after seeing the scars on Gersen's hands, Kranz had secured agreement from the client. Gersen and Gabrielle were to depart the next morning from the Avente spaceport.

Jaeger arrived at the appointed time, spotted Gersen, and seated himself at the table. He seemed, so Gersen thought, to be in a buoyant mood, as was often the case with old hands at the outset of a well-planned mission. They each ordered a wine from Chancy's celebrated list, then Jaeger handed Gersen a small canvas bag that contained a collection of tools.

"These are all the sorts of things one might expect a piano tuner to use," Jaeger explained. "All but one."

He extracted from the bag an item shaped like a common screwdriver except that, instead of a blade at the tip of its shaft, it had two thin filaments of some undetermined material.

"A contribution from Bert Stingley's shop," Jaeger said. "If asked, you can call it an instrument for testing the tensile quality of a piano string. But in fact, it is a signaling device. We will have placed a reception buoy out of range of any Grabhorne radar, but close enough to pick up the signal. Use this to let us know when you have disabled the cannon.

"We will have four personnel carriers, each with ten troopers, waiting for your signal — also beyond the range of Grabhorne radar, of course. When we know the cannon is out of action, we will launch the attack."

"A bold plan," said Gersen. "But what if this toolkit is confiscated? Or what if I am unable to get access to the cannon? We have to assume it will be well guarded, and I am but one man."

"We've thought of that. If we haven't received your signal within two weeks, we are going in anyway."

"A foolhardy undertaking, in view of what happened to the surveillance team."

"Of course, we are well aware of the danger. But all the troopers are volunteers. In fact, we had two volunteers for every place on the team. Ensign Tyng was much admired by her colleagues. And based on what you and Bert Stingley learned at Jarnell, we have put together a plan of attack that we think will minimize the danger. First, all that risk will be absorbed by the lead vessel. The cannon will only have time for one shot. By the time it can be re-loaded and re-sighted, the entire attack force will be within Grabhorne's atmosphere, and as you know, the Thribolt projectile will self-destruct if activated within the atmosphere. And second, the sighting system assumes its target will stay on course, as would be the case of a vessel that was unaware of the Thribolt's presence. Instead, however, our lead vessel will make regular small course corrections as it approaches; Stingley and I have devised a formula for this that we think will reduce the risk of being hit."

"I follow your logic," said Gersen, "but it is by no means certain. It will take a skilled pilot to command that ship. And a brave one. Have you selected an officer for the job?"

"We have," said Jaeger. "It will be me. Tomorrow will be Day One. If we have not received your signal, we will launch the attack at Grabhorne's sunset on Day 14."

There was little more to be said. The two men stood up, shook hands, wished each other luck, and departed into the darkness.

CHAPTER VIII

IPCC File #4278-B1956 Subject: Grabhorne

Grabhorne was discovered by (the late) locater Strod Vanderway, who filed a claim with the Interworld Locater's Guild in the year 1432. The source of the name 'Grabhorne' appears to have been whimsical, as there are no identifiable antecedents — neither persons, places, family pets, etc. — to that name. Vanderway described Grabhorne as the fourth planet of the star Hypnos, in sector B-127. Its diameter was listed as 7,100 miles, mass .88, and atmosphere .93 of Earth normal. A single large unnamed continent, comprising some 40% of the planet's surface, runs from pole to pole, with a mountain range ten degrees west of its central axis, running like a spine from north to south. The balance of the surface area is ocean, with the exception of several large islands. The equatorial zone is tropical and covered with dense rain forest; this thins into open savannah as the land mass approaches the southern and northern poles. (Note: Vanderway's description was largely confirmed by an IPCC expedition in 1535 — see below).

According to the *Popular Handbook to the Planets*, Grabhorne was settled by a splinter group of Ravatanga Zoroastrians around 1450; however, no trace of that settlement, if it ever existed, has been found. IPCC sources operating in the Beyond reported in the early 1500's that the planet had been occupied by one of the notorious Demon Princes, calling himself Malagate the Woe. These sources claimed that Malagate had established a plantation of 10,000 square miles, worked by 20,000 slaves, some of whom had been kidnapped from Mount Pleasant, and some from other locations. This information was picked up and published in Caril Carphen's popular book, *The Demon Princes*. As often happens, however, the information gleaned from IPCC operatives in the Beyond is necessarily a compilation of rumor, braggadocio, and invention. An IPCC expedition in the year 1535 — nearly a decade after Malagate's last known appearance and, according to rumor as well, his likely demise — discovered the remains of a settlement located at the 45th latitude north, the temperate zone, that was likely the one attributed to Malagate. This plantation, if that is what it had been, was smaller than what had been rumored, but still substantial. The IPCC team recorded what had once been an elegant mansion, approximately 2,000 acres of arable land, several workshops, and more primitive quarters estimated to have housed perhaps 5,000 slaves. There was no trace of any survivors, and their fate remains a mystery, although the team did note the presence of predatory creatures that would have been a threat to unarmed humans.

In 1549, a settlement called Willow Grove was raided, and a population estimated at 3-5,000 either killed or kidnapped. Sources in the Beyond attributed this assault to a criminal chieftain styling himself Mongo Malagate, possibly in league with some other leading criminals. While the origins of this new Malagate are unknown, the IPCC's working hypothesis is that he is connected in some way to the original Malagate the Woe. IPCC sources secured evidence that this new Malagate had established his base at Grabhorne, and an ill-fated surveillance mission confirmed this to be the case. At the time of this writing, plans are being developed to mount a rescue mission, although this is complicated by the fact that Malagate's headquarters are protected by a Thribolt cannon.

—⋙—

Day 1

Before first light, Gersen arrived at the general vessel terminal of the Avente Spaceport. A second self-drive taxi pulled up behind him, and Gabrielle Richet emerged. Together, they entered the building, presented their identification cards to the drowsy concierge, and gave him the vessel hull number that had been provided by Jasper Kranz. Per Kranz's instructions, they carried no baggage with them, although Gersen held the small tool bag that he had received from Jaeger the evening before. They boarded a spaceport van and headed out toward their waiting ship that, as they approached, Gersen could see was a late model Pharaon emblazoned with a purple and gold color scheme. Well, at least they would be traveling in comparative comfort, he told himself. The Pharaon would have owner and pilot's quarters, in addition to two guest compartments; atmosphere control and sanitary systems would be top-of-the line.

A gantry crane stood alongside the vessel and was lowering a boarding platform as they approached. A man hopped off the platform dressed in space gear with purple and gold insignia that suggested he was to be their pilot. He was of stocky build, bandy-legged, had a broken nose and a conspicuous white scar running down his left cheek.

"Darby? Richet?" he inquired, and when they answered affirmatively, "Come on board and let's get underway."

"What's our destination?" asked Gersen.

"You'll find out when we get there."

As the boarding crane raised them toward the main cabin door, Gersen looked toward the Jarnell-Distis hangar where *Quicksilver* was parked — a mute testimony to what he was leaving behind. The future holds two possibilities about when I'll be back, he told himself. One is three-to-four weeks; the other is never.

Their pilot depressed a lever to open the cabin door, but then stood blocking the entrance.

"No baggage," he said, and reached for Gersen's tool bag.

"These are tools I will need to tune the piano," said Gersen.

"If the boss approves, you can have them back."

"Who is the boss?"

"You'll find out when we get there."

Obviously, the pilot was not going to provide any useful information, so Gersen handed over the bag, and he and Gabrielle entered the vessel. The accommodations, as Gersen had expected, were reasonable. The owner's suite was locked and off limits, but he and Gabrielle each had a small cabin, and there was a galley adequately stocked with food and water. The pilot would have his own quarters adjacent to the control platform.

"I'll be up front for the duration of the flight. If there's an emergency, you can reach me with this call button. But it better be a real emergency; I don't like being disturbed."

"Understood," said Gersen. "What's your name, by the way?"

"Yatz," said the pilot, and departed for the flight deck, leaving a hiss of air as the door sealed itself behind him.

Gersen looked at Gabrielle and smiled. "Well, at least we got that out of him." Of course, to the questions that 'Yatz' had declined to answer, Gersen already knew the answers. The flight time would be something less than three days, and the 'boss' would be Malagate, or whatever identity Malagate was using. However, it did not hurt to ask questions to which you already knew the answer; you never knew what you might learn. Without delay, they heard the sound of equipment warming up — the whine of ion thrusters, the whoosh of cabin pressurizing systems, the clicking of circuits opening and closing. Gersen in his mind's eye could visualize Yatz at the controls, pushing buttons, moving levers, checking readings, waiting for clearance from ground control. Then the vessel gave the slight shudder that preceded lift-off, that Gersen always thought felt like a person waking from a deep sleep, and up they went. There was still darkness at ground level, but as the ship rose, Rigel appeared briefly on the horizon, then contracted quickly to a speck as they sped out of the Rigel system. There was a brief dizzying sensation as the Intersplit engaged, but that passed as quickly as it came on, and they were off toward Grabhorne — Grabhorne and whatever fate had in store for them.

Three days would pass slowly, Gersen knew, when there was little to occupy one's time. He and Gabrielle had changed into space garb, which they had found on board and which, Gersen noted with satisfaction, were made of *paraflax*, the easy-to-clean material the technology underlying which he owned. As a first order of business, Gersen inspected their quarters thoroughly and, somewhat to his surprise, found them free of listening devices. Despite being assured of the privacy of their conversation, Gersen opted not to tell Gabrielle about the two-week deadline imposed by Jaeger's schedule. Their plan was still the same — to convince their host that they were harmless, then exploit whatever opportunities arose. There was no need to impose on her the pressure of a time limit.

The two passengers then mapped out a routine of light exercises, the best they could devise in such comparatively cramped space. They consulted on menu planning with respect to the provisions that had been provided. It was inevitable, though, that once these tasks were out of the way, the conversation would turn to personal matters.

Gersen was fascinated by Gabrielle. She was hauntingly familiar; she sometimes reminded him of one lost love, and at other times, another. Finally, after one of their exercise sessions, when they were seated facing one another at the small table in the galley, he began the conversation this way:

"Tell me about your family at Willow Grove," he said.

"As I mentioned earlier, they are my adoptive parents — Claude and Monique Richet. They took me into their home when I was five, and loved me as their own, even though they had a daughter my age, my step-sister Madeleine. Since I never knew my real parents, or anything about them, Claude, Monique, and Madeleine were the only family I have ever had. This is why, if there is an effort to rescue them, I must do what I can to help."

"Where did the family live before they moved to Willow Grove?"

"In the neighborhood of Rouen, in western Europe. Claude and Monique were both instructors at the University there."

"That seems like secure employment," said Gersen. "What caused them to uproot themselves and move to another planet — Brandywine, I think, is where Willow Grove is located?"

"Is that so uncommon?" said Gabrielle. "People tire of the old ways, of being told how to think and how to behave. Is this not why so many planets have been settled by the folk of Old Earth? A new life, a fresh start, the challenge of building a model society from the ground up. Who can say? But Claude and Monique were determined, and Madeleine joined them with her fiancée, soon to be her husband, Henri."

"But you elected to stay?"

"I think I have already mentioned this. Music has always been my passion. At Willow Grove I would have had to give that up, except per-haps in some primitive way."

Gersen was observing her carefully, looking for familiar signs — her sometimes somber moods, interspersed with sudden flashes of joy at some memory or bit of cleverness; the quiet droop of her mouth becoming a mischievous smile. Then, at the risk of evoking some unwanted memory, he prodded her history further.

"You were five when the Richets adopted you. Surely you remember something from that time?"

She considered him quizzically, as if wondering why this subject mattered. Then she said, "I do remember one thing. I was in the care of an uncle. He is the one who found the Richets and placed me with them. But that was so long ago, and I was so young, that I remember little. In my memory, though, he was a kindly man."

"Can you recall his name?"

"It was a strange name. I have never heard one like it. But I remem-ber it because my parents told me I owed him a debt of gratitude. His name was Navarth."

Gersen had spent a lifetime concealing his reaction to surprising news. But the name *Navarth* coming as it did from the lips of Gabrielle, tested his control, striking him with tectonic force and flooding his consciousness with aftershocks. Navarth was the 'Mad Poet' who had accompanied Gersen to the domain of the third Demon Prince, Viole Falushe. Falushe had kidnapped the bewitching girl who had teased then jilted him as a teenager. Then through a process of auto-fertiliza-tion, Falushe had created several exact clones of different ages. One of those, named Drusilla Wayles, Falushe had placed in the care of Navarth, to be her custodian until Falushe should come to claim her.

Gersen had destroyed Falushe, and Drusilla, by then a fetching creature of twenty years, had begged him to take her with him. But he had declined, despite being smitten by her. There had been two remaining Demon Princes still to be hunted down, and his obsession to complete the task left no place in his life for romance — as much as he desperately wanted it. Life, he had always supposed, deals each person with many causes of regret. For him, the loss of Drusilla was the sharpest pang, even more so because it was brought about by his own volition. But the four-year-old version of Drusilla, who he thought of as Drusilla IV, and who he had left in the care of Navarth, was now sitting here and facing him. She was a mature and radiant version of the Drusilla he had given up twenty-five years earlier.

"You have a faraway look," Gabrielle interjected. "Have I said something to offend you?"

Gersen dragged his thoughts back to the present. "Not at all," he said. "Perhaps it was just that the name Navarth struck me as unusual."

Gabrielle showed one of her knowing smiles. "I think it is more than a peculiar name," she said. "You are a man of many secrets, Edgar Darby, or whatever your real name is. In any event, poor Navarth died not long after my adoption. My parents were forced to tell me, because Navarth had come to visit occasionally, and they had to explain why that would be no more. And that is the end of the story."

Life rarely gives us second chances, Gersen thought, and he must not fumble this one. He needed time to think, to absorb this revelation, but before he could change the subject, she said, "Call it a woman's intuition, but I suspect the name Navarth is not unknown to you. Am I correct?"

This was not a time for dissembling, Gersen realized with stark clarity.

"Yes, I knew Navarth," he said.

"Then you must know things that would help unravel the mystery of my origins. Who were my parents? Where were they from? How did I come into Navarth's care?"

Her expression conveyed an earnestness that he was not going to be able to deny. As simply as he could, and with deliberation, he told her the whole story — how his real name was Kirth Gersen, how Falushe had been one of five master criminals who had raided his family home when he was nine, and how he had committed himself to destroying each of them. Then he related how she, Gabrielle, had been the youngest of four clones created by Falushe; how Falushe had met his end; and how Gersen had consigned both her and the older Drusilla to Navarth's care.

"What became of her?" asked Gabrielle, referring to the older Drusilla.

"I don't know," said Gersen. "She is undoubtedly happily married, and living somewhere on Earth."

"Thank you for explaining these matters to me," she said. "It is a strange feeling, knowing that there exists an exact copy of myself somewhere on Earth."

"That should not trouble you," said Gersen. "Each of us is their own person, no matter what physical similarities we may have. It is well known, for example, that identical twins — who are perfect clones of one another — grow up to have quite different personalities. And as for you and the older Drusilla, I can assure you, for example, that she had no interest in music whatsoever. There is an obvious point of difference; I am sure there are many others.

"I can tell you one thing, though, she was a beguiling creature — and so are you."

Gabrielle smiled demurely, "No man has ever spoken words like that to me."

"I hope I did not offend you."

"I am not offended. What I can say in response is that I like Kirth Gersen better than Edgar Darby."

That seemed to settle matters between them. They each understood that there was a dangerous mission ahead, such that they could not be distracted by sentimental frivolities. Nevertheless, the rest of the flight was spent with a comfortable warmth that had not been there before. There was, as well, a certain unspoken intimacy derived from the knowledge that they each knew things about the other that no one else knew.

They discovered that the manufacturers of the Pharaon spaceship had kindly supplied the guest quarters with a chess set, and although neither Gersen nor Gabrielle were experienced players, it proved to be a useful way to pass the time. Gersen was pleased with Gabrielle's reactions — delight when she made a good move, self-effacing amusement when she unexpectedly lost a piece. All things considered, it was one of the most enjoyable periods of downtime in Gersen's experience.

Day 4

Gersen, though, always seemed to have a clock in his head, and he began to feel the growing tension as the time for action approached. Sure enough, there came the brief dizzying sensation as the Intersplit disengaged, then Yatz brought the ship into a slowing orbit around Grabhorne. The surface was much as Gersen remembered it from the IPCC expedition fifteen years earlier — a large single continent, with its north-to-south mountain range; dense jungle in the equatorial zone, and savanna in the higher latitudes. As the ship descended in tightening orbital circles, Gersen could make out specific features — the vast spread of agrarian acreage, the clustered rows of slave quarters, and the owner's mansion on a piece of high ground overlooking it all. Then Yatz put the ship upright into landing mode and settled her gently with a high-pitched whine of thrusters. As the ship was coming down, Gersen and Gabrielle had changed from their space garments into the simple street attire in which they had left Avente. Yatz emerged from the flight deck and punched in a code to open the main door. Yatz had also shed his space gear and was now clad in garments that Gersen construed to be a uniform of some kind — black trousers and boots, gray tunic, and crimson sash. The militaristic effect was accentuated by a combat-style projac holstered at his left side.

"Good flight," said Gersen amiably, to which Yatz grunted something unintelligible.

There was no gantry crane here on Grabhorne, so Yatz engaged the ship's auxiliary disembarkation platform and began to lower the three of them to the ground. As they descended, Gersen cast a quick look around to try to get his bearings. It was mid-afternoon, he guessed, and Hypnos, the pale white-blue sun of Grabhorne, was to the west. In that direction, parked some fifty yards away was another ship, a freighter with the same yellow and green markings that Gersen had observed on the Galactic Freight vessel at Hobson's Hole. This was unexpected, but on reflection, not surprising. Malagate could reap no economic benefit from his 'plantation' unless he had some means to export its production, and what better partner for that undertaking than Bruno Bolfo? But Gersen put these reflections aside because they were now touching down and a flat-bed vehicle was approaching. The driver was a hard-looking man in an outfit identical to that of Yatz, including side-arm, confirming that Gersen's speculation had been correct: this was the dress-code for Malagate's palace guard. I wonder, Gersen thought to himself, how many of them there are?

Yatz handed Gersen's tool bag to the driver and motioned the two passengers to board the vehicle, as he was evidently staying behind with the ship. Gersen and Gabrielle sat on the flatbed with legs dangling over the side, and Gersen whispered to her, "I hope Yatz appreciates that we left the guest quarters in ship-shape condition." Gersen could see the tension in her features and had hoped to lighten the mood, but her response was a tremulous nod. *Ten days to go*, he thought.

Their conveyance trundled in a northerly direction along a gravel path toward the high ground where a majestic building stood, dominating the surrounding area. Mansion, chateau, palace, fortress, or whatever it was, it was an impressive structure of two stories, accommodating perhaps twenty rooms, Gersen estimated, with round turrets at either end. A broad terrace surrounded by a balustrade projected outward, and ran from one end of the building to the other. At the eastern corner of this veranda was a metallic shed-like structure — a recent addition, probably, as it was clearly not part of the original design. Its approximate dimensions were just about the size to accommodate a Thribolt cannon.

To the east as well, the ground sloped gently downward, and Gersen could make out the tops of the structures that he had construed to be slave quarters when he had sighted them from the orbiting ship. He tapped Gabrielle on the shoulder and gestured in that direction. She nodded grimly.

As they approached the building, the gravel road forked, the driver swung left and came to a stop at a side entrance flanked by two more uniformed and armed guards. The door opened and a small woman with short gray hair and pleasant features emerged. "I am Enga," she said. "Welcome to Grabhorne Keep. Follow me and I will show you to your quarters." She led them down a corridor that was dimly lit by some invisible source, and showed them into a suite of rooms that included two bedrooms with attached bath facilities and a common sitting area. "Please wait here," said Enga. "The Baron will see you shortly."

Enga departed and Gabrielle was about to speak, but Gersen gave a swift negative shake of his head, reminding her to be aware of likely listening devices.

"Well, here we are," he said, affecting an affable tone. "I am eager to get to work on the piano, but I surely hope our employer will see fit to return my tools. In the meanwhile, we might as well look over our accommodations."

They proceeded to do just that, and a brief inspection disclosed that fresh clothing had been provided along with a supply of toiletries, linens and other basic necessities. Gersen also located several listening devices, and made sure that his positive comments about the furnishings were within hearing range. After that, there was nothing to do but wait.

"We should have brought the chessboard," Gersen said lightheartedly, as much for the benefit of eavesdroppers as for Gabrielle.

After about an hour that seemed interminably longer, Enga reappeared and said, "Follow me; the Baron will see you now." They proceeded down the corridor outside their quarters to a set of stairs that Gersen supposed were roughly at the center of the building. At the top of the stairs, Enga opened a door and ushered them into a great vaulted chamber surrounded by stained glass windows. Around the periphery were various sofas and chairs, and at the center stood the Broadwood Grand Piano. Enga then backed away and closed the door behind her.

Another door opened at the far end of the room and a tall man entered, dressed in elegant deep blue and wearing a red sash draped from his left shoulder to his right hip. Gersen's tool bag dangled from his left hand.

"Welcome to my humble home," he intoned in a resonant baritone. "I am Gyle Warweave."

For the second time in three days, Gersen was confounded. Gyle Warweave was the human *persona* that Attel Malagate had adopted, and as whom Malagate had died twenty-five years earlier. That Gyle Warweave was at the time forty-five to fifty years of age, Gersen had estimated. The same man today would be in his seventies. But the stately, handsome figure, strong and fit looking, with short-cropped black curls and harsh nose and chin who now stood before Gersen was not a day older than the Warweave he remembered. The solution to this enigma came to Gersen as a revelation — Mongo Malagate was a clone of Attel Malagate, and had adopted the identical human *persona*. Gersen quickly pulled himself together and replied, "It is a pleasure to meet you. I am Edgar Darby and this is my assistant Gabrielle Richet. Thank you for your welcome; our accommodations are quite satisfactory. I see that you have my tools."

Warweave pierced him with a hard glance of his dark eyes. "Ah yes, your tools," he said. "We needed to examine them — a necessary security precaution, I'm sure you will appreciate."

"I trust that you found nothing to cause alarm," said Gersen.

"Nothing of great importance, but my security people did wonder about this one." Warweave pulled the signaling device from the bag and held it in his immaculate hand with glossy fingernails.

"That," said Gersen, "is an instrument for measuring the tensile properties of piano strings." Gersen then launched into a well-rehearsed lecture on piano wires — how their length, tension, thickness, and metallic qualities combine to produce exactly the desired tones.

After less than a minute, Warweave waved him off. "I see the point," he said. "Well, one can't be too cautious where security is concerned." He placed the signaling device back in the bag and handed it over to Gersen. "When are you ready to begin?"

"Right away," said Gersen. "The sooner we begin, the sooner we complete the job, and I agreed to a fixed price arrangement with your representative."

Warweave chuckled softly, "Indeed you did. Very well, I shall leave you to your work."

"Just a moment," Gabrielle interrupted, then strode over to the piano and ran her hand over the polished mahogany veneer. "I know this piano. It is the Broadwood that was stolen from the Pontefract Museum."

Gersen was about to interrupt, but didn't. *What is she doing?* he thought.

"Yes, indeed, this is the Pontefract Broadwood. Do you think I stole it?" Warweave uttered an indulgent laugh, as if talking to a child. "Of course not. When I learned of the theft, I contacted the perpetrators and paid a considerable ransom."

Gabrielle, however, was not to be condescended to in this way. "Do you not suppose that by paying ransom you are simply encouraging more thieves?"

"That is the view that some have expressed, but let me ask you this: if your child has been kidnapped, which is your greater concern: discouraging further kidnapping or rescuing your child from brutes? No, my dear, in this case I could not allow myself to leave this precious object in irresponsible hands."

Not to be outdone by Warweave's facile response, Gabrielle pressed on, "Will you then return the piano to its rightful owner?"

"Most likely," Warweave replied, "provided of course that I am recompensed for the considerable expense I have incurred — with perhaps a bit extra for the effort. In the meanwhile, I find myself entitled to enjoy some pride of ownership, however temporary that may prove to be. Life is ephemeral, after all, and one must take one's pleasures where one finds them. And hopefully, one of those pleasures will be hearing the piano played, as I understand the sound that it produces is without parallel, especially when engendered by skilled hands."

Gersen at first had been alarmed at Gabrielle's seemingly confrontational posture; this was not at all the 'harmless piano tuner' motif that they had agreed. But then he began to understand what she was doing. Warweave/Malagate was toying with her as with a pet. The net effect would make him more rather than less comfortable with their presence, as he was clearly awarding himself the upper hand in this colloquy. As a Star King, Gersen reflected, Malagate knows nothing of human genders, nor especially of the art of female psychology. This could turn out to be a significant point in their favor.

"I hope my performance will not disappoint you," said Gabrielle.

"We share that hope," said Warweave. "Let Enga know when you are ready." Then he wheeled about and exited the way he had come in.

Gersen and Gabrielle were now alone with the Broadwood in the great vaulted chamber. Gersen glanced surreptitiously around the space, looking for listening devices or places where they could be concealed. He also assessed that anything in this enormous room would be too far away to pick up muted conversations. The one remaining alternative was the piano itself. He put a finger to his lips and pointed that way; by now Gabrielle had been with him long enough to know what he was doing. The two of them moved their hands and eyes with deliberation around the Broadwood, as would a surgeon examining a patient before an operation. They found nothing to cause concern. To be doubly sure, Gersen depressed a series of keys in no particular order, while he whispered to Gabrielle.

"We should use the background sound of random notes to muffle our conversation. The man with whom you just engaged as Warweave is actually Mongo Malagate."

"I guessed as much," said Gabrielle. "But how can you be sure?"

"It's a long story," said Gersen. "But trust me, I am sure. Of course, we don't want him to know we are aware of his disguise. Continue to think of him as Warweave. But remember, he is dangerous."

Then they set about the actual job for which they had been hired — checking and adjusting string tensions, smoothing hammer felts as necessary, and so forth. It was tedious work, Gersen reflected, and he was glad not to have to make a living this way.

While they worked, Gersen pondered their recent encounter. If he had recognized Warweave as Malagate's persona, was it possible then that Malagate had recognized him as Kirth Gersen — perhaps concealing that information until he could put it to some advantageous use? After all, Mongo Malagate had sent his henchman, Sligo Patch, to interrogate Rundle Deterras about Gersen. Upon reflection, however, the fact that Mongo knew the name did not mean that he could recognize the person. Clones do not inherit the memories or knowledge of their precursors. Far more likely was that Attel Malagate, before his demise, had provided Mongo with certain information — not only about Gersen and Deterras, but most certainly as well about Teehalt's

Planet, and Attel Malagate's plan to use that as the home base for a new master race of Star Kings. Attel might even have provided Mongo with Kirth Gersen's physical description, but that would have necessarily been sketchy, at best, since Star Kings were supposedly unable to differentiate between one human and another. For the same reason, Mongo would scarcely have been able to recognize Kirth Gersen, based on twenty-five year old sketchy details. Therefore, Gersen concluded that his identity as Edgar Darby was safe for now.

Day 5

Not only was the task of piano tuning tedious, but Gersen was ever-mindful that the deadline for Jaeger's assault was looming, and he was making no progress in finding a way to disable the Thribolt. For one brief moment, it seemed that fate had presented him with exactly the opportunity he needed, but that chance evaporated almost as quickly as it had appeared. Enga had been serving Gersen and Gabrielle meals in a small dining area adjacent to their quarters. On their second evening, they discovered two additional guests at the table. One was a frail, sparse-haired man with bird-like features, who introduced himself as Alistair Sand. The other was a skinny blond eight-year-old named Kara, with eyes that looked red from recent crying. Gersen introduced himself and Gabrielle, then said, "We are piano tuners. What, may I ask, brings you to Grabhorne?" Although, of course, Gersen already knew the answer.

"I am providing technical assistance," Sand answered evasively, speaking with a nervous tick, and undoubtedly aware that he was being monitored.

What luck! was the thought that flashed through Gersen's mind. His plan had been to disable the Thribolt operator, and with this flimsy-looking character, that could be done with the flick of his wrist. Then he asked, "How long do you plan to be here?"

"Not much longer. I am training several of the Baron's men. That task is nearly complete and when it is, Kara and I will be returning to our home planet."

Bad news, thought Gersen. If replacements had been trained, disabling Sand would accomplish nothing, except to expose his and Gabrielle's identities — a likely death sentence. On his own, Gersen might take that risk, thinking that he could escape and evade retribution until Jaeger's arrival. But he could not expose Gabrielle. Instead, he must find some other way.

After two more days of painstaking work, they advised Enga that the Broadwood was ready to be played. Another day passed, however, with no reply. Then Enga approached them at the evening meal, and said, "The Baron will hear you play tomorrow."

Day 9

At the appointed hour, Enga escorted Gabrielle and Gersen to the vaulted chamber where the piano stood. As before, Enga departed and there was nothing to do but wait. Then Warweave made his entrance in the manner of a celebrated actor appearing on a stage. He was grandly attired as before, his suit perhaps a deeper blue, but still with its crimson sash. His deep-set black eyes looked them over, and for a moment Gersen imagined the sensation that a rodent must experience under the gaze of a hungry serpent.

"Congratulations," Warweave intoned in his resonant baritone. "You have worked efficiently, a behavior much to be admired."

Then he nodded to Gabrielle, "I understand that you are ready to perform."

"If you are ready to listen," said Gabrielle.

"By all means proceed." Warweave settled himself into one of the comfortable arm chairs at the periphery of the room, with the air of a gourmet awaiting service at a celebrated restaurant.

Gabrielle took up her position on the piano bench, gently stretched her fingers, paused for a brief moment's concentration, then ran her hands over the keyboard. The piece she played, Gersen would later learn, was a well-known exercise by the pre-Apocalyptic composer, J.S. Bach. The effect, in Gabrielle's skilled and gentle handling, was mesmerizing. Gersen found himself entranced by the melodic progression of notes. For Warweave, though, the effect was even more pronounced.

Warweave had closed his eyes; his head lolled backwards, almost as if asleep. His customarily stern expression had settled into a mask of rapturous contentment. It was a miraculous transformation, Gersen felt, that this cold-blooded monster could be so swayed by music. And this result was not just from the elegance of the composition, but equally due to the artistry of Gabrielle's performance.

Gabrielle continued through several pieces, finished with a flourish, and rose from the bench. Warweave's eyes popped open and he sat upright, his hands applauding softly.

"Well done," he said. "Perhaps you will perform again for me tomorrow."

"If you wish," said Gabrielle, "but I have a favor to ask."

"Of course, my dear, if it is not unreasonable."

"Edgar and I would like to venture outdoors."

"Are your accommodations not satisfactory?"

"The accommodations are fine, but we feel like prisoners here. We have not seen daylight in several days."

"Very well. I will arrange for one of my companions to accompany you tomorrow morning." Evidently 'companions' was how Warweave referred to his security forces.

"Why is a guard necessary?"

"A standard security precaution. I would not want you to be injured or become lost."

"We would not want to divert one of your guards from their normal duties."

Warweave uttered another of his sardonic laughs. "This will not be a problem, there are more than enough companions."

"Oh? How many do you have?"

"At the moment, perhaps one or two more than a hundred."

"My goodness...why so many?"

"I have various interests in the Beyond, which, as you likely know, can be a dangerous place. A hundred or so may seem excessive here on Grabhorne, but when help is needed off-planet, it is convenient to have ample companions on hand. Also, there is more for them to do here than you might imagine. For example, we share Grabhorne with several species of formidable predators, and companions patrol the border of our property daily, keeping the beasts at bay. In any event, there is no inconvenience in providing you with an escort. I will assign Yatz to the task, since you already know him. He will call for you in the morning. And in the afternoon, perhaps you will play for me again."

"A fair bargain," said Gabrielle. "In the meanwhile, Edgar and I need to spend some time with the piano. During that last piece, there were a few notes I felt needed adjustment."

"I detected nothing amiss," said Warweave, "but you are the expert. How much time do you need?"

"An hour should be sufficient."

"Enga will fetch you then. Until tomorrow."

Warweave then swept out, leaving Gersen and Gabrielle to themselves.

"What adjustments are necessary?" whispered Gersen.

"None really, but I thought it would be useful to have a conversation."

"You are a clever creature," Gersen said, "in addition to a beguiling one."

"Well, at least we will be allowed outdoors tomorrow. I thought it would help to get the lay of the land."

"Undoubtedly it will. Did you see Warweave's reaction when you played?"

"I only had a glance," said Gabrielle, "as I was concentrating on my performance."

"He looked to be in some sort of trance-like state. It reminded me of what was formerly said of opium users."

"I learned in my music studies that certain compositions, played in certain ways, stimulate a dopamine release in certain listeners. It is a powerful hormone that infuses a person with a sense of well-being."

"If that is what I observed, the effect was quite intense. Perhaps this is a sensitivity of Star Kings not previously known. We will see whether it shows itself again tomorrow."

Day 10

The next morning, Yatz was waiting in the flat-bed wagon, and signaled them on board. They rumbled down the gravel path on worn-out air cushions, with Hypnos rising at late morning attitude on their left. The Pharaon spaceship was on the field where it had landed, but the Galactic vessel had departed. One less variable to keep in mind, mused Gersen. Once past the landing field, the path ran through dense vegetation, which soon became tall trees. Dappled splotches of Hypnos light filtered through the leaves, and the hoots and chirps of unfamiliar creatures sounded in the distance. Presently the path forked. Yatz steered left, eliciting a dismal moan from somewhere deep in the portion of the forest they were skirting.

Yatz proceeded a short distance to where the woods had been cleared and cultivated fields spread out in all directions. Yatz turned north and ran along the planted area until they came to the rows of rough-planked structures that Gersen recognized as slave quarters, although at the moment there was no sign of habitation. Gersen tapped Yatz on the shoulder.

"Who lives here?" he asked.

"Workers," answered Yatz.

Eventually they turned left and headed back to the gravel path that led to Warweave's palace. As they approached, Gersen once again noticed the rectangular structure at the east end of the terrace. He once more caught Yatz' attention and pointed to the object, "What is that?" he asked.

"Off limits," Yatz replied, his most comprehensive answer of the day.

After a simple lunch, Enga led them back to the vaulted chamber where they waited until Warweave arrived.

"I trust you enjoyed your outdoor excursion," he said.

"Very refreshing, thank you," said Gabrielle, "but we have some questions."

"All things at their appointed moment. First, your performance."

Warweave settled into the same chair as before and Gabrielle began to play. Gersen marveled at her skill. The notes came clean and crisp and filled the air with a charmed fountain of sound. Warweave was entranced as before, his eyes closed and his head lolled back. When the performance came to an end, it seemed that his mood had mellowed.

"You had some questions?" he asked.

"Yes. Yatz drove us past enormous tracts of planted fields. Are you using slaves to operate your lands?"

"Slaves?" Warweave snorted. "By no means, my dear. My workers are indentured servants. They sign a contract that requires them to work for a term of years, to fulfill an obligation. When the contract is completed, they are free to go. This is not slavery, but a straightforward commercial arrangement."

"What is the nature of the obligation?" Gabrielle persisted, "and what is the length of the contract?"

"That varies from case to case. It would be misleading to generalize."

"I would like to confirm this indentured servant status for myself. If the situation is as you say, the workers should be free to speak with me."

Gersen was growing increasingly concerned. Gabrielle was pressing her luck, but he suppressed his instinct to intervene and held his tongue. Warweave was visibly coming out of his mellow mood, but nevertheless seemed to take Gabrielle's doubt as a game in which he held the winning hand.

"It will be arranged," he said. "Tomorrow, Yatz will take you to meet representatives of the workers' committee."

"Please instruct Yatz that Darby and I are to consult with these representatives in private."

Warweave's black gaze turned cold, but he still seemed to view himself as the cat and Gabrielle the mouse.

"As you wish," he said, then rose and exited the chamber.

Day 11

The next morning, Gersen arose early and slipped out to the sitting area he shared with Gabrielle. He opened the outer door a crack so that he could scan the length of the dimly lit corridor. Yatz had all but confirmed the location of the Thribolt cannon when he declared the east portion of the terrace to be 'off limits.' And where could Alistair Sand be training replacements, but at the Thribolt cannon itself? If this reasoning was correct, he should observe Sand leaving his own quarters and heading toward the terrace.

For what seemed like an eternity, the corridor was empty, but Gersen continued his scrutiny with the patience of a hungry predator. Then one of Warweave's companions came quietly down the hallway, stopped at a door, rapped softly, and Alistair Sand emerged. The two figures then proceeded back in the direction from which the guard had come. Gersen eased his own door open and followed at a discrete distance. Presently Sand and the guard came to the stairway that, Gersen knew, led up to the vaulted chamber where the Broadwood piano stood. But the guard turned right instead, tapped some codes into a key pad, and a door swung open to the outside. Gersen followed as closely as he dared, but by the time he reached the exit, the door had closed. Lacking the code to open it, he spun around, re-traced his steps, and returned to his own quarters.

Gersen took a seat, stared into the darkness, and pondered his situation. Jaeger's ships were in place and waiting, a safe distance from Grabhorne's radar. They would time their assault to arrive at sundown on the day of receiving Gersen's signal, or on the 14th day if no signal had been received. When their approach was detected, Sand would be summoned. That is when Gersen would intercept him. The odds that he could succeed were unknown, but they were the same whether on the 14th day or earlier. When there was no advantage to delay, Gersen always favored action. He would send the signal today.

CHAPTER IX

The best laid schemes o' mice an' men
Gang aft agley,
And leave us naught but grief an' pain
For promised joy.
   — Robert Burns

———✖———

Hypnos, the sun of Grabhorne, had favored Gersen and Gabrielle with a clear, bright mid-morning on this their eighth day here. They were riding on the flat-bed vehicle driven by Yatz, on their way to meet with the workers' committee — the concession that Gabrielle had extracted from Warweave the day before. Gersen for his part was energized. He had a plan of action, and the period of tedious confinement in Warwave's palace, unable to communicate freely except with words muffled by piano tones, would soon be over. He reached into his pocket and extracted the signaling device — a small tool resembling a screwdriver, except that instead of a blade it ended in two filaments. All he needed to do was depress the inconspicuous bulb at the end of the handle for a count of five, and the signal would be sent. It would first travel to a tiny satellite that Jaeger had placed deep in the Hypnos system, appearing no different to Grabhorne's radar than a random piece of space debris. Then the signal would be relayed to Jaeger's waiting fleet in deeper space.

Gersen took a breath, depressed the activation bulb, and counted. Then he slipped the little gadget back into his pocket and smiled, imagining the release of tension among the forty waiting troopers. They, after all, had been cooped up in their four ships for as long as he and

Gabrielle had been virtual prisoners here. The assault, by agreement with Jaeger, would begin approximately nine hours from now. On their approach, however, Jaeger's fleet would be spotted by Grabhorne's radar. Some sort of alarm would be triggered, and Alistair Sand would be summoned to operate the Thribolt cannon. That outcome Gersen must prevent, by whatever means he could devise. Jaeger had a plan to evade the Thribolt projectile, but the success of those tactics was far from certain, and failure would mean instant death for Jaeger and the nine troopers on board his ship. The loss of a quarter of the assault force, as well as its commander, would also jeopardize the mission, perhaps irretrievably. After all, if Warweave's statement about the number of his 'companions' was accurate, the IPCC forces were already outnumbered by better than two-and-a-half to one, and any deterioration in those odds could be catastrophic. Success or failure, therefore, lay squarely on Gersen's shoulders.

Sitting by Gersen's side, Gabrielle was grim. He understood full well the reason. Her family had been among the victims of Malagate's raid on Willow Grove. There were only two possible outcomes for them, neither of them good. Either they had not survived, or they had been enslaved. Willow Grove had been a tight-knit community, and members of the workers' committee likely knew their fate. But he must warn her to be cautious. Warweave's permission to meet the workers had been granted all too easily, Gersen reflected; one or even all the committee members could well be informants. Gabrielle must say nothing to reveal her identity, as that would alert Warweave and likely thwart Gersen's plan.

Gersen glanced over Yatz' shoulder as their vehicle approached the rough-hewn barracks that were enclosed by a metal fence, where in an open gate five male figures awaited their arrival. Yatz, per his instructions, halted out of range of hearing, grunted "Go," and gestured toward the waiting men. As they approached the group, Gersen grasped Gabrielle's arm and slowed their pace.

"Careful," he said in low tones. "Do not reveal your identity, there could be informants here."

Gabrielle turned her head and looked surprised. She had obviously been expecting something different — identifying herself and inquiring about her family. There had not been a chance before now to mention Gersen's concern about informants without being overheard. But then she showed a look of understanding as the import of his warning sunk in. As much as she wanted to learn the fate of her family, that would have to wait.

"Understood," was her hushed reply.

"Be patient," Gersen added, "events are moving forward."

Another couple of paces further and this time she grasped Gersen's arm.

"The one second from our left," she whispered, "is my brother-in-law, Henri."

They arrived before the waiting group, where Gersen was struck by the starkness of their appearance. They wore drab gray pajama-like attire; they had a gaunt, malnourished look, and their features were so lacking in animation that it was difficult to tell them apart. Gersen's gaze briefly shifted from the waiting figures to the cultivated lands spreading out as far as the eye could see — how many hours under the blazing sun had they toiled to plow and plant those fields? Then the one in the center of the group, possibly the elder, stepped forward.

"I am Willard," he said. "The Baron's orders are to tell you whatever you wish to know."

"I am Edgar Darby," said Gersen, "and this is my assistant Gabrielle. We have only a few questions, and will not require much of your time. We understand that you are indentured servants. Is that correct?"

"Yes," said Willard. "You understand accurately."

"What, then, are your terms of service?"

"That varies from case to case," Willard replied. "It would be misleading to generalize."

This was the same answer — the exact words, in fact — that Warweave had given earlier to Gabrielle. The committee had obviously been instructed meticulously about what to say.

"Do you expect to be free when your term of service is complete?"

"Yes," said Willard. Perhaps it was Gersen's imagination, but there seemed a deep sense of desolation in that single word, as if Willard knew it was untrue, and had no hope of altering their fate.

"Thank you," said Gersen. "You have told us what we wanted to know. We will leave you to your own affairs." Then Gersen hesitated as if a new idea had occurred to him, and added, "We would like to consult with one of your members in private." He scanned the five forlorn figures as if trying to select one at random; it was remarkable, he thought, that such deeply tanned features could not obscure their ashen looks. Then he pointed to Gabrielle's brother-in-law.

"You," he said. "What is your name?"

"Henri Dassault."

"Step over here for a moment, please." Gersen motioned Henri to move out of hearing of the others. It seemed that Willard was about to object, but his instructions obviously failed to cover this eventuality. He said nothing, and Henri did as he was told.

"Show no sign of recognition," Gersen said, "and listen to me carefully. At dusk this evening, a liberation force will land. There will be a battle, and assistance would be valuable. Can you find three others who are reliable?"

"Yes, I think so," said Henri, still bewildered.

"Say nothing of this. Just tell the three to be ready for my visit after sunset. And assure the others here that we just asked you the same questions we asked beforehand, and you confirmed the answers. Understood?"

Henri nodded tentatively.

Then Gersen raised his voice so that he could be overheard by the rest of the group. "Thank you for confirming Willard's answers. And thank you, Willard and the others, for your time."

Gersen wheeled about, grasping Gabrielle's elbow and turning her with him, and the two walked purposefully back to the waiting vehicle. Before they arrived within Yatz' hearing range, Gabrielle turned toward Gersen so that her lips could not be read.

"At last," she said.

That afternoon, Gersen and Gabrielle were summoned to Warweave's presence. As they arrived at the stairs leading to the vaulted chamber, Gersen glanced covertly to his right and confirmed the location of the exit and the keypad that would open it. *Five hours from now*, he told himself.

Warweave effected his customary self-satisfied, elegant arrival, while Gersen and Gabrielle attended by the Broadwood like servants waiting for instructions.

"I trust your interview with the workers' committee was satisfactory," said Warweave.

"They confirmed what you told us," said Gabrielle, then added, "precisely." If Warweave noticed the pointed irony of Gabrielle's final word, he showed no reaction. Instead, he seemed well pleased with the state of affairs.

"Since that trifle is now behind us," he said, "let us move forward with today's recital."

"One moment," said Gabrielle. "We were hired to tune the piano, and I was to demonstrate the satisfactory performance of that task by playing it. The piano is tuned; the results are now confirmed. Our contract is fulfilled and we should be discussing arrangements for returning to Avente."

"You do not wish to play?" said Warweave in a tone, Gersen imagined, of feigned surprise.

"It is not a question of whether I wish to play or not," Gabrielle replied. "It is that our contract is fulfilled."

"That is one possible interpretation. But let us not blemish an enjoyable afternoon of music by engaging in tiresome negotiations."

Gersen imagined that Warweave/Malagate had no intention of allowing them to return to Avente, either now or later; but there was no point in carrying this conversation further as all would be resolved in a few hours.

"For the sake of harmony," he said, "Gabrielle will play and we will take up the issue of the contract at a later date."

"A sound proposal," said Warweave, and settled back into his chair.

What Gersen hoped would be their final session with Warweave had been completed smoothly. It was now early evening and Enga had set out a modest supper in the dining area, where they had been joined by Alistair Sand and little Kara. Gersen forced himself to produce a few shards of vacuous table conversation, but his mind was drawn elsewhere, to a kaleidoscopic whirl of mixed emotions. One of these

was relief that they were done with Warweave and his unctuous condescension. Warweave would be revealed as Malagate and shortly killed
or captured. Second was the need to clear his mind for the action that
lay ahead. If Jaeger timed his assault to occur at sunset, his fleet would
be within Grabhorne's radar range approximately half an hour before
that — any minute now, in fact. And third, but by no means least, were
his thoughts about what the future held for Gersen and Gabrielle
together. The notion that in Gabrielle he had found the possibility of
romance that all his life he could only dream about, was now firmly
locked in his imagination. Were there reciprocal ideas on her part?
Once they were clear of the present entanglement, he would make his
feelings known. She seemed to have an ability to read his thoughts, and
some of this she must already sense. But whether she saw a life ahead
together, as he did, would only be revealed in time…

Suddenly the air was shattered by the ululating wail of a siren.
Alistair Sand sat bolt upright, eyes bulging as if in shock, his nervous
tic oscillating rapidly. Then the door burst open and one of Warweave's
companions stalked in — a burly thug, flat-faced and scarred. He
grasped Sand by the shoulder and hauled him upright.

"Duty calls," he growled, then turned Sand around and marched
him out.

Gersen stood, glanced at Gabrielle. "Wait in our quarters," he said.
"You should be safe there."

She leapt up, embraced him and whispered in his ear, "I trust you."

He slipped out the door and down the dim-lit corridor as if on
winged feet, rapidly closing the distance between himself and the two
others. There was no need for silence, as the siren was drowning everything else out. The guard and Sand stopped at the exit door, and the
guard punched in the codes. As the door began to swing open, Gersen
came up behind him, locked his right arm around the thug's thick
neck, and grasped the bicep of his left arm which then braced itself
against the back of the guard's bristled head. Then Gersen tightened
hard, twisted, heard the snap of separating vertebrae, and the guard
dropped to the floor like a sack of stones. Gersen stooped and removed
the dead guard's belt and holstered projac, then fastened it around his
own waist. He withdrew the projac and quickly examined it. It was a

standard issue, one that he knew well, and fully charged according to its meter. He flipped off the safety catch and slipped the weapon back into its holster.

Now out on the terrace, Sand fixed Gersen with a bewildered stare. "The cannon," he pleaded, "I have to operate it. They will do horrible things to Kara if I fail."

"Don't worry," said Gersen. "I will take care of that. Let's go to the cannon."

As the two proceeded along the terrace, Gersen glanced back over his right shoulder. Hypnos was coming down. *Fifteen minutes to sunset,* he thought.

Gersen, guiding Sand by the shoulder, arrived at the large rectangular shed that occupied the east end of the terrace; its door also had a keypad. Gersen prodded Sand forward and instructed him to enter the necessary codes. Sand started to comply, but with hands shaking so badly that Gersen wondered whether he could finish. Then there was a shout from the direction from which they had come, and two more guards plunged out onto the terrace. Gersen drew the projac off his hip, dialed the power to high, and launched a bolt of pure energy that carved a melon-sized hole through the midsection of the attacker on the left. The devastation of the assailant caused Gersen to realize that he was over-using the weapon, likely due to his anger at the ugly threats to little Kara. He dialed the power back and sent another stream of heart-stopping energy into the chest of the other guard, who collapsed forward and lay twitching on the deck. Gersen wheeled around, and saw that the door to the cannon's shed had opened. Sand had entered and was reaching for the second keypad that Gersen knew from his briefing at Jarnell would give access to the cannon's control panel. Projac still in hand, Gersen shoved Sand aside and aimed a concentrated beam at the keypad itself, melting it into an unusable pool of slag. No one now — neither Sand nor any of his trainees — could operate the Thribolt. Gersen's primary mission was complete.

No time to waste, though, with self-congratulations.

"What have you done?" Sand pleaded. "What will happen to Kara now?"

"Nothing will happen to her," said Gersen. "You can't be blamed if the controls are not accessible. Return to your quarters and look after your daughter."

His features white with fear, Sand stumbled off in that direction. Gersen followed until he came to the two downed guards whose projacs he removed, flipped off the safeties, and tucked them into his waistband. *Not recommended procedure*, he thought, *but sometimes circumstances require exceptions.* Then he placed both hands on the balustrade, vaulted over, landed nimbly as a cat, and began jogging toward the workers' barracks. Hypnos, off his right shoulder, was now a shimmering blue white disc sinking into the far horizon.

As Gersen closed the distance to the workers' housing, the terrain sloped gently downward, allowing him to pick up the pace. This also provided a view out over the rooftops of the barracks, where he could see four ships with black and silver IPCC markings descending into the open fields. They briefly reflected the fading light of Hypnos, which then went dark just as they settled to the ground. *Immaculate timing*, Gersen thought. But his reflections on Jaeger's navigational prowess quickly faded, as there were two more guards at the gate to the workers' compound. They spotted Gersen just as he saw them and began to draw their weapons. Gersen snatched the two projacs from his waistband, threw himself to the ground, and fired. With a hiss of energy, both beams found their target, and both guards went down. On occasion in the past, Gersen had wondered whether all the effort learning to shoot left-handed was worthwhile, but those doubts had just been crisply answered.

Four still figures waited at the now-unguarded gate, as Gersen pulled up breathing hard. He could not make out their features in the gathering darkness, but as he approached more closely, he recognized Henri. The other three presumably were those whose help Henri had enlisted.

"Gabrielle is back in Warweave's palace, safe in her own quarters," he told Henri. "What of Madeleine?" referring to Gabrielle's step-sister and Henri's wife.

"She is back with the other workers," said Henri, "safe as well, at least for now."

"What about your parents?"

"Dead," replied Henri. "They were executed along with all the others deemed too old to work. Our son, Jono, as well did not survive the raid."

Gersen felt himself grimace at this news. It would be devastating to Gabrielle. But these thoughts would have to wait.

"Are these men ready to take on Warweave's companions?" he asked Henri.

"They are. This is Jason…Luke…Bernard," said Henri, as each man nodded in response.

Gersen handed one of his two extra projacs to Henri and the other to the one named Jason. Then he stooped, relieved each of the two dead guards of their weapons and passed them to Luke and Bernard.

"Do each of you know how to handle these things?" he asked. All four nodded affirmatively.

"Set the power control to half; that is enough to take out a target if you hit him in the right place, and we need to conserve our fire power. You each have enough for maybe twenty shots, so make them count. Aim for the midsection."

Gersen could see that the four were following his words closely, and they wore expressions of grim determination. Henri was not the only one to have lost loved ones, he imagined.

"Do you know where the companions' quarters are?" he asked.

The others nodded.

"That's where we will find our targets. You can't see them from here, but beyond your barracks, four IPCC ships have just come down, carrying forty troopers. They will bear the brunt of the fighting. But Warweave has over a hundred armed men. Our job will be to even the odds a bit. Ready?"

With Henri leading and Gersen at his side, the group marched off along the fence line, heading in the general direction east of Warweave's palace. Glancing to his left, Gersen noticed the shape of Warweave's Pharaon in the distance, standing where it had been parked, and reflecting the pale light from Grabhorne's moon, Miel, that was rising in the east. The image seemed to shudder, and then to Gersen's dismay it began to rise, slowly lifting off then gaining speed.

Gersen muttered a bitter expletive. His plans had not allowed for Warweave to escape. But this was no time for self-recrimination.

Warweave — or Malagate — would soon lose everything, and the slaves of Grabhorne would be free. In the moment required for these fleeting thoughts, the Pharaon had disappeared into the night sky, and was lost among the myriad points of starlight.

Gersen proceeded alongside Henri toward the companions' living quarters. Presently, Henri paused and pointed to a building dimly visible in the dark. "There," Henri whispered, "that is the first of several where they live."

Gersen motioned the group forward to the windowless side of the building, then peered around the corner to what he imagined was the front. There he could see several figures emerging, still half-dressed and struggling with gear. Gersen fired off two hissing bolts that sent two of the companions to the ground; any others still inside would now be wary.

He grasped the one called Jason by the arm, and positioned him at the same spot from which Gersen had fired. "Stay here," he said, "and shoot anyone who tries to leave. You others come with me."

Gersen led the group along the back of the structure until they came to the side of the next building in line, then he repeated the sequence until each of four exits was covered by Henri and his three volunteers. Gersen had no way of knowing how many of Warweave's thugs were still bottled up inside their barracks, but possibly enough, he hoped, to make a difference. In any event, it was the best that could be done with four untrained recruits.

Leaving the group with clear instructions, Gersen returned the way he had come. Most of the companions, he supposed, would likely be setting up defensive positions somewhere near the palace. Moving slowly because the footing was uncertain, he began to make out the looming shape of the east side of the palace, and proceeding further, a flurry of activity at the base of the terrace. He dropped to his knees and crept closer. As the moon was rising and visibility was improving, he could discern various figures of companions, moving about in a state of agitation, with shouted orders stirring them to action. Then the full moon emerged from behind a cloud and he could clearly see that the companions were setting up a line of five anti-armor weapons. The tripod bases were being secured by iron spikes driven into the ground by sledge-hammers; the barrels were being placed on swiveling mounts, and their sighting optics fastened into place. *This was serious business*, Gersen grasped, and he hoped Jaeger's people were prepared.

Then one of the companions shouted a warning and flung his arm out toward the south. All heads turned and Gersen turned with them, to discover a fleet of airborne personnel carriers heading in their direction. The companions sprang into action, with gunners taking sights and spinning dials, and others loading high-energy cartridges into the breeches of the guns. Gersen felt his insides tighten; this did not look good for the assault force, but against so many dozens of the heavily armed defenders, there seemed little he could do.

Then he heard a high-pitched vibrating sound and the moonlit air was full of glistening drones, each with pointed tips and carried by four rapidly oscillating wings like dragonflies. The flock merged into a stationary formation, hovering some fifty meters distant, as if waiting for a signal. Then the heavy rifle nearest in line to Gersen fired, and a fireball of pure energy sizzled though the air, scattering drones as it passed through their formation and slamming into the hull of the nearest personnel carrier. There was a great snapping sound; the energy ball diffused leaving the hull of its target intact, but the disabled carrier slowly settled to the ground.

As if goaded into action, one of the drones abandoned its hovering formation and sped with whirring wings toward the gunner who had fired the heavy rifle, plunging its sharp tip into the unfortunate gunner's chest and exploding in a cloud of blood and bones. There followed a brief silence, as if the combatants had been awe-stuck by the shocking damage. Then, seemingly on signal, the entire fleet of drones swarmed forward and began attacking other targets. The companions fought back with desperation, picking off drones with handgun and rifle fire, but the line of defenders was filled with more grisly explosions as drone after drone evaded the defensive hail of energy bolts and found its target.

Still crouching low and to the side of the growing chaos, Gersen saw that the personnel carriers were landing; IPCC troopers came spewing forth and charged into the melee, loosing energy bolts with deadly accuracy as they rushed forward. The companions were so intent on repelling the swarming drones that they scarcely noticed these new attackers. By the time they did, it was clear that further resistance was futile, and hands were being flung up in surrender. A few sporadic shots hissed through the night air, then all was quiet. The battle had ended almost as quickly as it started.

Some twenty surviving companions were now on their knees and handcuffed; the rest were strewn about the ground in rag-doll postures. Gersen pulled himself upright and began walking toward the field of combat. The first trooper to see him levelled his rifle and shouted, "Halt! Hands in the air!"

Gersen did as he was told. Even though he was not wearing the uniform of a companion, he could not depend on an agitated young trooper to make that distinction. His would-be captor stepped forward with a pair of cuffs, but as he did so, a new voice rose above the din — one that Gersen knew full well — and ordered, "Stand down, trooper! That man is one of us!"

The trooper lowered his rifle with a sheepish expression on his face.

"Sorry, sir," he said. "Are you Darby?"

Gersen gave a quiet laugh. "I used to be," he said. "But no harm done."

Jaeger then stepped forward with hand extended. His tunic was splattered with filth, but his customarily stern expression wore an uncharacteristic smile.

"No trace of a Thribolt projectile," he said. "Was that your doing, or did my evasive tactics work?"

"No projectile was fired," said Gersen. "Sorry I didn't give you a chance to test your helmsmanship."

"Well done," said Jaeger. "That's one test I'm happy to have missed."

"The mission has succeeded," Gersen replied, "in all respects but one. Malagate escaped. I saw his ship lift off just before the fighting started."

"Do you have any idea where he was going?"

"None at all."

"We've pulled his fangs, though. I doubt he will be reappearing any time soon."

Still gripping Jaeger's hand, Gersen explained that the four volunteers were holding a group of Warweave's underlings at bay. Jaeger summoned a squad of troopers, and they proceeded toward the companions' barracks, where they relieved Henri and his fellows, and returned to the palace with a dozen more companions disarmed and cuffed.

With that responsibility fulfilled, Gersen now found himself anxious to give the good news of their victory to Gabrielle. He explained that desire to Jaeger.

"Of course," said Jaeger. "Take this squad of troopers. They will sweep the palace clean of any of Malagate's thugs we haven't yet accounted for."

Gersen and the troopers climbed over the terrace balustrade, past the bodies of the guards Gersen had dispatched, and into the building. Gersen picked two men to accompany him, and sent the others to scour the rest of the building. He proceeded down the same dimly-lit corridor, retracing his steps from only a few hours earlier, with the memory of Gabrielle's last embrace uplifting his thoughts. He entered the suite of rooms that he and Gabrielle had shared, and what he discovered there would displace that happy memory with desolation. There were four dead bodies sprawled on the floor, in positions that told of violence — two were Malagate's men, Sand and Enga were the others. Kara was huddled in the corner sobbing softly. Gabrielle was nowhere to be seen.

Gersen searched from room to room with a growing sense of hopelessness, first the quarters he and Gabrielle had shared, then the spaces occupied by Sand and Kara. But in the end, the conclusion was unavoidable: Gabrielle was gone. As gently as he could, he extracted from little Kara a sense of what had happened. Five companions had arrived and ordered Gabrielle to leave with them. There had been a struggle. Gabrielle had dealt with two of her assailants, but the others had overpowered her and bound her arms. Sand and Enga had tried to intervene, and both were killed. Gersen examined the dead companions, and one broken neck and another crushed windpipe supported Kara's account. It was cold comfort, he realized, but Gabrielle had comported herself well.

Gersen took a last look at the signs of struggle, then realized he had no desire to ever see this place again, nor could he leave Kara here alone. He hoisted her on his shoulders and made his way back to the terrace and outside. There he found a group of troopers erecting tents for the night, with Jaeger and Henri in some final stage of consultation. They both regarded him quizzically. *Where was Gabrielle?* said the expression on their faces.

"Malagate abducted her by force," he replied to the unasked question. "I saw his ship lift off just before the battle started, although I did not realize at the time that Gabrielle was his captive. I don't know where he went, but he must have a bolt-hole somewhere. With your permission, Commander, I would like to interrogate the prisoners. One of them must know his destination."

"First thing in the morning," said Jaeger.

"Then we need to make arrangements for Kara here. A tent full of battle-happy troopers is not the best place for her to spend the night."

"I'll take the girl to Madeleine," said Henri, referring to his wife and Gabrielle's sister. "We lost our own son, Jono, in the raid on Willow Grove. He was just about the age of this one, and Maddie will be happy to have a child to care for."

"Thank you for that," said Gersen, thinking how often fate worked in unexpected ways. "One final matter, there are two civilians in the palace who will need proper burials."

"It will be dealt with," said Jaeger.

Gersen rose at first light and began the process of interrogating prisoners, delivered to him one at a time by a squad of troopers. Almost as soon as he began, he could see that this was going to be a fruitless and dispiriting undertaking. The first man in had a lean, lanky body and a face so hollowed that it looked cadaverous, with hair hanging in unkempt festoons.

"You can help yourself," Gersen began, "if you will tell me what I need to know. Where did Malagate go?"

The prisoner squinted and spat drily. "How would I know?" he said. "But do you think I would tell you if I did?"

The rest of the interrogation proceeded in that vein, with threats and blandishments alike met with curses and smirking insults. The closest Gersen came to anything of substance was when one of the prisoners said, "Ask Yatz." Yatz, however, was not among the captives and Gersen assumed that he had left on Malagate's ship. Gersen nevertheless persisted, until the last prisoner was led away and he was no wiser than when he started.

That evening found Gersen sharing a libation with Jaeger in the latter's tent. This would be Gersen's final night on Grabhorne, as Jaeger had offered him a place on one of the IPCC vessels that would be returning the next day to Avente with the wounded. The two men sat on folding chairs with metal frames and fabric webbing, with a small bamboo table between them. Jaeger was still wearing the dirt-splattered tunic from the day before, open at the collar in a gesture of informality. His features had the drawn look of one who could use a good night's sleep. Perhaps it was Gersen's imagination, but the iron gray of Jaeger's hair seemed to have advanced another shade toward white. He extracted a small leather flask from his pack, poured out two measures into silver shooter's glasses, and handed one to Gersen.

"The role of military governor is new to me," Jaeger began. "Here in the Beyond there is no judicial framework. For better or for worse, my judgements are absolute. Today, I followed for the most part the wishes of the workers. They shared with me certain details of their suffering at the hands of Malagate and his underlings. I've seen my share of evil-doing in my career, but some of the things I heard today push the boundaries of depravity."

Gersen was not inclined to hear the details, but Jaeger clearly wished to unburden himself and Gersen was the only plausible audience.

"Malagate's introduction to the Willow Grove community was unthreatening. He told them of the predation of pirate bands in the Beyond and offered to protect them. They accepted because his stories of the dangers were horrific and the fees he proposed were modest. Then the fees kept increasing. Willow Grove was an agricultural community with negligible export earnings. When they could not pay in currency, Malagate demanded slaves. When the community declined, his raiders took them all. He forced them to sign contracts as 'indentured servants' to cover the debts he claimed they owed, and executed those too old or feeble to work off their share of the supposed obligation.

"His regime here on Grabhorne was merciless. Production quotas were imposed and shortfalls increased the term of the indentures. It was for Malagate a cruel game, pretending that his captives were contract workers when in fact they were slaves.

"His 'companions', as he called them, made no pretense of equable behavior, and they devised a particularly monstrous punishment for anyone who displeased them. The wilds beyond the plantation are inhabited by voracious predators, who the companions kept at bay by regular hunting expeditions along the perimeter, creating an invisible boundary that the beasts quickly learned not to cross. Workers deemed guilty of even minor infractions were taken beyond those lines and left to fend for themselves. None ever returned.

"Today it fell to me to decide the fate of the companions we hold as prisoners. I repeat that this is the Beyond and there is no protocol to deal with such matters. Therefore, the companions will be loaded on to transport vehicles, taken well past the boundaries of their own creation, and left to the same fate as their Willow Grove victims."

Here Jaeger paused, and emptied the balance of his glass. He took a deep breath and continued.

"Now on to more pleasant matters. I advised the workers' representatives that I could arrange transportation at no cost to them back to Willow Grove. But the consensus of the group is that they prefer to remain here on Grabhorne. The climate is more salubrious, they say, and the soil more fertile. The vast plantings that they themselves have labored to create will soon become a bumper crop. They will have vehicles, machinery, workshops, a power plant, and above all weapons confiscated from their former captors. I will see that Grabhorne is registered in their name; they will have a law enforcement arm that will become an IPCC affiliate. In this way, we add one more civilized community to the Oikumene, and take another small step toward conquering the Beyond."

There will always be a Beyond, Gersen mused, but kept this reflection to himself.

"That ends the account of my day's activity," said Jaeger. "What are the plans of Henry Lucas?"

"A simple enough question," said Gersen. "I intend to track down Malagate and rescue Gabrielle."

"By no means an easy undertaking. Where will you begin?"

"My first thought is Ghnarumen — the planet of the Star Kings."

"Not likely, if you want my opinion," said Jaeger. "It is well known that the race of Star Kings held Attel Malagate to be a renegade. If Mongo Malagate is a clone, he would be most unwelcome on Ghnarumen. Besides, Ghnarumen is off-limits to humans. Even if you discovered that Malagate had somehow sheltered there, you would be helpless to apprehend him."

Gersen nodded glumly. Jaeger was correct and he had little more to say. He stood and looked to the open flap in Jaeger's tent.

"Good luck," said Jaeger. "If I can help, you know where to reach me."

Gersen stepped out into the cool evening, and gazed at the star-filled sky.

You cannot appreciate the vastness of space, he thought, *until you have lost someone dear to you out there.*

CHAPTER X

Oranges and lemons
Say the bells of Saint Clemens

You owe me five farthings
Say the bells of Saint Martins

When will you pay me?
Say the bells of Old Bailey

When I grow rich
Say the bells of Shore Ditch

    — Anonymous

          —⚏—

The morning sky on Grabhorne was dismal overcast, portending likely rain. The IPCC ship that would transport Gersen back to Alphanor was standing in the field where Malagate's Pharaon had previously been parked. Gersen waited nearby and watched as the four wounded personnel whom he would accompany on the flight were loaded onto the ship's auxiliary boarding ramp. Several of the troopers who had served as stretcher bearers paused to wish Gersen well and shake his hand. His role in disabling the Thribolt and thinning the defenders' numbers had circulated through the ranks and prompted congratulations. He accepted the good wishes gracefully, although he would have preferred to remain alone with his reflections. He was not a person accustomed to recognition of any sort, favorable or otherwise; moreover, from his personal point of view, the mission had ended badly. He had never expected Malagate to flee, especially when protected by the Thribolt cannon and over a hundred heavily armed companions. Nor had he anticipated the abduction of Gabrielle. These were failures of anticipation for which he held himself account-able, and for which he would now dedicate himself to making amends.

As the ramp was being lowered for Gersen's turn to board, a vehicle pulled alongside. The driver was Henri Dassault, Gabrielle's brother-in-law and Gersen's former comrade-in-arms. Henri alighted from the driver's seat and extended his hand.

"I've come to say good-bye," he said, "and to thank you on behalf of all of us. I understand that Commander Jaeger has informed you that the Willow Grove survivors have elected to remain on Grabhorne. The prospect of returning to our former home on Brandywine was too painful to endure, with everything we worked so hard to build now having been destroyed. Instead, we will make a fresh start here, and capture much of what our forced labor has created. We will call our home New Horizon, and Willow Grove will exist only in memory.

"I thought you would want to know, as well, that Maddie and little Kara are doing well. They are good for one another, as Kara had earlier lost her mother and Maddie, as you know, had lost her son."

Gersen nodded his appreciation for this news, and started to step toward the ramp that had just been lowered to take him on. But he could see by Henri's troubled look that he still had more to say.

"I myself had mixed feeling about the decision not to return to Willow Grove. The exact fate of our son Jono remains unknown. It is assumed that he perished during Malagate's raid, but no one among the survivors was witness to that fact. Ever since our confinement here on Grabhorne, I have told myself that if I ever had the chance, I would return to Willow Grove and search for Jono. The idea is bred of wishful thinking, I know. The chances of a nine-year-old surviving on his own seem next to none. But now that we have been released from bondage, I am faced with that decision — to return to Willow Grove or not. I am sharing this with you because you are in large measure responsible for allowing me to make this choice; you are also close to Gabrielle, and Jono is her nephew.

"But I have decided to remain here for two reasons. First, I can't leave Maddie alone with her new responsibility. Second, I have been elected Chief Constable of the New Horizon Law Enforcement Office.

Jason, Luke, and Bernard will be my deputies, and Commander Jaeger has assigned one of his lieutenants to supervise our training. I could scarcely turn down this assignment in view of all that's happened. Besides, the effort to recover Jono would only lead to further heartbreak for both Maddie and me."

Gersen nodded his understanding. He grasped Henri's hand once more, and said, "I am sure you have made the correct decision."

Then he stepped up on the ramp, surveyed the scene around him as it lifted him to the ship, and reflected on the harsh reality that sometimes in life there is no perfect decision.

Once clear of the Hypnos system, the ship's Intersplit engaged, and all passengers settled in for the three-day voyage. Gersen had been accorded an officer's cabin, where he spent a few hours in privacy taking stock of his situation. He would soon be back in Avente as Henry Lucas, a person of incalculable wealth. Jaeger had offered him the help of the IPCC, arguably the most powerful entity in the Oikumene. But what good was all that wealth and power if they could not be put to use on the only thing that now mattered?

Within two weeks of his return, it would be time to depart for the semi-final Bunter races, assuming that Jehan Addels had secured a membership in the Lyonnesse Stable. Knowing Jehan, that was a virtual certainty. But somehow the notion of negotiating with Bruno Bolfo for the Jarnell stake had lost all interest for Gersen. His goal was to recover Gabrielle, and all else was a distraction.

He stretched out on his bunk and laced his hands behind his head. Something was tugging at his consciousness — something he had overlooked. What was it? Bunter races? Jarnell? Then suddenly it came to him: there was one person most likely to know where Malagate had fled — that was Bruno Bolfo. Gersen had seen one of Bolfo's freighters parked in the field next to Malagate's Pharaon. He had reasoned that Bolfo's Galactic Freight was transporting Grabhorne's export goods for Malagate. But now that he considered matters, the relationship was undoubtedly deeper than that. Bolfo had likely been a partner in the raid on Willow Grove, as his fleet would have been needed to transport the captives.

The way forward was now clear. He would travel to Rosalia for the semi-final races, and there he would encounter Bolfo. By one means or another, he would extract from Bolfo the whereabouts of Malagate. Now that he had a plan of action, Gersen settled into a needed sleep.

A few hours later, Gersen was awake and rested. His plans had taken on some new dimensions. He rose, mopped his face with a damp towel, and sauntered toward the ship's cockpit. There he discovered the pilot — with the name 'Borg' stitched on the chest of his tunic, and silver lieutenant's bars on his shoulders. Lieutenant Borg was a lean young officer with wavy blond hair and glittering blue eyes. The ship being on auto-pilot, Borg had nothing much to do, and looked up with an embarrassed smile from the hand of solitaire he had been playing.

"Welcome to the flight deck, Mr. Lucas. As you may know, life here is ninety-nine percent stultifying boredom and one percent howling panic."

Gersen gave a soft laugh, "I fully understand. I've done a bit of piloting myself."

Borg's expression changed to one of interest in the possibility of talking shop with a fellow rocket-jockey, as the young pilots called themselves. "Really? Are you flying anything currently?"

"In fact, I am."

"What model, may I ask?"

"Actually, my little bird hasn't been given a model designation yet. It's an experimental craft, a joint venture between Distis and Jarnell."

Now he had Borg's full attention. "Experimental, you say? Tell me about it. I'm always interested in keeping up with the latest flying kit."

"I call the vessel 'Quicksilver'," said Gersen. "It's powered by Jarnell's new Intersplit-LF."

By now, Borg had spun around in his pilot's swivel chair, and he regarded Gersen eagerly. "The LF? I've read about that in the spacecraft trade mags. I didn't know they had actually put it in a ship."

"I guess I am a sort of test pilot," said Gersen.

"I saw a report last week that speculated the LF would produce one-point-seven times standard velocity. An incredible performance boost! Is it really that fast?"

Gersen was amused. It hadn't taken long for the one-point-seven estimate he had given to the UTCS to make its way into the social media rumor loop. Of course, the actual performance of his *Quicksilver* was considerably better than that. But he was getting into the zone of confidential information and needed to change the subject. So he said, "Well, you know how these things get exaggerated. It sounds romantic, I know, moving at these speeds. But the Model 9B, that was real flying. Not today's push-button stuff. I spent my share of time wandering about in those old rattle-traps but, truth to tell, I sort of miss those days. But tell me something, Lieutenant, what is your IPCC OS* when you're not piloting?"

"I'm a drone operator."

"Was that you running the drones in the Grabhorne set-to?"

"That was me."

"I have a question, then. You had them lined up in a tight formation, about fifty meters from the enemy, but then they paused, as if waiting for something. What was that all about?"

"Commander Jaeger was sitting next to me. He told me to hold off, thinking that when the enemy saw what they were up against, they likely would surrender. Would have saved a lot of blood and guts, for sure."

"I see," said Gersen. "But then one of Malagate's men fired the heavy rifle. I have to say, I thought the personnel carrier that got hit was done for."

"Our APC's† have a new outer skin made of carbon-xcalium alloy. Only a few microns thick, very light, but does a great job diffusing energy. So, no real problem there, other than a few of our people being shaken up by the blast. But at that point, the Commander turned me loose. The lead drone attacked the gunner who had fired the shot, and just before impact, sent a signal to the rest of the fleet, to identify and eliminate all similar targets. You saw what happened next. Anyone near one of those heavy rifles was the first to go. After that, it was just a mop-up operation."

---

* Occupational Specialty

† Armored Personnel Carriers

"Mission accomplished," Gersen agreed. Then, seeing that he had successfully changed the subject, added, "Would you mind if I used your star-finder? I have a trip in mind I'd like to pencil out."

"Sure thing," said Borg, and gestured to the ship's Nav station. "Help yourself."

Another well-padded swivel chair served the Nav station, and Gersen settled down to work. Borg, he supposed, would be quite curious as to where Henry Lucas planned to take his ultra-speedy vessel, but was far too disciplined to ask, and so, instead, turned back to his hand of solitaire. Gersen activated the screen and began to punch in coordinates from memory. During his recent nap, his mind had been at work, as often happened when he slept. The first problem to be solved was how to use the two-week hiatus between the time he landed at Avente and the time he would need to depart for Rosalia. It was intolerable that he should remain idle then, while Gabrielle was still a captive. While it was impossible to know with any certainty where Malagate had fled, two possibilities had occurred to him. And then, even if both of these proved fruitless, there still might be time to visit Willow Grove and search for the lost child Jono. Even if that did not involve rescuing Gabrielle, it was something of which she would approve. Now to see if the star-finder would confirm that such an itinerary was feasible.

The first set of coordinates was for the massive dead star where Attel Malagate's henchman, Hildemar Dasce, had set up his hideaway — a place as remote and forlorn as could be imagined. Gersen believed that Attel Malagate had known the location of this place and, if so, quite possibly so did Mongo Malagate. Gersen shuddered at the thought that Mongo had taken Gabrielle here, remembering that this is where Dasce had sequestered the unfortunate Pallis Atwrode, and where Dasce had performed unspeakable acts of lechery upon her innocent person. Thank heavens, thought Gersen, that both Malagates were Star Kings and thus devoid of human sexuality. In that sense, at least, Gabrielle was safe.

The second set of coordinates was for Teehalt's Planet. Mongo Malagate had expended great effort to discover its location. He had not obtained that information from Gersen, but had he possibly found some other source? And if so, that might be his current place of refuge. A remote possibility, but still one that must be investigated.

The third coordinates were ones that Gersen did not have in his head, but would pull them up from the ship's star-finder. These would locate Brandywine, the planet of the Eos star system, and the former home of Willow Grove. If his search of Dasce's hideaway and Teehalt's Planet proved unproductive, there still might be time to land at Willow Grove and search for Jono.

Using the ship's navigation capability, Gersen now made some calculations. From Alphanor to Dasce's star was 30 degrees off the rhumb line to Teehalt's Planet, then 30 degrees back to arrive at the latter. Then the trip to Brandywine and onward to Alphanor would entail similar angles in reverse — almost a perfect parallelogram if laid out in two dimensions. With *Quicksilver*'s speed, he could visit all three destinations, although with little time to linger, and still be back on Alphanor in time for the trip to Rosalia. Three long shots, to be sure, but better by far than spending two weeks sitting idly at the Hotel Credenza in Avente.

His work completed, Gersen rose and stretched, feeling satisfied with the results.

"Get what you needed?" asked Borg.

"Yes, I did. Thank you."

"We still have a couple of days to kill," said Borg. "The troops are going to play a few hands of cards, if you'd care to join us."

"For money?"

"Well, yes, but low stakes. Those are our rules."

Gersen in fact was an accomplished card player. His grandfather had trained him thoroughly from an early age, not to make him a gambler, but to teach him the value of calculating odds. "I appreciate the offer to join," he said, "but I have a proposal. Suppose we agree to pool the total winnings and use them to fund a memorial plaque for the fallen troopers, including those on the surveillance vessel."

"Great idea," said Borg. "I'm sure the others will agree."

There would be eight players in all — in addition to Gersen and Borg, three caregivers (one of whom spelled Borg on the flight deck), and three wounded well enough to play. They formed themselves into round robin groups of four. Even with low stakes, Gersen managed to lose enough to fund an attractive plaque, raising his bets on weak hands, and folding early on strong ones. The challenge was to do all this without the others seeing through it. At the end, they had passed the time pleasantly, there was a substantial fund, and everyone had stories to tell about how they had bested Henry Lucas at cards.

Consistent with his plan, Gersen wasted little time in Avente; in fact, his residence there consumed barely half of Alphanor's twenty-nine-hour day. His driver-cum-security man, Bane, met him at the IPCC terminal shortly after mid-day, transported him to the Credenza, and returned him to the Avente spaceport at dawn the next day. There, *Quicksilver* was fully prepped and waiting. During his brief stay at the Credenza, he had contacted Jehan Addels, donned civilian clothes, and enjoyed supper out on the hotel terrace.

"Welcome back," said Addels, responding to Gersen's call. "I trust your trip was successful."

"In some respects," said Gersen, "but not in others. I'll fill you in on the details when I see you. I can tell you this much, though, I have some new reasons to meet with Bruno Bolfo. Are the arrangements in hand for the semi-final races?"

"Indeed, they are," said Addels. "In fact, you are now the Managing Partner of the Lyonnesse Stable. The opportunity arose, the price seemed reasonable, and I thought it wouldn't hurt to raise your profile in the racing community."

"I agree," said Gersen. "Well done. Now tell me about your security situation. Any threats?"

"None whatsoever. I took your advice and laid on some formidable protection. To Bolfo, or his agents, it was clear I was no sitting duck."

"That's good to hear," said Gersen, "because I'd like to take Kim off your hands. I could use his company for another trip I have in mind."

"Another trip? My goodness, you are on the move these days. How soon do you need him?"

"Have him take the afternoon shuttle to New Concept. I'll pick him up at the spaceport there in two days' time. Can he leave today?"

"Of course, if that is your wish. Will you be long? Remember, we need to depart for Rosalia in two weeks."

"No worry on that account. I've laid my itinerary out carefully, and an encounter with Bolfo is now a high priority."

"Understood," said Addels, "but just remember, when you sup with the devil—"

"Yes, I know," Gersen laughed, "—use a long spoon."

With Kim at his side in the cockpit of *Quicksilver*, Gersen studied the looming mass of Dasce's dead star, with its red dwarf companion pulsing flares of dark color on the horizon. Gersen knew the terrain quite well from memory, but what he did not know was whether Malagate had taken refuge here and, if he had, what armaments he might have installed against unwanted visitors. *Quicksilver*, as well, with her size and elegance, would present an easy target. Rather than expose her to risk, Gersen settled into a gentle drift, safely on the dead star's dark side. Then he and Kim donned air-suits and clambered aboard *Quicksilver*'s auxiliary flyer.

They descended toward the surface, then skimmed along as low as possible to avoid detection. The ground below was a confusion of dissipated star-stuff, a dark spongy surface in varying shades of maroon, umber, and gray. Ahead were low black hills dotted with volcanic craters, some still active and some long dormant. Still clinging as close to the ground as he dared, Gersen arrived at the plateau formed by a titanic lava flow that he recognized as the approach to Dasce's encampment. Ahead stood the remains of a long dead volcano in whose crater the hideaway had been established. Then, off to the side, he spied the small space boat that had stood abandoned for the twenty-five years since Gersen had taken Dasce prisoner. All was as Gersen remembered and, importantly, there was no other vessel in sight—not Malagate's Pharaon or any other. This was strong evidence, it seemed to Gersen, that Malagate was not here. He was tempted, therefore, to proceed no further. He had no desire to revisit the site of Dasce's bestial predations, and thereby revive unwanted memories. But he had come this far, and must persist until all hope of finding Gabrielle at this place had been exhausted.

Not far from the abandoned space boat was the air-lock of the tunnel that would lead to the interior of the crater where Dasce had created his secret compound. Gersen parked his flyer, opened the hatch, and motioned to Kim to follow. The lever to operate the air-lock still functioned; they entered, closed the door behind them and proceeded cautiously in the gloom. At the end of the tunnel, they emerged into the ancient volcanic crater, dormant now for untold ages, some fifty meters across and surrounded by sheer walls of striated volcanic glass. Overhead was the webbed dome constructed of thin cables supporting a transparent film, through which the glowering reddish illumination of the companion dwarf seeped through, shrouding the entire enclosure in semi-darkness. The air generator had ceased to run — the domed film now sagged for lack of pressure; the rank vegetation of Dasce's planting had withered and died; the small pond of water had evaporated and was dry. The cage that had held Robin Rampold prisoner for seventeen years stood empty at the center of the crater, and to the side were the cluster of black tents that had served as Dasce's living quarters, and where he had kept Pallis Atwrode hostage.

It was clear that no living creature — human, Star King, or otherwise could inhabit here, but to be absolutely sure, Gersen glanced inside the tents. Finding them empty, he motioned Kim back to the tunnel. They proceeded hastily to the air car, and within less than an hour from the time they had left *Quicksilver*, they were back on board.

One possibility, thought Gersen, however remote, was now eliminated.

Gersen guided *Quicksilver* away from the gravitational pull of the dead star, feeling at the same time the emotional tug of long-abandoned memories. This was not a venue he had ever expected to see again, and now that he had, he was reminded why. He turned to Kim, who until now had made no comment.

"Well, Kim, we've crossed that off the list. What did you think?"

"A place of much evil," Kim replied. "I could smell it."

No more needed to be said. Gersen punched in the coordinates for Teehalt's Planet, and they were on their way.

Quicksilver sped at unimaginable velocity though the vastness of space, passing thousands — no, millions — of stars that shined and glittered unmindful of their transit. It was a passage that no man prior to Lugo Teehalt, then Kirth Gersen (twice) had ever made before. Gersen and Kim passed the time in conversation, in exercise in *Quicksilver's* small but efficient gym, and in quiet contemplation. Eventually, the ship's instruments advised that they were nearing their destination — a warm, golden-white star with three orbiting planets. The Intersplit, on automatic, shut down; the target star glowed on the viewscreen dead ahead. The ship flew on using ion drive and travelling the million miles remaining at the comparatively leisurely pace of 100,000 miles per hour. As they neared the solar system, the three orbiting planets came into view. The nearest to the sun was small and hot, a fuming cinder; the farthest out was a gloomy ball of ice; the third was sparkling green, blue, and white — betokening lush vegetation, great oceans, and snow-capped peaks and poles. This planet, so Teehalt, its discoverer, had observed, was much like Earth before the infection of humanity. It was a world fresh, natural, and unmodified.

Gersen guided *Quicksilver* into a shallow orbit, observing that nothing had changed since his last visit nearly twenty-five years earlier. He had left two humans — each with consuming hatred for the other — Hildemar Dasce and Robin Rampold. Dasce, in revenge for some long-forgotten insult, had captured Rampold, transported him bound to the dead star, and kept him in a cage to be regularly tormented, both spiritually and physically, for seventeen years. Gersen in turn had captured Dasce and released Rampold, and carried the two with him to Teehalt's Planet, along with the three officials of Sea Province University — Warweave, Deterras, and Kelle — one of whom Gersen planned to expose as Malagate the Woe. The gambit was successful, Malagate was killed, although in the turmoil, Dasce escaped carrying Gersen's projac. Upon departure, Rampold had insisted that he remain and when, a year later Gersen returned, he found that Rampold had turned the tables and had tricked and captured Dasce. What was now the status of these two — after a twenty-five-year hiatus? Gersen had no idea. Rampold was tough-minded and resourceful, but Dasce was an evil trickster. Of one thing, though, Gersen could be certain: there was a projac on the planet, and whether it was still possessed by Rampold or had passed into Dasce's hands, was highly uncertain. Caution, therefore, was warranted. And what of Malagate? Could he be here, too? And, if so, how armed? And on whose side, Rampold's or Dasce's? There were many questions to be answered.

Gersen decided, once again, to keep *Quicksilver* out of sight. He placed her into a distant orbit across the poles, and therefore unobserved from the locations most likely to be occupied. He and Kim once more boarded the auxiliary flyer — no air-suits needed this time, as the planet's air was fresh and clean. Together the two descended toward the river valley where the Sea Province ship had landed, and where he had last seen Rampold. Gersen circled cautiously, looking for Malagate's Pharaon, but saw no ship of any kind. If Malagate was on the planet, it was not here. He therefore guided the flyer down and landed.

The valley was as lovely as before. The air was cool, with a grass-scented freshness. Beyond stood forests of tall dark trees. Presently, they came to the river that ran through the valley, and encountered near the river bank a cluster of strange, unworldly inhabitants that Teehalt had designated Dryads. They stood near the forest, with swaying frond-like limbs, seemingly indifferent to the presence of these off-world intruders.

Gersen and Kim proceeded along the river bank until they came to the place where Gersen remembered Rampold had built his camp, and where he had captured and penned Dasce. Gersen drew his projac and Kim did the same. As they approached the camp, Gersen could make out two figures — one on a bench in a cage of stout wood poles, and the other reclining on a settee outside a small log cabin. Gersen called out, "Rampold! Hallo, it is Kirth Gersen!"

There was no answer, nor did the reclining figure stir. Gersen with deliberation approached closer, keeping a careful eye on the occupant of the cage, who also remained unmoving. Then he discovered why Rampold had been unresponsive. His once bronze and fit figure had shrunken to a desiccated, bleached-out corpse. He evidently had been dead for some time, but decomposition in the planet's atmosphere worked differently than on Earth. What remained of Rampold was a mummified version of the original.

Then Gersen turned to the cage. Inside was what was left of Dasce, deceased and shrunken as well, but unmistakable with his purple skin tone and rangy form. Upon inspection, there were signs that Dasce had expended superhuman efforts to escape. The cage poles had been scraped by fingernails, the ground that held them clawed. But Rampold's construction had resisted Dasce's most strenuous efforts. It quickly became clear to Gersen what had happened. Rampold had contracted a fatal ailment of some kind — perhaps some residual effect of his many years of privation at Dasce's hands, perhaps some poisonous local substance he had unwittingly consumed. Knowing that he was going to die, he reclined upon the settee in front of his cabin, where his final look would be of Dasce in the cage. Dasce for his part had depended on Rampold for food and water. Not long after Rampold died, he too succumbed to starvation and dehydration. Thus, the two old enemies died facing one another in hatred, and since the planet's atmosphere apparently had preserved them, they would remain that way forever more.

Gersen and Kim returned together toward their flyer, passing the dryads who waved their fronds indifferently, and lifted off the planet back to *Quicksilver*. Gersen piloted the ship several more times around, searching through the macroscope for every possible spot where Malagate might have landed. Finding none, he turned the ship and headed outbound, engaged the Intersplit, and was gone.

Although *Quicksilver* had left Teehalt's Planet light-years back in her wake, Gersen's experience there had left him in a somber mood. He could not wrench his mind free of the sensation that, for all her natural beauty, there had been a sinister feeling to the place. Lugo Teehalt had been murdered because he tried to prevent the planet from being exploited. Attel Malagate had been obsessed about acquiring it, but instead had perished there, and now, for all Gersen knew, Mongo Malagate was similarly obsessed. The dryads, through their very indifference, seemed to be mocking vanity, whether that of Star Kings or of humans. And the final scene of Dasce and Rampold, with their unseeing eyes locked in hate, was not one easily forgotten. Was he now done with Teehalt's Planet, or would there somehow be another chapter?

Gersen breathed an exasperated groan and forced these dismal reflections from his mind. He had one final stop to make on this brief expedition. It would be the longest of long shots for young Jono to have survived and, if he had, for Gersen and Kim to find him. The odds favored heart-break as Jono's father Henri had foretold. Nevertheless, they had to make the best of it. He turned to his console, pulled up the *Popular Handbook to the Planets,* and located the entry for Brandywine:

Brandywine is the fourth orbital planet of the smallish, pale yellow sun Eos. It has a diameter of 7,800 miles and a mass of .84 Earth standard. Discovered in the year 1484 by locater Volodny Krimp, the planet remained unexploited for nearly fifty years, for reasons that are revealed by even the most casual examination. It is a spare planet, with long, dry prairies, sparsely inhabited by various types of rodents and small reptiles, who subsist by feeding upon one another. Its geophysical attributes have much in common with the least popu-lated territories of Earth. That is, soil conditions are sandy and only lightly supplied with such nutrients — nitrogen, potassium, phospho-rus — as are needed to support robust plant life; rainfall is erratic; the atmosphere is thin, at sea level approximating the oxygen content at 8,000 feet on Earth. Accordingly, agricultural production can be sustained only through considerable effort, and crop yields necessar-ily vary from year to year. Consistent with these conditions, wildlife must be hardy to survive. The most common forms — rodents and small reptiles — have already been mentioned. Most populous among larger ruminants is the mofu, a hairless quadruped resembling a small llama. The most successful predator is the gnax, a creature with the stature of a medium-size Earth canine, but more closely resem-bling a large rat. The gnax typically run in packs of twenty-to-thirty individuals, feeding on any unfortunate victims they chance to find.

As noted, Brandywine lay unexploited for half a century after its discovery; Krimp died, the royalty entitlement passed to his estate and was progressively lowered by his heirs. The relatively modest royalties were undoubtedly what ultimately attracted a group of set-tlers, who rationalized the unproductive conditions of the planet as being conducive to the development of strong and resilient character. Eventually, several thousand of these like-minded pioneers founded the community of Willow Grove in the year 1528.

Here the Brandywine entry in the *Handbook to the Planets* terminated, and evidently had not been updated since Malagate's raid.

Quicksilver's arrival at the Eos system was an unwelcoming experience. The sun was small, pale, and lusterless. Brandywine was mostly an expanse of scrub-covered prairie interspersed with low hills. Gersen coached Kim on the proper technique for placing the ship in a series of descending reconnaissance orbits. Kim was a quick study, and Gersen imagined he would be piloting on his own in not more than a year's time.

On their third pass around the planet, they located the remains of the Willow Grove settlement. The dwellings were collapsed and burned; the few pieces of farm equipment were overturned tangles of twisted metal; the fields were reverting to weed and scrub. After a brief discussion, Gersen and Kim decided to leave *Quicksilver* in orbit, and do their exploration in the flyer. If Jono were alive down there somewhere, he might mistake the larger ship for a raider vessel, reducing even further their slim chances of finding him.

They landed the flyer on the outskirts of the former settlement and began to wander through the wreckage, intermittently calling out for Jono. Everywhere they looked, in addition to the ruins of what had once been comfortable family dwellings, they saw the scattered remains of humans. The deceased had been savaged and torn by scavengers. The bones were recognizably human, but there was not even a partially complete skeleton that could be identified. With bitter irony, Gersen found himself relieved, because had there been any intact remains, he would have wanted to give them a decent burial. But there were far too many to permit that act of respect in the limited time they had available.

During the seven hours of daylight that remained, the two laid out a systematic walking route that covered the entire settlement. By the time Eos began to touch the horizon, the conclusion was unavoidable: if Jono was alive, he was not here. Rather than returning to *Quicksilver* for the night, Kim suggested that they remain on the ground and build a fire. If Jono was anywhere within range, this evidence of human presence might encourage him to investigate — if not tonight, then perhaps in the morning. The idea was persuasive; they took out bedrolls from the flyer and stood watches while they fed the fire from a large pile of timber they had collected from the ruins. There was no moon; the air was chill; it was a disheartening vigil. For Gersen, it was a mostly sleepless night; he imagined it was the same for Kim. What bestial urges, he wondered, had led Malagate and his minions to inflict this carnage? And what did that mean for Gabrielle, who was now in Malagate's hands?

The pale sun produced wan light below the horizon. Kim brewed tea and set out a modest breakfast from the flyer's stores. Just after dawn, a wild cry split the morning air, to be followed by a full chorus of yelps and screams. There being nothing better to do, they boarded the flyer, checked their weapons, and moved off in the direction of the sound. About a quarter mile distant was one of the low hills they had earlier observed from the air. Kim pointed in that direction.

"That way," he said. "Something going on over there."

Gersen guided the flyer closer, and as they approached, they could make out a tumble of boulders at the base of the hill. Closer still, they could see movement among the boulders, and the source of the frenzied noise was a pack of what the *Handbook to the Planets* had called *gnax*, dog-sized rodents, shrieking and squealing in frantic activity. Then Kim tugged at Gersen's arm and pointed to the ground below the pack. There could be seen some half dozen fallen *gnax*, with arrows protruding from their corpses.

"Arrows coming from above," said Kim.

Kim pointed again, this time to a spot near the top of the boulder heap, some forty feet above ground level. Up there was an opening in the rocks like a small cave, with the *gnax* at that level furiously trying to gain entrance. But they were being repelled by a pointed stick being thrust from inside the cave. *There was a human in there.*

Gersen withdrew his projac and started to take aim. But Kim waved him off, and pointed instead to the lower level of the seething pack.

"Shoot the ones down here. Not up there. Might hit the boy. I'll get him."

Then Kim reached into his boot and withdrew a glittering double-edged blade. He vaulted from the flyer and began to climb, moving fast and with astonishing dexterity. Gersen meanwhile began picking off *gnax* lower down, without the risk of hitting whoever was in the cave.

Finding themselves assaulted from behind, the *gnax* began to retreat, reaching the bottom of the rockpile and scampering away, with Gersen dispatching the stragglers.

Kim meanwhile had reached the level of the cave entrance, where the handful of remaining pack leaders had been so obsessed with their quarry in the cave that they failed to notice that their followers had deserted. Kim plunged among them with his blade flashing, and almost as quickly as it started, the furious melee was over, leaving a scattering of dead *gnax* strewn among the rocks. Kim could be seen hoisting himself level with the cave entrance and speaking with whoever was inside. Then the arms of a young boy flew around Kim's neck. Kim lifted him free and caried him past the bodies of the *gnax* to where Gersen was waiting by the flyer. The boy was rail thin and filthy; his clothes were tatters. But he was smiling. He was still clinging to Kim, who bore his light frame effortlessly.

"He knew my name!" the boy announced to Gersen.

"Jono!" said Kim, triumphantly.

The return to Avente was by far the most enjoyable part of the trip. Kim's culinary skills were on parade, with Jono consuming four full meals in a twelve-hour interval, and sleeping the other twelve. By the time of their arrival, Gersen and Kim told one another that they could already see the boy's emaciated frame filling out. Jono was brimming with curiosity, and Kim obliged by showing him around the intricacies of *Quicksilver*. They had, of course, informed the boy that his parents were alive and well and he would soon be joining them. But they asked no questions about his time alone on Brandywine. Kim, Gersen knew, had suffered a similar experience on his home planet, Solitaire, and had never shared the details. Some things in life, Gersen was aware, go best unremembered.

Upon their arrival at Avente, Jono moved in to Kim's suite at the Credenza, and as long as they were there, the two were constant companions. Meanwhile, Gersen contacted Lieutenant Borg at IPCC headquarters. He learned that regular shuttle flights to Grabhorne had been scheduled until the IPCC mission was deemed complete. The next flight out was the day before Gersen and Kim were to leave for Rosalia and, yes, of course they had space for Jono.

On the whole, Gersen was forced to deem the last two weeks successful. He had eliminated the only two possibilities he could think of for finding Malagate, and against all odds he and Kim had rescued Jono. He would soon be encountering Bruno Bolfo, and that would give him new direction.

CHAPTER XI

Excerpt from the *Popular Handbook to the Planets* entry on Rosalia:

Rosalia is the third and only habitable planet orbiting the pale green-white star Xantos 297. Rosalia was discovered by the legendary locater, William Whipsnade, or 'Wild Willie,' as he was known to his fellow locaters. With a diameter of approximately 7,600 miles, the planet is slightly smaller than Earth (7,915 miles), but has double the land mass, roughly 115 million square miles. The balance of the surface area, in excess of 74 million square miles, comprises a complicated system of seas, bays, channels, and straits surrounding the planet's eight continents and innumerable islands. Wild Willie had been notably susceptible to the charms of the many comely women he encountered in his interplanetary wanderings, and to memorialize some of these pleasant episodes, he named the planet Rosalia, and the eight continents Ottilie, Eclin, Koukou, Yellow Nelly, La Mar, Trinky, Hortense, and Almyra. Port Mona, at the head of Maybelle Bay, became the site of the planet's first city and the location of its spaceport.

Rosalia's terrain exhibits considerable variety — from fertile valleys to dense forests, snow-capped mountains and parched deserts. The local fauna is deemed, at least comparatively speaking, not hostile to human presence, although a species generically labelled waifs — tree-waifs, water-waifs, and desert-dwelling wind-waifs — seem to enjoy tormenting human interlopers, sometimes with unpleasant effects on the unwary.

Wild Willie was distinctive — unique perhaps — among locaters in that he was a so-called 'wildcatter.' That is, he explored at this own expense and risk, as opposed to the customary practice of locaters to secure funding from large estate houses, in exchange for the lion's share of the rewards from a successful discovery. It was perhaps an urgent need to replenish Whipsnade's dwindling bankroll that prompted his somewhat novel approach to liquidating his interest in Rosalia.

After registering his claim, Whipsnade blocked off the planet's land surface into segments of a hundred miles to a side — that is, ten thousand square miles each — and proceeded to hold a grand auction. Here, the record becomes somewhat confusing, because 115 million square miles blocked off in this way would produce 11,500 segments. While some bidders acquired more than one segment, it was subsequently determined that not all the available land had been sold. Moreover, significant trading had occurred between the original owners, with those transactions being only sketchily documented. Some fifty years after the auction, long after Wild Willie had disappeared into the murky reaches of the Beyond, the 160 landowners — ranchers, as they referred to themselves — decided to conduct an audit to confirm who owned what. The largest tracts, such as Willow Glen, Stronsi, and Aigle-Mort ranches covered over a million square miles each; smaller owners such as Black Lilly and Iron Triangle measured only a hundred thousand square miles or even fewer. Wild Willie's record-keeping was discovered to have left much to be desired, and in the end, the auditors could ascribe ownership to only about sixty percent of the land mass. The 160 landowners exhibited small desire to acquire more, so it was agreed to assign the unclaimed portion to a public trust, under the auspices of an elected Board of Civil Regulation. The BCR, as it came to be called, was also given responsibility for public infrastructure, such as the spaceport and the post office, as well as constabulary functions.

—◊—

On the final day of their flight to Rosalia, Gersen was observing Jehan Addels, seated in the lounge chair opposite him in *Quicksilver*'s small but comfortable common room. Addels' head was buried in a text.

"Excuse me, Jehan," said Gersen, "what are you studying so closely, if you don't mind my asking?"

Addels' head popped up, with an expression that conveyed possible annoyance at having his concentration broken. But then his features relaxed. He now had an audience for some things he wanted to say.

"I don't mind at all. I've been examining the by-laws of the Intergalactic Bunter Consortium. After all, now that you are the Managing Partner of one of the member stables, we had best know the rules."

"Just so," said Gersen. "Have you learned anything of interest?"

"Quite a few things, actually, but before we get to that, I have some background material you might find useful. I took the liberty of using your UTCS account. I hope you don't mind."

"Not at all," said Gersen. By long-standing practice, he and Addels had shared access to the same UTCS account. If there was something in particular that Gersen wanted blocked, he could so instruct the account manager. But as a practical matter, anything he was unwilling to share with his very long-standing and trusted confidante, he would not put on UTCS to begin with.

Addels tapped in some codes on the room monitor, and a female voice announced herself.

"Greetings, gentlemen," said Eleanor, "what a pleasure to find you together."

"Hello, Eleanor," said Gersen. "Addels says you have some information of interest."

"About the Bunter Consortium?"

"Yes."

"Very well. What I have on file is a compilation of what was available here at UTCS, and what was augmented by Mr. Addels through his own research. Where would you like to begin?"

"At the beginning," said Addels. "Mr. Lucas has been out of touch, and I have not yet brought him up to date."

"Certainly, sir," said Eleanor and then began to expound with the intonation of a lecturer addressing attentive students.

"The popularity of bunter racing has grown enormously during the last quarter century. The sport originated on Cadwal, where bunters are indigenous. Bunters are large, foul-tempered beasts that have been known to inflict serious injury or even fatality on humans, except when their eye-stalks are covered in which case they become docile and can be ridden for sport. Bunter-riding was an amenity offered to the more adventurous visitors to Cadwal's wilderness lodges, and it was perhaps inevitable that riders would challenge each other to race. Those with the financial means to do so began to breed bunters as racers, and to stage inter-lodge competitions. Matters came to a head, however, when these racing enthusiasts — now stable-owners — sought to establish a formal facility where organized events could be held on a regular basis. Despite energetic lobbying by its sponsors, the proposal was turned down by the Cadwal Board of Supervisors as being contrary to the planet's Charter, which restricts human infringement on the planet's natural state.

"The Board's decision was the source of considerable unhappiness, as the proposal's sponsors were eminent citizens in their home worlds, unaccustomed to such rejections, especially when the racing facility was thought to provide manifest economic and cultural benefits to Cadwal. The tension was relieved when the firm of LB Ventures, an engineering, construction, and transport enterprise of considerable galactic repute, offered to host the racing facility on Rosalia. Many years earlier, the founder of LB, Lewyn Barduys, had offered to expand the network of wilderness retreats on Cadwal, but when that proposal was turned down, Barduys set out to create his own chain of lodges on Rosalia, where he had significant connections, as well landholdings of his own. LB's offer to create a racing facility was enthusiastically accepted by the stable-owners, and within a fortnight, the entire population of racing bunters was shipped off to Rosalia on LB's transport vessels. Some Cadwallians muttered privately that the Board had squandered a superb opportunity; the Board itself, however, seemed relieved and quite content to wash its hands of the whole matter.

"Shortly after the establishment of the sport at Rosalia, it was discovered that the Cadwal bunter could be cross-bred with a related species from Solitaire. The result was a beast of exceptional speed and endurance, not to mention ferocity, as the Solitaire bunters were carnivorous, and this trait was retained by the offspring of the inter-species breeding. The gain in racing performance, however, was deemed well worth the extra security precautions, and racing experienced an explosion in popularity.

"LB Ventures, therefore, undertook to enlarge on its original design, creating the current Rosalia Intergalactic Racecourse on a site approximately ten miles northwest of the Port Mona Spaceport. The facility consists of a 2.5-mile track with luxury seating for more than 10,000 spectators, along with hotel accommodations, retail concessions, and so forth. At the same time, the Intergalactic Bunter Consortium was formed; the number of members or 'stables' thereafter grew rapidly, and is now fixed at thirty-two, each representing a different planet. These include twenty-four from the Rigel Concourse, three from the Vega system, Earth itself, Rosalia, of course, then Methel, Murchison, and Sasani."

At the mention of these last three names, Gersen became alert. He knew all three well, and they prompted many interesting memories.

"As might be imagined," Eleanor continued, "the breeding, training, and campaigning of racing bunters is quite an expensive undertaking. Only the wealthy have the capacity to indulge in the sport and, even then, the cost exceeds what most individuals are willing, or have the capacity, to bear. Stables, therefore, are permitted to take on partners. However, as you will see, the ownership of racing bunters has come to carry with it significant social status. Therefore, to maintain the proper aura of exclusivity, stables are allowed no more than fifty partners. One of these must subscribe to at least a twenty-five percent interest, and thereby becomes Managing Partner.

"Each stable may enter one or more of its bunters in a series of monthly races. At the end of the year, the top-performing sixteen bunters (limited to one per stable) are formed into two groups of eight each for the semi-final event. The top four from each group then compete in the final race.

"For large portions of the Oikumene, these end-of-season events have become the social highlight of the year. Anyone who considers themselves anyone wants to be there. Spectator seats, therefore, are tightly rationed, allowing 300 places per stable. Stables may allocate these places as they see fit, but assuming fifty partners, the average would be six places per partnership interest. Since the opening of the Racecourse, the 9,600 seats (300 times 32 stables) have never been under-subscribed, even though the cost per seat is quite high — 1,000 SVU for each of the final two events. This provides the Bureau of Civil Regulation — or BCR as it is colloquially known — with nineteen-point-two million SVU just from the two end-of-season events, not to mention hotel and restaurant taxes, and so forth. When LB Ventures completed the facility, ownership was transferred to the BCR in exchange for a note in the amount of LB's costs. That note was paid off from revenues after only five years of operations. I should point out, finally, that, due to the cosmopolitan nature of the racing enthusiasts, all wagers and admission charges are now denominated in the inter-planetary currency, the Standard Value Unit, or SVU. Not long after adoption of the SVU by the racers, Rosalia's previous indigenous cur-rency, the Sol, had all but disappeared.

"Gentlemen," said Eleanor, "that completes the information I have on file. Any questions?"

"Yes," said Gersen. "You said the seating capacity of the Racecourse was 10,000; if the thirty-two stables account for 9,600, what happens to the remaining 400 places?"

"Good question," said Eleanor. "Those are taken up by leading citi-zens of Rosalia, at much reduced rates."

"Thank you, Eleanor," said Addels. "That was an excellent summary. We will dial you in if there is anything further."

"Happy to be of service," said Eleanor, and the screen went blank.

Addels shut down the monitor and looked across at Gersen. "I dis-covered a few things in the course of my negotiations for the Lyonnesse interest that you might find useful."

"By all means," said Gersen.

"In addition to competing for bragging rights, the stables engage in quite energetic rounds of wagering. It seems to be a sort of 'put your money where your mouth is' syndrome. I discovered this somewhat indirectly when I wanted to understand why Jared Oopf, the former Managing Partner of Lyonnesse, was in financial straits. Of course, I insisted on reviewing the stable's financial records, but found nothing out of the normal course of business.

"In order to earn more, I arranged a dinner with Ariel Selp who, in addition to being Managing Partner of the Aloysius Stable, is a fellow member of the Abacus Club in Pontefract. Ariel advised me, in strict confidence — one club member to another — that the source of Oopf's financial distress was a series of increasingly large, losing wagers. Ariel went on to advise that high stakes wagering has become virtually an integral part of bunter racing. There is no formal requirement, of course, but it is considered unsportsmanlike not to participate, with an attendant loss of social status.

"Of course, all of this may be irrelevant to your hoped-for encounter with Bruno Bolfo, but I thought you should be aware of the game you are, putatively at least, about to be playing."

"Thank you, Jehan. I will keep these matters in mind." Gersen spoke with a casual tone, but his mind was already working on how all this could be useful.

The Rosalia spaceport was densely packed with row after row of elegant private spacecraft. Fortunately, a spot had been reserved for *Quicksilver*, and she stood proudly in their midst like a queen attended by courtiers. Gersen, Addels, and Kim were met by the Rosalia Regency courtesy vehicle and conveyed briskly and comfortably to their lodging. The Regency was reputed to be Rosalia's finest, with a massive translucent atrium, pink marble floors, and dining and refreshment nooks with strolling musicians. The place was buzzing with excited race-goers. When Gersen checked in at the reception desk, he was handed an envelope which contained a business card and accompanying note. The card, printed in glittering raised letters, stated:

HON. ELLWOOD CLATTUC
SUPERVISOR, ROSALIA CONSTABULARY
PORT MONA, ROSALIA
Ch. B-0001

The note read as follows:

Dear Mr. Lucas,
Welcome to Rosalia. If during your stay I may be of
assistance, please feel free to contact me.
Sincerely, E.C.

Gersen was intrigued. He punched some codes into the viewscreen in his room that would give him privileged access to selected IPCC files. Ellwood Clattuc, he learned, was a descendant of an eminent Cadwal family, that had for three generations held the position of Supervisor of Bureau B, the Cadwal Police. However, how and why a descendant of this illustrious clan had come to hold a similar position on Rosalia was not revealed. Yet another unanswered question was how and why this high-ranking bureaucrat had become aware of the presence of 'Henry Lucas.' But the offer of assistance was welcome. As soon as he settled into his new quarters, he decided to contact Clattuc. He tapped in the codes on his room monitor and was promptly put through.

"Welcome to Rosalia, Mr. Lucas," said Clattuc, a man not far from Gersen's age, with close-cropped graying hair and neutral skin tone. He was seated at a desk, so Gersen was unable to judge his stature, but his shoulders were square and he wore a comfortable smile.

"Thank you," said Gersen. "I appreciate your offer of assistance. But how, may I ask, were you aware of my presence on Rosalia?"

"As you might imagine," said Clattuc, "we have a list of all the stable MPs. But the special attention in your case was due to a note from Miles Jaeger. Jaeger and I have cooperated for many years. He speaks highly of you and, as you undoubtedly know, he is not one to make cloying statements."

"Understood," said Gersen. "There is, in fact, a matter where your advice would be appreciated. I am hoping when here to arrange a meeting with a certain Bruno Bolfo. Does that name mean anything to you?"

"It does, indeed. He runs Galactic Enterprises, and his bunter, Black Hole, is one of the favorites in the coming races."

"I have some business with him that will require a meeting. However, my experience in the past is that his negotiating tactics may be less than gentlemanly. Therefore, I am hoping to find a neutral location, one that will be free of 'hidden persuaders,' if you catch my meaning."

"I do," said Clattuc. "You are well-advised to be cautious. We've had Bolfo on our watch list for some time, but he has given us no cause for action, at least not here on Rosalia."

"Can you recommend a neutral, but safe venue for a meeting?"

Clattuc thought for a moment. "I would suggest a place called 'Linger Longer.' It's a pleasant little café not far from your hotel. The proprietor is a retired Constabulary man. He keeps it free of listening devices, as well as undesirables. I think it will suit your purpose, and if you advise us when the meeting is to occur, we can arrange for some extra security."

"Thank you very much," said Gersen. "I hope that won't be necessary, but will keep it in mind. One final question, if I might?"

"By all means," said Clattuc.

"I am informed that the Clattuc family are eminent functionaries on Cadwal. How did you happen to wind up in the Rosalia hierarchy?"

Clattuc smiled softly and shrugged his shoulders in a gesture of one experienced in the whims of fate.

"Cadwal," he said, "is governed by strict and sometimes seemingly perverse rules. The number of positions in the bureaucracy is fixed by Charter, and those who miss out on claiming one of those positions can only remain on the planet as 'collaterals' — in effect, second-class citizens. Alas for myself, although I passed the qualifying exams with high marks, the post of Supervisor of Bureau B was claimed by my elder brother, Glawen, the third generation of the family to fill that slot. Fortunately for me, there is a history of good relations between the Clattucs and the Barduys family that owns LB Ventures. Through that connection, I was offered a position on Rosalia, and here I am."

"I am happy that things worked out well for you," said Gersen.

"Quite well. Of course, there have been times when I miss the old planet, but to tell the truth, life there had become a trifle stale. The entire population comprises fewer than a thousand families, and they are crammed into a rigidly allotted space of five hundred square miles, which on Rosalia would be a single tiny ranch, inconsequential, really. Here, there is endless variety and more than one's share of challenges."

The two exchanged a few more pleasantries, then broke off the connection. Gersen was feeling optimistic. The first step of a plan of action was falling into place.

The next morning, Gersen and Addels, with Kim driving, departed the Rosalia Regency in a hired slidecar, heading west toward the bunter stables. Gersen found himself trying to suppress the feeling that he was now a racing impresario. His Lyonnesse stable owned a thoroughbred called 'Moonbeam,' one of the top-several entries in the finals. A huge crowd would be brimming with excitement, and if Moonbeam won? He would be in the winner's circle, receiving the adulation of ten thousand cheering fans. He gave his head a quick shake to rid his mind of these thoughts. They had nothing to do with what he was here on Rosalia to accomplish. Once beyond town limits, Kim accelerated and went racing along past mile after mile of open savannah, with waving grasslands roamed by occasional herds of long-legged bong birds. Within twenty minutes they were at their destination.

The bunter training and stabling facility consisted of thirty-two rows of stables, three training tracks and several dormitory buildings for the grooms, stable hands, and trainers. Kim cruised down the line of stables, and pulled up at the one whose sign read 'Lyonnesse.' Outside a young man was waiting, an almost perfect replica of Kim.

"My cousin Kwan," said Kim. They exited the vehicle, Kim and Kwan embraced, and Kim made introductions.

"Would you like to visit Moonbeam?" asked Kwan.

Gersen nodded affirmatively, and Kwan slid open the stable door. The group was greeted by an overpowering stench, causing Gersen to sense his nose wrinkling.

"Don't worry," laughed Kwan, "you'll get used to it."

There behind a heavy metal barrier stood the magnificent Moonbeam, huffing and snorting as though the scent of humans was as unappealing to him as vice versa. Gersen had seen photographs of bunters and read descriptions, but none had done justice to the awesome presence of the real thing. Moonbeam's back was a hand's breath higher than Gersen was tall, and the creature's head, extending from a bulging muscular neck, was even higher. The head was less crocodilian than some descriptions pictured it, rather more lizard-like, Gersen thought, but nevertheless the jaws were formidable. The eye-stalks were covered by leather caps, as the beasts became passive without sight. Moonbeam began to settle down a bit, but was still making moaning and coughing sounds, and shifting from one pair of its six legs to another. Its hide was a sickly greenish-yellow, covered with folds and wrinkles. It was, thought Gersen, both formidable and hideous. Gersen quickly found that he'd seen enough, and was eager for fresh air. He thanked Kwan for the presentation and suggested they adjourn.

Once outside, Gersen said, "Moonbeam is an impressive beast, for sure. How do you feel about your chances in tomorrow's race?"

"We will win," said Kwan without hesitation. "Our toughest rival is Supernova. He is faster than Moonbeam, but his rider, Tywald Slant, does not know how to win."

"Please explain," said Gersen.

"At the start, Tywald becomes excited. He urges Supernova to top speed. Supernova leads the pack until the last quarter-mile or so, then he tires. I will have conserved Moonbeam's strength, and we will pass him before the finish."

"Sound tactics," observed Gersen. "What about the finals?"

"A different story, I am afraid. Black Hole is fast and strong, and his rider, Myron Jolt, knows how to pace him. Black Hole has won every race he's run this year, and I fear he may be too much for Moonbeam. Now, if I could ride Supernova in the final, matters would be different. I believe that Supernova, properly ridden, could defeat Black Hole."

"Not much we can do about that," said Gersen. "You'll just have to do the best you can."

Xantos 297 rose into a clear bright sky on race day. Gersen and Addels met for an early breakfast; Kim had stayed behind at the stables to assist his cousin Kwan. The hotel lobby was already alive with activity, as race-goers decked out in their celebratory finest paraded about hoping to see and be seen. Gersen's Managing Partner status entitled him to special transportation, and an exclusive entrance to the race course. The spectator stands were protected from the weather by multi-colored awnings; bright pennants fluttered in the breeze. The stands were quickly filling out with excited spectators, for whom viewing one another was as much a sport as viewing the races. The men were decked out in jaunty jackets and natty neckware, the ladies in silk and linen frocks and floppy hats. Gersen and Addels were escorted by a red-and-gold clad usher to their seats in a private box over-looking the finish line. Gersen had been provided with a roster of the participating Managing Partners, as well as a seating plan. There were thirty-six boxes, each accommodating six persons, arranged in three rows (A, B, and C) of twelve each. Thirty-two of the boxes were allocated to the stables, and four were reserved for Rosalia dignitaries. Lyonnesse Stable was in the middle row (Row B), Box 6. Gersen scanned the list of MPs looking for names he recognized, and found two of immediate interest. The first of these was:

BOX B-5 MURCHISON STABLE, SUPERNOVA
MP OLIVIER GASCOYNE
OCCUPATION: MERCHANT
SABRA, MURCHISON, SAGITTA 203

Gersen cast a cautious glance to his right, and there in Box B-5 was an older version of the Gascoyne he had encountered briefly many years earlier. He was a handsome, well-built man with curly hair and a dashing mustache, once a glossy black but now an elegant gray. He was dressed in a dapper lavender suit and scarlet kerchief. Seated next to him was an attractive blonde companion, perhaps twenty years his junior, dressed in yellow silk and a floral hat.

Gersen's gaze went back to his roster, but not for long, as a plan was forming in his mind. He rose, exited his box, and stepped over to B-5.

"Mr. Gascoyne?" he inquired. "Allow me to introduce myself. My name is Henry Lucas."

"Ah, yes, Mr. Lucas. The new MP of Lyonnesse," replied Gascoyne, exhibiting the friendly self-confidence that Gersen remembered from their brief encounter in the past. Gersen had not given his name at that time, nor did Gascoyne seem to recognize him now. Just as well, he told himself.

"I am pleased to make your acquaintance," Gascoyne continued.

"Our two bunters look to be the best of the first race. I wish you luck, although of course, I expect my Supernova to win, ha ha."

"I wish you luck as well," said Gersen. "I wonder if I could prevail upon you to join me for lunch tomorrow. I have a proposal you might find interesting."

"A proposal, you say? Well, I am already interested. Besides, I could hardly turn down an invitation from a fellow stable MP."

"Excellent," said Gersen. "Do you know the Linger Longer café? Not far from the Rosalia Regency."

"I don't know it, but I can certainly find it. What time?"

"Shall we say half an hour past noon? And if you don't mind, I would like to include my associate, Mr. Jehan Addels of Braemar Investments."

"Braemar, eh? This must be serious business. Well, the more the merrier," said Gascoyne. "And good luck again."

"What was that all about?" asked Addels, after Gersen returned to their box.

"That was Gascoyne, the MP of Murchison Stable. I'm going to offer to buy Supernova tomorrow."

Gersen turned his attention away from Addels' raised eyebrow, to his left, Box B-7, which the roster had assigned as follows:

GALACTIC STABLE, BLACK HOLE

MP BRUNO BOLFO

OWNER, GALACTIC ENTERPRISES

SUL ARSAM, SASANI, AQUILA GB 1201 IV

The box was empty. Evidently, since the first race was about to begin, Bolfo did not plan to attend, as Black Hole was entered in the second race. Nevertheless, Gersen had already learned something useful. Sul Arsam was the terminal formerly used by Interchange, the agency that served as a broker between kidnappers and those wishing to ransom their victims. It was here, so many years ago, that Gersen had fleeced the criminal Kokor Hekkus, and gained the enormous sum of money that Addels had subsequently multiplied several times over. Gersen allowed himself a private smile. This information suggested that it was Bolfo who had been the proprietor of Interchange. If the plan that had formed in Gersen's mind came to fruition, he might get the best of Bolfo once again.

Gersen's thoughts were interrupted by the clarion sound of trumpets signaling the start of the first of the two semi-final races. Those who had been wandering about the stands, purchasing refreshments, or visiting the lavatories, were hastening to their seats. The bunters were being led out, still with their eye-stalks capped, and therefore passive. Once they were all in the starting gates, the eye-caps were removed, and they began to bellow and stamp, and crash against their enclosures trying to attack their neighbors.

The crowd was hushed. Then a bell clanged, the gates opened, and the bunters charged out. This is what they had been trained for: if they ran hard, they would be fed delicacies. The plunging, bellowing multi-colored herd of beasts was now accompanied by a great roar from the stands, with everyone cheering on their favorites. Exactly what they were cheering for, though, Gersen could not discern, as the racers were churning up such a cloud of dust that it was impossible to make out the order of their progress. As the cloud reached the far side of the track, though, Gersen could see the reddish shape of Supernova clearly in the lead, as Kwan had foretold. Gersen found himself bemused that 10,000 spectators would don their finest, shell out 1,000 SVU each, and scream themselves hoarse, just to observe the progress of a distant cloud of dust. Soon the cloud reached the far turn and was plunging toward the finish, with Supernova still out front and hugging the rail. Then emerging from the pack appeared the yellow-green shape of Moonbeam, on the outside and gaining fast. Moonbeam drew up to half a length behind, then closed to even, and the two bunters were matching stride for stride, straining with every ounce of energy they could summon. Seemingly inexorably, Moonbeam began to pull ahead, and crossed the finish line first by half a length.

The pitch of crowd noise now sounded a subtle change of tempo, a blend of exultation from the winners and despair from the losers. Winning tickets were being waved joyfully in the air, while losers were being torn to shreds and scattered. Meanwhile, the bunters had been slowed to a walk by their riders, and were milling about in a disorderly mass, grunting, kicking and snapping at each other. Dozens of handlers leapt on to the track waving morsels at the end of sticks. As the bunters thrust out their heads to gobble up these snacks, handlers on either side deftly attached leather caps to their eye-stalks. And almost as if by miracle, the herd relaxed into a quiescent state and allowed themselves to be led off to their quarters. The spectators began to disperse, some to simply stretch their legs, others to mingle with friends and acquaintances, still others to catch a midday meal, as the second semi-final race would not begin until early afternoon. Gersen decided to be among the latter, as they had access to an exclusive dining area reserved for Managing Partners. He motioned to Addels and they departed.

The two made their way to the MPs' cafeteria, which they found to be catered by Fortunato's, one of Port Mona's finest eateries. Gersen was pleased to find that in addition to a list of celebrated wines, they offered a selection of imported beers and ales. He ordered a glass of *Smade's Own* along with a salad of local greens. After their order arrived, Addels regarded him curiously, "Would you mind elaborating on what you said earlier about offering to buy Supernova?"

"Of course," said Gersen. "My logic is quite simple. Kwan seemed confident that if he could ride Supernova, he could defeat Black Hole in the final. I wish to put that idea to the test."

"Kwan is a fine fellow, to be sure, but there must be more to your idea than allowing him to win a race."

"There is, indeed. During our travel here, you told me that the running of bunters is very much a matter of bragging rights, reinforced by sizable wagers. Bolfo thinks that his Black Hole cannot be defeated. I am guessing there may be some advantage to be had in knowing otherwise."

Addels made something of a skeptical face, and Gersen guessed that he was about to caution about using a long spoon when supping with the devil. Gersen laughed softly and said, "No cause for alarm, Jehan. We are in the early stages of the game, and undoubtedly there will be many twists and turns before the end."

Just at that moment, they were interrupted by a visitor at their table, who could only have been one of the MPs in that this facility was exclusively for their use.

"Excuse me, are you not Henry Lucas? I apologize for interrupting, but I wish to introduce myself. I am Aldo Privet of Methlen Stable."

The visitor was a man of late middle age, tall and somewhat slender although with a rather prominent potbelly. He carried the aristocratic look of self-confidence that Gersen had once found annoying among the Methlen upper crust. "Yes, I am Lucas," he said. "How may I be of service?"

"Once again, my apologies for interfering with your lunch, but it is a matter of some urgency. To be brief, I am the Chief Executive of Chanseth Bank on Methlen. We have been trying to locate the owner of Kotzash Mutual. We have traced it from Cooney's Bank to Universal Trust, in which you are reported to be the principal."

"I see," said Gersen. "But what possible interest do you have in Kotzash?"

"I will be candid, Mr. Lucas. A monster vein of duodecimates has recently been discovered on Dar Sai, and upon investigation, it has been revealed that Kotzash holds lease rights to the tract, in perpetuity. We would be prepared to pay Universal a handsome price for that interest, or, if you prefer, enter in to a joint venture to exploit the discovery."

Gersen gestured toward Addels. "This is Jehan Addels. He is the man you need to talk to on such matters. He has full discretion. But, of course, nothing can be done in the middle of these races. Contact Mr. Addels at the Rosalia Regency and he will consider any proposals."

"Very well and thank you," said Privet, and backed away. He returned to his seat a few tables over, and joined a matronly woman of about his age, whom Gersen recognized as Jerdian Chanseth, the lovely young girl over whom he had been over-the-heels smitten so many years ago on Methlen. But now, she was overweight and rather sour-faced, as if her wonderful life on Methlen had not gone quite as well as she had expected. Privet, then, must be the same 'Aldo' who had competed for Jerdian's affections (unsuccessfully, as Gersen recalled), but apparently had wound up marrying her and succeeding her father as CEO of Chanseth Bank. Ah, thought Gersen, the unpredictability of life.

"How do you wish that I deal with this Privet fellow?" came Addels' voice, interrupting Gersen's musing.

"Duodecimates are enormously valuable," said Gersen. "Do a deal, if there is one to be done. But protect our end of it as if you were watching your children's nest egg. I have no desire to do Privet any favors."

"Understood," said Addels, and the two adjourned to the track for the second race.

The afternoon event went much as the earlier one, with surging, bellowing bunters, the roaring crowd, the race itself largely hidden in a cloud of dust. But in the end, Black Hole had won, rather easily so it seemed. Just before the race, Bolfo had appeared and seated himself in Box B-7. He was a tall individual, dressed in carefully tailored medium gray, with immaculately trimmed hair to match. His features were patrician — lean and with an aquiline nose; his gaze from under heavy brows was penetrating and cold. There was no chance to speak with Bolfo, however, as there were five hard-looking black-clad subalterns seated around him in the box, and the moment Black Hole crossed the finish line, Bolfo got up and left.

"Mr. Lucas?" came the voice of one of the red and gold clad ushers. "If you would be so good as to accompany me, I will escort you to the awards ceremony."

Gersen followed the usher and shortly found himself on a podium in the company of seven other MPs, all owners of the top four finishers in the two semi-final heats. These would be the competitors in the following week's final race. Gersen was positioned in the center of the group as the winner of his semi-final event; Gascoyne, in second place, was on his right, and on this left, as winner of the other semi-final, was Bruno Bolfo.

"Congratulations, Lucas," said Gascoyne in his customarily pleasant tone. "You ran a fine race, but I'll have another shot next week. Are we still on for lunch tomorrow?"

"We certainly are," said Gersen. Then the talking stopped, as the Event Officer, the Rosalia Supervisor of Tourism, was delivering a congratulatory speech, and attendants were hanging medals on ribbons around the necks of the winning MPs.

When the ceremony was over, Bolfo turned to Gersen and addressed him: "I have been looking forward to meeting you, Henry Lucas. We have some interests in common, I think." Bolfo's manner of speaking was silky smooth, but somehow reminded Gersen of a spider in its web. His smile was no less unsettling.

"We do?" said Gersen, trying to inject a note of diffidence, that he had earlier decided would be his posture.

"I am referring to our respective interests in Jarnell. Neither of us can act without the other on the stake that is soon to be offered."

"Yes, I suppose there does seem to be something of an impasse," said Gersen.

"Are you a betting man, Mr. Lucas?"

"That depends, I suppose, on the nature of the wager and the size of the stakes."

"I am proposing that we wager on the outcome of next week's race. Your bunter versus mine. And your Jarnell interest versus mine."

"My goodness," said Gersen, as if taken aback. "That is quite a bet. The Jarnell interest is worth many times the value of the entire thirty-two stables, with the racecourse thrown in for good measure."

"Be that as it may," said Bolfo, "I see no other way to resolve the impasse. There are times in life, Mr. Lucas, when one has to roll the dice."

Bolfo was obviously trying to goad Gersen, by challenging his pride, into making a bet that Bolfo was confident he would win. *The hook was set*, Gersen thought. *Now to play the fish.*

"This is quite a daunting proposal, Mr. Bolfo. I will have to think about it. I will give you an answer in two days' time, as tomorrow, I have another engagement."

Bolfo allowed himself to show a slight grimace. He obviously did not like the delay. "I can't imagine what engagement could be more important than this matter."

Gersen allowed himself a touch of indignation. He was, after all, Henry Lucas, reputedly the wealthiest man in the Oikumene. "I am not in the practice of breaking engagements once they are made, as you would not care for me to do, if you were the other party. Shall we say, the café Linger Longer, at half past noon, day after tomorrow?"

Gersen could see that Bolfo did not care for the venue, and was about to suggest an alternative, but then thought the better of it, as his quarry was becoming touchy.

"As you wish, then," said Bolfo, and departed from the podium.

CHAPTER XII

Excerpt from *Curious Creatures of the Galaxy* by Atka Mip,
Entry 139 'The Bunter':

> The Bunter is a large hexapod often bred for speed and endur-
> ance. The creature is noted for the splendor and vivacity of its
> appetite, which is closely allied to that of humans, to which, how-
> ever, it is inferior in scope, for it sticks at bunter.

—⚬—

Linger Longer was a pleasant little café located in a small stand-
alone building within walking distance of the Rosalia Regency.
The décor had an Old Earth feel to it, with flower arrangements
on the tables, and hand-painted wall murals of nautical scenes and
country life. The proprietor, Yon Yarnall, was slender and bustling,
not quite what one would expect of a retired police official. Yarnall's
principle of operation seemed to be that all restaurant staff performed
all functions at all times, whether these entailed taking orders, delivering meals, bussing tables, and so forth. Although there was no obvious
order to the operation, everything worked — no glass was left unfilled,
no order untaken, or place not cleared promptly.

Yarnall greeted Gersen personally, as Supervisor Clattuc had fore-
warned him that Henry Lucas was a friend of the Rosalia Constabulary
with confidential matters to transact, and seated Gersen and Addels at
an out-of-the way corner table. Within a minute of the appointed time,
Gascoyne arrived. Although not clad in the natty attire of race day, he
was nevertheless in a well-tailored outfit of quality fabric, connoting
an individual of discrimination. The group exchanged a few bromides,

placed orders from a crisply efficient waiter, then Gascoyne got down to business, "I believe you have a proposal to make," he said.

"Yes," said Gersen. "I won't waste words. I want to buy Supernova."

Gascoyne uttered a hearty laugh. "Surely, you are joking!"

"Not at all," said Gersen. "I am quite serious."

"Well then, in that case, let me explain something of my philosophy of commercial transactions. As you perhaps saw in the roster of Managing Partners, my occupation is listed as 'Merchant.' That is a profession that I, too, take quite seriously. It means that I am in the business of buying and selling things. When I seek to buy, I offer a fair price; when I seek to sell, I ask a fair price. Nothing more, nothing less."

Gersen, when he heard these pious philosophic underpinnings of Gascoyne's profession, could scarcely conceal a knowing smile, because the merchandise in which Gascoyne transacted was human. That is, he was a slave trader. He specialized in providing workers for the manufacturing facilities on Murchison, for which his Ten Point Guarantee was a recognized mark of quality. He was widely known as one of the biggest and most successful in his field, a distinction supported by the fact that his profession accorded him the wherewithal to indulge in bunter racing. Of course, Murchison was in the Beyond, and there were no prohibitions against Gascoyne's particular form of commerce. Nevertheless, hearing Gascoyne expound on the ethics of his profession forced Gersen to stifle a laugh.

Instead, he replied, "Of course, Mr. Gascoyne, I would not seek to pay other than a fair price for Supernova. Suppose I offered one million SVU. Would that meet your requirements?" Gersen noted that this figure caused raised eyebrows not only from Gascoyne, but from Addels as well.

"A million, eh? That is a handsome sum, I can't deny it. There is a problem, though. As a racer, Supernova may well be worth a million. Certainly, that is a respectable offer and shows that you are a serious person. But for breeding purposes, Supernova is worth considerably more than that. Since you are new at this game, Mr. Lucas, let me explain: the value of top-performing bunters as breeding stock is the reason so many stables are willing to invest heavily in raising, training, and campaigning racing bunters. If done properly, it can be a profitable business."

Gersen was tempted to reply that this was merely a case of stables trading SVU among themselves, but he could also see matters from Gascoyne's point of view. He was beginning to feel a flicker of discouragement, that perhaps his elegant plan was running on the rocks.

But then Jehan Addels cut in to the discussion: "As a matter of curiosity, Mr. Gascoyne, what would a top-performing bunter like Supernova be worth as breeding stock?"

Gascoyne thought for a minute. "I would say, conservatively, three million SVU."

"And suppose Supernova won the final event at the end of the week? That would improve its value would it not?"

"The final? By beating both Black Hole and Moonbeam? Not very likely, of course, but I would say double that amount — six million."

"In that case," said Addels, "I have a way for you to turn Supernova into seven million. Are you interested?"

"You certainly have my attention," said Gascoyne.

Addels was now in his element, putting the details of a transaction together in ways not previously considered. He fixed Gascoyne with his icy pale blue eyes, and began laying out his argument. "I have made a careful study of the by-laws of the Bunter Consortium. There are no prohibitions against one stable leasing a bunter from another, and entering that bunter in any race, including the final events of the year. Provided, of course, that the bunter in question is so qualified.

"Therefore, I propose that Lyonnesse Stable lease Supernova for a single day — that being the day of the final race, of course — for the lease rate of one million SVU. At the end of the day, you have Supernova back, and you are still able to cash in on all its breeding value."

Gascoyne was tugging at his chin. "Interesting," he muttered. "But where does the seven million come from?"

"Supernova will be ridden by the Lyonnesse jockey, Kwan. I mean no offense, Mr. Gascoyne, but you have seen with your own eyes that, with Kwan on board, Moonbeam beat Supernova, even though most knowledgeable observers would rate Supernova the better beast. That is the result of superior riding technique. No offense to Murchison's jockey, whose name escapes me —"

"Tywald Slant," Gascoyne added.

"Yes, Slant. In any event, no offense to Slant, but we are confident that with Kwan riding, Supernova will beat Black Hole, and become this year's overall top bunter. By your own estimation, Supernova's breeding value in that case would rise to six million. Then add that to your one-day lease fee of one million, and there you have it — seven million. How does that sound as a fair-minded appraisal of value?"

Gascoyne broke into a broad grin, "It sounds like we have a bargain!" But then his brow furrowed. "But I would not like to be among the spectators with no bunter in the race."

"No problem there," said Addels. "We will lease you Moonbeam for race day, at a lease rate of one SVU."

"Mr. Addels," said Gascoyne, as he extended his hand to both parties at the table, "I can see why Mr. Lucas values your advice. You know how to put together a transaction."

"I will have the necessary paperwork sent over to you tomorrow," said Addels.

The next day at the same time, Gersen was alone at the same table at Linger Longer waiting for the meeting with Bruno Bolfo that had been agreed at the semi-final awards ceremony. Gersen had alerted Supervisor Clattuc, and he was pleased to see four obvious Constabulary men occupying a table by the door. Gersen noted that theirs was the only table that lacked a flower arrangement, evidently to avoid any obstructions in the event of a cause for action. Whatever else happened between himself and Bolfo, there would be no physical coercion.

After a short time, Bolfo appeared at the restaurant's entryway. He paused there for a moment, scrutinizing the interior. Behind Bolfo, Gersen could make out the figures of several of the thugs who had shared Bolfo's box at the racecourse. Bolfo's gaze fell on the constables' table, then he glanced back at the figures behind him and gave a negative shake to his head. The thugs faded out of sight, just as Yarnall came hustling over to see to Bolfo's needs, and promptly guide him to Gersen's table.

Gersen rose and extended his hand. Doing so was offensive to his instinct, but it was important that Bolfo not detect any antagonism. Bolfo's grip was cool, neither weak nor strong, and felt like dry parchment to the touch. The two men took seats; a waiter in a crisp white shirt and a black apron promptly appeared with an order pad, but Bolfo waved him off, and turned to Gersen, "You said you would have an answer for me. Do you?"

Gersen once again feigned hesitancy, as if thinking out loud. "As you stated," he said, "we are at an impasse. Neither side can act without the other, and neither wishes to concede. I wish there were another way, but just to make sure I understand your proposal, would you repeat it for me?"

"It is simple enough," said Bolfo, barely concealing his impatience. "We make a wager on the outcome of the final race. You back the Lyonnesse bunter; I back the Galactic entry. The stakes are our respective Jarnell interests, which are twenty percent each."

"And suppose that neither bunter wins?"

"That seems unlikely, since both were semi-final winners. But for the sake of completeness of the wager, if neither stable wins, the wager is void. Neither party is better or worse off than before."

This of course was exactly where Gersen had hoped to be in this discussion, but he continued to show reluctance. "I don't know…such a large bet…it seems imprudent…"

"Come now, Mr. Lucas. It is well known that you are a man of means. This would be a wager you could easily afford to lose. So if you cannot bring yourself to make the bet, it is not the money, but simple cowardice. Besides, that 20% stake should have been rightfully mine long ago."

"Oh?" Gersen was in fact a bit surprised, although this remark by Bolfo reinforced what he had suspected ever since he saw Bolfo's address on the roster of Managing Partners. The address had been Sasani, which had also in former times been the home base of Interchange. Had Bolfo been the proprietor of that enterprise, which facilitated kidnapping for ransom throughout the Galaxy, and from which Gersen had deceptively extracted a large fortune?

"Yes," confirmed Bolfo. "When that twenty percent stake became available, I was in the leading position to be the buyer. But I had a sudden and altogether unexpected setback that prevented me from consummating the purchase. Then your representative — that Addels fellow — appeared and snatched the Jarnell interest out from under me. Only later did I learn that he was acting on your behalf. But who were you? Up to that time, you had been unknown in the financial world. No one could determine, then or now, the source of your sudden wealth. I have often suspected that there must be some connection, that is, between my enormous loss and your mysterious gain. But I never could prove anything. Even so, it seems just, does it not, that fate has given me this chance to win my twenty-percent interest back?"

"But you could also lose," said Gersen.

"That's the chance I take," said Bolfo. "Now then, enough of this idle banter. You owe me a decision."

"Very well," said Gersen. "I will accept the wager. But on one condition."

"A condition? No games, please. This must be a straight wager."

"My condition has nothing to do with the terms of the wager."

"Well, then, what is it?"

"I want to know where to find Mongo Malagate."

"Malagate!!?" Bolfo's palms were on the table and he pushed himself up and forward. "What does Malagate have to do with this?"

"Nothing, in so many words. But Malagate has taken something precious from me, and I want it back."

"And what makes you think I know where Malagate can be found? And, for that matter, that I would tell you if I did?"

"I have my reasons for thinking you know where Malagate is, and they are not relevant, any more than your reasons for suspecting I had something to do with your financial setback. Neither sets of reasons matter. What does matter is that I want the chance to recover something from Malagate, and you want the chance to recover something from me. This is the condition on which I accept the wager."

Bolfo fixed Gersen with his cold, dark stare. Then he said, "Very well, Mr. Lucas, I will tell you where to find Malagate, when we have formalized our wager. Obviously, it needs to be in writing, and enforceable."

"Obviously," Gersen agreed. This was going as well as he could have hoped. "Addels will see to the necessary paperwork. I suggest we meet back here in two days' time in order to complete the formalities."

Without another word, Bolfo rose and departed.

Almost immediately, Yarnall the proprietor, who seemed to be aware of all goings on in the café at all times, appeared at Gersen's table with a concerned look on his face.

"Your guest left without ordering. Was there a problem, Mr. Lucas?"

"Not at all, Yon. I suppose he was just not hungry. But now that you mention it, I am famished. What do you recommend?"

"Perhaps a freshly made mollusk bisque, Mr. Lucas. Shellfish harvested this morning, and the recipe is a specialty of the house."

"Perfect. And a tankard of Smade's, if you please."

"Right away, sir. And I'm glad to hear there was not a problem."

"No problem at all, Yon. None at all."

The next two days were busy ones for Jehan Addels. Despite his personal misgivings about the prudence of the wager Gersen was proposing, once he had committed himself to a course of action on behalf of his friend and client, there was no holding back. The day after the meeting with Gascoyne, Addels had produced, and submitted to Gascoyne for signature, the documents necessary to commemorate the lease of Supernova to Lyonnesse Stable for the final event, and the simultaneous lease of Moonbeam to Murchison Stable. The lease payment of one million SVU had been drawn on Henry Lucas' personal account, in his capacity as MP of Lyonnesse. That phase of Gersen's gambit was thus firmly bedded into place.

The enforceable documentation of the wager between Henry Lucas and Bruno Bolfo was considerably more complicated, and required all of Addels' legal and financial dexterity to pull together. Nevertheless, at the appointed hour, with the results of his intense period of labor enclosed in a slender leather case, he arrived at Linger Longer. He paused briefly at the entrance, noted the Constabulary men at their table, and proceeded to the corner of the room where Gersen was waiting. By prior agreement with Yon Yarnall, they would not be disturbed while their meeting was in progress. Instead, the table had been provided with a pitcher of water and four glasses. After only a brief interval, Bruno Bolfo appeared. He was alone this time, gave no notice of the Constabulary contingent, and strode over to the table. There were no handshakes or bromides. There was no need to introduce Addels, as Bolfo knew quite well who he was.

"Are you ready to proceed?" said Bolfo.

"We are," said Addels, then reached into his case, extracted two documents, and placed one each in front of Gersen and Bolfo. "This is a simple memorandum of the wager. It is the first of two undertakings you gentlemen will need to execute. As you can see, this one lays out very simply the terms you have agreed. It will not be enforceable, however, without the second document. Please read it, and when you are ready to sign, we will invite Mr. Yarnall to serve as a witness."

Both parties briefly read the terms, signified their readiness to sign, and Addels motioned to Yarnall, who was standing ready at a discrete distance. Gersen and Bolfo signed, Yarnall witnessed, then asked if he could refill anyone's water glass. There being no requests, he silently retreated. Addels then withdrew a second set of documents from his case.

"These will make the terms enforceable. And to assist in that purpose, I have asked a representative of the law firm of Glyphon and Blum, Mr. Tobias Wormley, to join us."

"One moment, if you please," Gersen interrupted, and turned to Bolfo with a hard look. "Mr. Bolfo, I think now is the time for you to meet my condition."

Bolfo reacted with an expression of amused condescension. "I find it odd, Mr. Lucas, that a man of your wide knowledge and many connections would need an answer to such an obvious question. However, since you insist, you will find Malagate at the most likely place imaginable — that is Ghnarumen, the planet of the Star Kings!"

Gersen found himself suddenly off-balance. Ghnarumen, after all, had been his first instinct. But Miles Jaeger had persuaded him otherwise. Jaeger's reasoning — that Malagate was considered a renegade among the Star Kings and therefore unwelcome on their planet — had been persuasive. Now Bolfo was refuting that logic. Was Bolfo playing some game?

"How can that be?" he challenged Bolfo. "It is well known that Malagate is a pariah among the Star Kings."

"The internal politics of the Star Kings are none of my affair," said Bolfo. "But Ghnarumen is a big planet. Malagate has based himself in a region remote from the Star King population."

"How do you know that?"

Bolfo laughed indulgently. "The answer to that question should be obvious. I know where Malagate is because one of my freighters made a delivery to him only last week. A very strange delivery, in fact. An antique instrument for playing music, something called a 'piano.' Now, I've told you more than enough to satisfy your condition." Then Bolfo turned to Addels, "Summon this Mr. Wormley."

Addels glanced at Gersen for confirmation, and Gersen nodded affirmatively. There was no way for Bolfo to have invented this statement about the piano. It meant not only that Malagate was on Ghnarumen, but that he had Gabrielle there, and had arranged for her to play for him. This news had many dimensions that he would have to sort out later, but he had got from Bolfo what he wanted.

Addels touched a button on his communicator, then distributed the second set of documents to Gersen and Bolfo. "These, gentlemen, are irrevocable powers of attorney. Please read them carefully. By executing them, you will be granting Mr. Wormley's firm the power to dispense with your Jarnell shares pursuant to the terms of the wager. It makes no difference where those shares may be held at present, because the power of attorney gives Wormley's firm the authority to require changes directly to Jarnell's shareholder records."

As Gersen and Bolfo were scanning their documents, Wormley arrived. He was a short, plump man of middle age dressed in conservative business attire. He was carrying a small satchel from which he withdrew a metal impression seal. When the parties were ready, he instructed them to sign; he counter-signed, stamped both the power of attorney and the wager, and placed all materials in his satchel.

"That completes the transaction, gentlemen," said Addels. "Mr. Wormley will record these documents with the judiciary on Alphanor, that being the location of Jarnell's headquarters. I should advise, for the sake of completeness, that Mr. Wormley will assess a modest fee, to be paid by the winner of the wager."

Bolfo rose to his feet, looking content with the state of affairs. The old expression about the look of the cat that swallowed a canary came to Gersen's mind. He found himself bemused that such a sinister figure could look so smug. Obviously, Bolfo believed that Black Hole's victory was a sure thing, and that he had taken advantage of the naivete of Henry Lucas. *Let him enjoy his moment,* Gersen thought. Bolfo gazed briefly at his two interlocutors, then spun on his heel and left.

The afternoon following the successful execution of his wager with Bruno Bolfo found Gersen strolling along the Beach Road that skirted Port Mona's eastern shore. Although events were playing out as well as he might have hoped, Gersen nevertheless found himself in a sour mood, and thought that some ocean air might sooth his troubled spirits. It was now mid-afternoon and Xantos 297 was casting shadows through the groves of Sasandar trees on his left, while painting a bright sheen on the calm expanse of Maybelle Bay to his right. There was no sound but the soft lapping of surf on sand and occasional bird song from the overhanging branches.

Yes, he considered, he had enticed Bolfo to make a bet Bolfo would likely lose. And yes, as the winner, Gersen would secure Bolfo's twenty percent interest in Jarnell, and clear the way to acquiring a further forty-five percent. By now, Wormley would have turned the executed documents over to the local judiciary, to be forwarded via secure courier to their counterparts on Alphanor. It would not be possible for Bolfo to renege on the wager, even if he wanted to. And yes, he had induced Bolfo to reveal the whereabouts of Malagate — a surprise, but upon reflection, one that should not have been unexpected. But the source of his discontent was that despite having played the hand to perfection, he seemed no closer to rescuing Gabrielle than he had been before, and that was the only thing that truly mattered.

Malagate had somehow managed to deal with the objections of his fellow Star Kings, and sequester himself, with Gabrielle apparently his captive, on Ghnarumen. Ghnarumen, in turn, was forbidden to human visitors. How was Gersen to overcome that seemingly insurmountable obstacle? It was certainly not so easy as simply ignoring the Star Kings' prohibition, as such a violation could have unforeseen, but potentially disastrous consequences. A conflict between humans and Star Kings could not be ruled out, with Gabrielle's safety being especially at risk. No, he must find some way to enlist the cooperation of the Star Kings. But how? They were a mysterious race. There was no obvious way to communicate with them, much less to secure their help. There was a sad irony in his present circumstance. If events progressed as planned, he would soon control eighty-five percent of Jarnell, arguably the most profitable enterprise in the Oikumene. But without Gabrielle, that wealth and power had no meaning.

These glum thoughts were interrupted by a soft humming on his communication device. Thinking it was an unwanted call, as only a handful had the codes to reach him this way, he glanced casually at the screen. It was Clattuc, though, the Supervisor of the Rosalia Constabulary.

"Is that you, Ellwood?" Gersen inquired.

"Yes. There has been a development you may want to know about. Violence. A fatality. And two of your people are involved."

"My people?"

"Their names are Kim and Kwan. We are holding them here at head-quarters pending a full investigation. I thought you would want to know."

"I certainly do. Thank you for advising me. I would like to see them, if possible."

"I thought as much. Where are you now?"

"On Beach Road. About a mile south of Marcie Way."

"Keep walking in that direction. I'll send a vehicle to pick you up."

The Constabulary driver met Gersen at the intersection of Beach Road and Marcie Way, and whisked him straight to headquarters. There, he was ushered into Ellwood Clattuc's office, a large, elegant room with an ovoid sandalwood table large enough to accommodate ten people. At one end sat Kim and Kwan, looking vaguely sheepish.

Clattuc rose and extended his hand. "Sorry to have troubled you," he said. "But you will be pleased to know that our investigation is complete, and your two folks are in the clear. In fact, based on the evidence, I've been tempted to offer them employment with the Constabulary.

"A body was discovered in the area outside the Lyonnesse bunter stable. Kim and Kwan were at the site. Protocol required that we bring them in for questioning. Fortunately, the security camera at the site was operative, and the video confirmed their story. Perhaps you would like to view it, as it is self-explanatory."

"Certainly," said Gersen.

Clattuc activated the office viewscreen on the wall above the table, and the recorded video began to play. The first frame showed Kim and Kwan standing outside the stable in casual conversation. Then three figures came into view, wielding what appeared to be bats of some kind — approximately three feet long and thicker at the end than at the handle. Gersen immediately recognized the bat-wielders. They were Bolfo's henchmen.

The first strode up to Kwan, cocked the bat behind him, then swung a vicious arc aimed at Kwan's knees. Kwan leapt into the air, the bat passed harmlessly beneath him, and Kwan aimed a kick at the now off-balance assailant, knocking him to the ground. As the second man tried to repeat the attack on Kwan, Kim caught the bat on the back-swing and used the batsman's momentum to topple him over. The third assailant then swung at Kwan's head. Kwan ducked under the blow, and the bat instead struck the skull of the first thug who was just stagger-ing to his feet. The force of the blow sent a gush of blood and brains spewing from the shattered cranium, and the victim collapsed into a senseless heap. The other two assailants turned and hastened away, out of the camera's range. The video stopped, with Kim and Kwan staring in seeming disbelief at the fallen man.

"Those were Bolfo's thugs," said Gersen. "I recognize them from the racetrack, and later from the entrance to Linger Longer."

"Yes," said Clattuc. "The constables I stationed at the restaurant also identified them. Your folks are free to go. They defended themselves skillfully, by the way."

"Is there a cause of action against Bolfo?" Gersen asked.

"Doubtful. The assailants, if we can find them — which we probably cannot — will deny they were acting under Bolfo's orders. We will try to pick them up, of course, but they likely have already departed on a commercial outbound flight. There are several such flights daily during race week. Do you have any idea what this attack was about?"

"I can make a good guess," said Gersen. "They were going after

Kwan, and targeting his knees. Kwan is the Lyonnesse jockey. Bolfo and I had made a bet on the outcome of the race. Bolfo thinks his Black Hole is a sure thing, but it appears he was trying to improve his odds by disabling our rider."

"There is still a day remaining before the race," said Clattuc. "It might be prudent for us to provide security. Although, I must say Kwan and Kim seem able to look out for themselves."

The next day passed uneventfully; the threat of further violence did not materialize. Xantos 297 set gracefully, there was a brief rain shower overnight, and race day dawned crisp and clear. The rain had damp- ened the track, not enough to compromise the footing, but enough to put down the dust. Now was the grand finale of the bunter racing season, the pinnacle of life for the socially inclined. All week long, Port Mona had been buzzing with activity. A dozen commercial flights a day crowded the spaceport, with those privileged to hold tickets to the finals displacing those only favored with the semis. This year for the first time, enormous screens had been erected outside the racetrack, doubling the number of viewers to be accommodated, with a conse- quent doubling of hotel occupancy, restaurant seatings, and retail sales. It was now or never for the Rosalia merchant clan.

The Rosalia Regency was even more alive with energized racegoers, if such a thing were possible. Gersen and Addels avoided the crush of public spaces until the last possible moment, then worked their way through the crowded lobby to their waiting transport. The racecourse, when they arrived, was already filling rapidly with gentlemen in dandy day-coats and ladies in daring frocks. On their way to Box B-6, Addels excused himself, said he would meet Gersen at the box, and pushed his way through the pullulating masses in the direction of the betting windows. A puzzling development, thought Gersen, as Addels was not a betting man. When Gersen arrived at B-6, Gascoyne, already in B-5 with his lovely companion, winked broadly and offered a thumbs-up sign. In due course, Addels arrived but provided no explanation about his recent whereabouts. The stands were nearly full, the sense of antici- pation in the crowd growing palpable. Then the deep plangent gong tone sounded, calling out the bunters. Just at that moment, Bruno

Bolfo arrived at Box B-7. He gave no notice of Gersen and Addels, but instead sat staring straight ahead, his aquiline profile looking even more severe than usual. Gersen saw that only three of his thugs were in attendance. A noticeable reduction in force, Gersen noted, and allowed himself a private smile.

The bunters had been pushed, pulled, and prodded into the starting gates, and had begun to moan and thrash about once their eyestalks were uncapped. Then the starting bell rang loud and clear, and off they went. Moonbeam, with Tywald Slant on board, sprinted into the lead. Black Hole, unaccustomed to not being first, leapt ahead to catch up. All the way to the far turn, it was Moonbeam and Black Hole, head-to-head, seemingly in their own private race and two full lengths ahead of the pack. With no cloud of dust obscuring things, Gersen had a clear view with his field glasses, and it looked to him as though the two leading bunters were oblivious to the guidance of their riders, and instead were striving against each other with neither willing to give ground. Supernova, under Kwan's guidance, seemed to be cruising along effortlessly, although a good three lengths back.

Then the racers reached the marker for the final quarter-mile. Black Hole and Moonbeam, though still leading and matching one another stride for stride, were noticeably slowing, it seemed to Gersen. Now on came Supernova, accelerating and lengthening its stride. The gap behind the leaders closed from three lengths, to two, then one, with Supernova pulling out ahead of the followers. With fifty yards to go, Supernova pulled even with Moonbeam and Black Hole, both frothing at the mouth and being furiously whipped by their riders, Tywald Slant and Myron Jolt.

At the twenty-five yard mark, the outcome was not in doubt. Gersen glanced to his left and saw that Bolfo's fists were clenched and his features locked in a rictus grimace. Then the crowd erupted in a thunderous roar as Supernova crossed the finish line, the winner going away. Gersen and Addels exchanged a hearty handshake, and Gersen looked to his right at Gascoyne. The merchant was embracing his lady friend, but signaling to Gersen over her shoulder with seven extended fingers. Gersen then turned to his left, but B-7 was empty, its occupants having disappeared into the crowd.

For a long moment, Gersen stood watching the bunters, now with eye-stalks capped and being led away, while he savored the satisfaction of being the overall winner. He had accomplished everything on Rosalia he had set out to do. At the same time, there was an emptiness; Gabrielle was as far away as ever. Then he felt a tug on his sleeve.

"Excuse me, Mr. Lucas," said one of the brightly clad ushers, "you are wanted in the MPs' lounge. There's been a protest and the race committee is meeting to consider it. There is a need for haste, sir, because the crowd is waiting for the winners to be officially announced."

Gersen stepped promptly out of the box, and followed the usher to the MPs' cafeteria. When he arrived, a group had already assembled. The chair of the committee introduced himself. It was Ariel Selp, MP of the Aloysius Stable and, Gersen remembered, Addels' fellow Abacus Club member from Pontefract. Others that he recognized were Bolfo, of course, Gascoyne, and Privet from Methlen.

"Fellow MPs," Selp began, "we are here to consider a protest filed by Mr. Bolfo of Galactic Stable. He acknowledges that Supernova won the race, but asserts that Supernova is the property of Murchison's, and therefore Murchison's should be deemed the winning stable. I will now entertain arguments for and against the protest."

"I have nothing more to say," said Bolfo in an imperious tone. "The facts are clear. Supernova is Murchison's beast, and therefore Murchison's is the winning stable."

At that moment, Jehan Addels entered the room. "Excuse me, Mr. Chairman, I wish to speak on behalf of Lyonnesse Stable. I will make three points which I believe will expedite your decision."

"Very well, Jehan. Your legal reputation precedes you."

"Point Number One. I have here a valid lease, signed by Mr. Gascoyne as owner of Supernova, leasing Supernova to Lyonnesse for one day, that being today.

"Point Number Two. Here is a copy of the by-laws of the Consortium. They clearly state that any stable is able to enter any bunter provided that bunter is qualified. In the case of Supernova, qualifications are not in dispute.

"Point Number Three. Here is a copy of a wager between Mr. Bolfo of Galactic and Mr. Lucas of Lyonnesse, which unambiguously specifies that the wager is between the bunter entered by the respective stables, without naming the bunters individually. In view of points one and two, the bunters that are subject to the wager are plainly Supernova and Black Hole.

"I believe those considerations should put the matter to rest. However, should there remain any doubt, I checked with the race technicians before arriving here. The contest for second place, as we all saw with our own eyes, was between Moonbeam and Black Hole. The result was a photo finish, and Moonbeam was judged the winner by a snout. If the committee disagrees with me and concludes that Supernova on race day was a Murchison's beast, notwithstanding the valid lease, then by the same logic Moonbeam was a Lyonnesse beast. Mr. Bolfo's protest thus becomes nuncupatory."

Selp called the race committee into a huddle, they conferred barely a moment, then Selp announced, "The unanimous verdict of the committee is that Supernova and Lyonnesse are first, Moonbeam and Murchison second, Black Hole and Galactic third. Now let us proceed without delay to the awards podium where the racing fans are waiting."

Gersen and Addels waited until the room had cleared, then followed the others out.

"Well done, Jehan," said Gersen. "This outcome cost me a million SVU, but the look on Bolfo's face almost made it worthwhile."

"Actually," said Addels, with an uncharacteristically coy expression, "the result has cost you nothing. The odds on Supernova to win were three-and-a-half to one, and I placed a bet of four hundred thousand on your behalf on Supernova."

With that Addels produced a bank draft drawn on the Rosalia Parimutuel account made out to Henry Lucas in the amount of one million SVU.

"Jehan," said Gersen, "sometimes you outdo even yourself."

That evening, Gersen hosted a celebratory dinner that included Addels, Kim, and Kwan, together with Gascoyne, his lady friend, and the Murchison jockey, Tywald Slant. All were in high spirits, and there was much good-natured jesting in which even the normally reserved Addels took part. There were a few too many champagne toasts, and

Gersen was relieved to retire for the night. However, there was a message from Ellwood Clattuc waiting on his hotel room monitor. He splashed cold water on his face to clear his head, and returned the call.

"Sorry to trouble you, Henry," said Clattuc, "but Bruno Bolfo is dead. I thought you would want to know."

"How did it happen?" asked Gersen.

"Not in a pretty way. He seems to have been devoured by that bunter of his — Black Hole. I know that seems extraordinary. The security camera at the site had been disabled, but we have two corroborating eyewitnesses. Apparently, Bolfo was so outraged by the loss in today's race that he intended to punish the losing jockey by feeding him to Black Hole. Something went wrong, though, and Bolfo himself became the meal. We have a recording of the witness's testimony. If you like, I can patch it through to your viewscreen."

"Not the best way to put myself to sleep tonight, but I suppose I had best see it."

Gersen waited while Clattuc set up the feed, then an image came on the screen of a sloppily dressed young man with a flat face and pointed chin, and a tangled knot of red hair. He was sitting at a table kneading his hands together, with his gaze wandering about nervously.

"Please state your name for the record," came the off-camera voice of the interviewer.

"Gideon Pond. People call me Giddy."

"And what is your employment?"

"I'm a stable hand."

"What do your duties consist of?"

"I clean out the muck when the bunters are out."

"Were you on duty earlier today?"

"Yes, I was."

"Did you witness what happened to the victim, Bruno Bolfo?"

"I wish I never had, but yes, I did."

"Tell me for the record what you saw."

"A black van pulled up beside the stable, and five people got out. I recognized Mr. Bolfo. I had seen him a couple of times around the stable, but everyone knows who he is. The other one I knew was Black Hole's jockey, Myron Jolt. His hands were tied behind his back, and a gag was stuffed into his mouth. He was making all kinds of noise through the gag, like he was crying something out. He was shaking his head back and forth, his eyes looked really scared.

"Mr. Bolfo was the one in charge. He was ordering the other three to bring Myron over to the stable door. Myron was struggling really, really hard. He didn't want to go. But the three guys dragged him over there. His yelling was getting louder. What was happening was that they were going to shove him in there with Black Hole. Now, I've worked around the stables for over a year, and I can tell you all these bunters are nasty creatures. Especially when they don't have their eye caps on, and especially when they're hungry. It being race day, I knew that Black Hole hadn't been fed.

"Next, I need to tell you about the stables. There is an outer door that slides open. Then inside, there is a heavy metal gate that keeps the bunters locked in their pens."

Gersen remembered exactly this arrangement from his visit to Moonbeam earlier. The outer door slid open to give human attendants access, but the bunters were still secure behind the metal gate.

Gideon Pond continued. "There was Mr. Bolfo at the sliding door, waiting for the others to drag the jockey up. Bolfo then slid the door back and motioned the others forward. But when they looked inside the open door, they backed up fast. The inner gate had been left open, and Black Hole was peering out. Mr. Bolfo was shouting at them and waving them to come forward, but then Black Hole's head came out, grabbed Mr. Bolfo by the shoulder, and dragged him inside. There was screaming like you can't imagine, blood and bits of flesh flying out the door. Then the screaming stopped, but I could still hear the sound of chewing. Good heavens! I will never forget those sounds — the screaming and the chewing. The three other guys dropped Myron Jolt, jumped in the van and drove away. I ran up and slid the outer door closed. At least for a time, it was strong enough to keep Black Hole penned up, especially while he was busy with his dinner. Then I untied Myron Jolt, and called the police."

There was nothing else of consequence on the video. Ellwood Clattuc came back on, "Myron Jolt corroborates the story. The unsolved mystery is how or why the inner gate happened to be left open and, for that matter, why Black Hole was without his eye caps. But he was one hungry beast, that's for sure. There was barely enough left to identify the remains. Some of our guys suspect that one of the Galactic workers might have set the trap, possibly even Jolt himself, knowing how Bolfo liked to punish those who failed him. We will never know. Nor, to tell the truth, do we really care. Any questions?"

"None at the moment," said Gersen. "Thanks for letting me know, although I suspect you've cost me a decent night's sleep. If I think of anything further, I'll call you in the morning."

Gersen shut down the monitor, shook his head in wonder, and retired for the night.

CHAPTER XIII

Excerpt from *The Devil's Dictionary* by Ambrose Bierce:

LOGIC, n. The art of thinking and reasoning in strict accordance with the limitations and incapacities of human misunderstanding. The basic of logic is the syllogism, consisting of a major premise, a minor premise, and a conclusion — thus:

Major Premise: sixty men can do a piece of work sixty times as fast as one man.

Minor Premise: one man can dig a posthole in sixty seconds; therefore —

Conclusion: sixty men can dig a posthole in one second.

From *Better Understanding of the Institute* by Charles Bronstein (68):

The Institute from its earliest days has sought to counteract the false promises of technology. When humans rely too heavily on automation, their own skills atrophy from disuse. To take one small but relevant example, in the pre-Apocalyptic era, the concept of so-called 'artificial intelligence' was popularized. Computers were thought to be able to replicate intrinsic human creations such as, for instance, essays on various topics. In the early phases of this fad, critics remarked on how indistinguishable from the human product were the results of computer composition. This was until it was observed that the similarity was not so much a case of the computers being intelligent, but rather that the human screeds they were replicating were dim-witted.

—ᴍ—

The blue-white fading light of Rigel was giving way to the soft glow of lanterns strung above the outdoor terrace at Chancy's Tea House, at Sailmaker Beach, Avente, Alphanor. Three men of unexceptional appearance were gathered in casual posture around a table in the corner. The speaker, of late middle age with close-cropped iron gray hair and a strong jaw, was Miles Jaeger, holding the rank of Commander of the IPCC.

"That's quite a story," he was saying. "Just out of curiosity, what was the fate of this Black Hole creature?"

"He was euthanized," answered Kirth Gersen, known to the public as Henry Lucas, who, for his part, was a man of sixty whose lean but solid frame could have passed for fifteen years younger. "The Rosalia authorities make that a requirement for any bunter who has tasted human flesh. It is considered to be habit-forming."

"Understandable," said Jaeger, "but they should have given the creature a medal first. Bolfo was a villain, best out of the way."

"That brings us to the purpose of our meeting," said Gersen. "As you know, Bolfo operated a fleet of space freighters under the business name Galactic Freight. It occurred to my colleague here, Jehan Addels, that Bolfo might have died intestate. I will leave it to Jehan to tell you the rest."

Here, Gersen nodded to the third man at the table, a slender individual with a narrow face, weak jaw, and icy pale blue eyes. This was Jehan Addels, Gersen's (or Lucas's) long-time friend and financial advisor.

"I travelled to Sul Arsam, on Sasani," Addels began. "And there I discovered that Bolfo had indeed died intestate. Furthermore, the potentially endless chain of possible inheritors was completely vacant. Therefore, under the interplanetary rules of judicial protocol, Bolfo's property was subject to escheat — that is, assumption of ownership by the state. The Sasani authorities had no idea what to do with the business, for reasons I will explain in a moment, so I bought it for a nominal sum in the name of Braemar investments."

"What did the property consist of?" asked Jaeger.

"Only two assets of significance. Galactic Freight, and Galactic

Insurance. Galactic Freight owns twenty-seven space freighters. Galactic Insurance writes policies against freight losses, mostly due to hi-jacking."

"Clever," said Jaeger, "since Galactic Freight itself is a well-known hi-jacker."

"It is the freight operation that we feel is a matter of mutual interest," Addels continued. "If weeded of its criminal elements, it could become a productive, not to mention profitable business. It was the problem of weeding that gave the Sasani authorities pause."

Now Gersen interjected. "This is where the IPCC comes in. These twenty-seven freighters are registered in as many different jurisdictions. Jehan can provide you with the complete roster. An unknown number, but we assume at least half, are operated by criminal elements. What we would like the IPCC to do is track them down, eliminate the criminals, and help turn Galactic Freight into a legitimate business."

"That certainly is within our capability," said Jaeger, "but, as you know, the IPCC is not a charitable organization. How do you propose to handle the costs?"

"Jehan has suggested, and I have agreed," said Gersen, "that we will turn Galactic Freight in trust over to the IPCC. Jehan calculates that the profits from a successful enterprise would pay many times over for the costs of cleaning it up."

"A generous proposal," said Jaeger. "I will take it up with our board, but I am confident they will agree. And New Horizon on Grabhorne will be among the new business's first freight customers. The community is making great progress creating a new life for themselves. And young Jono is reunited with his parents, by the way, and all are prospering."

"That is welcome news," said Gersen, "but one other point before we leave the topic of Galactic Freight. I told you about our winning jockey, Kwan. He wants to be a space pilot. He has passed the licensing requirements. When you clean up Galactic Freight, you will undoubtedly have plenty of openings for honest and capable pilots. Please give Kwan fair consideration."

"Of course," said Jaeger. "What then will happen to Lyonnesse Stable?"

"I am returning it to Jared Oopf, the original MP. With the prize money from the first-place finish, and the breeding value of Moonbeam as runner-up, he can easily return what I paid for the Managing Partnership. And it is understood that when Kwan leaves to pursue his piloting career, Lyonnesse will replace him as their top jockey with Myron Jolt, who will be looking for work now that Galactic Stable has been disbanded."

Jaeger rose to his feet. "Many loose ends appear to be getting tied up."

"Before you go," said Gersen, "there is one final matter — for me, the greatest loose end of all. Bolfo before he died confirmed that Malagate has taken refuge on Ghnarumen. I mean to track him down and rescue Gabrielle. But I have no way to communicate with the Star Kings. It is widely understood that there are Star Kings resident in human populations. But exactly where is unknown. Perhaps this is an area where the IPCC has information."

"I will inquire," said Jaeger. "You will hear from me as soon as I have anything useful to report. Good evening, then."

Jaeger departed the terrace, leaving Gersen and Addels by themselves.

"Jaeger is correct about the loose ends," said Addels, "but there is one important one still to be addressed. That is the matter of the Jarnell shares."

"Yes," said Gersen, "and that is now a matter of high priority, as I have urgent business I wish to take up with Jarnell. The sooner I can deal from a forty percent ownership position, the better."

"Glyphon and Blum have the necessary paperwork. There is no reason why the shares cannot be transferred tomorrow."

"Excellent. But one thing bothers me. Does not Gyphon and Blum represent the group of shareholders seeking to dispose of their combined forty-five present interest? And does that not create a conflict, because by consolidating our shareholding with Bolfo's, a significant buyer is removed?"

"All true," acknowledged Addels. "I had this out with the Glyphon folks before retaining them on our behalf. I pointed out to them that the forty-five percent interest could not be sold without the agreement of both Braemar's and Bolfo's interests. And as long as those were separate, agreement would never be reached. Now we will be the sole buyer, the price will have to be negotiated, and at the end of the day, they will have to accept our offer. But Glyphon's commission will still be substantial. It's a case for them of half a loaf being better than none."

There being nothing further to discuss, Gersen and Addels summoned their waiting driver and returned to the hotel Credenza.

By the afternoon of the next day, Gersen had received updates on two important matters. The first was from Jehan Addels.

"Congratulations," Addels began, "you now control forty percent of Jarnell. The transfer went very smoothly. My sense is that all parties were happy to have Bolfo out of the picture. The Gyphon and Blum people are eager to know when we want to begin discussions on the purchase of their clients' forty-five percent stake."

"I have a more pressing matter on my mind at the moment," said Gersen. "I'll let you know when I am ready."

"Very well," said Addels. "It doesn't hurt to build a bit of anxiety in the sellers' minds."

The second call was from Miles Jaeger.

"I'll begin by confessing that the IPCC file on Star Kings is rather thin. In fact, other than the two Malagates, we have no record of a Star King being involved in any criminal activity. Either they are as innocent as angels, or they are very careful about hiding anything that would catch our attention.

"I did learn one thing that surprised me, however. We have picked up reports that the Institute has a Star King serving of a very high Phase — high eighties, or even low nineties. That seems quite extraordinary, but our sources are deemed reliable."

Gersen was surprised as well. The Institute was an organization whose secrecy was matched only by its exclusivity. To rise to the highest Phase was understood to require decades of diligent exertion. Gersen himself had reached phase eleven at the age of twenty-four before resigning. How a Star King had managed to join their ranks and rise so far was indeed a mystery.

"A thought-provoking report," he said. "What can you tell me about your sources?"

Jaeger allowed himself a soft laugh, "Unfortunately, nothing, for reasons you know well."

"I understand," said Gersen, smiling as well. "You can't blame me for trying, though. Thank you for the information, anyway."

Gersen broke off the connection. Life, he reflected, was often like a chess game. You had to play your pieces one move at a time, with an eye to how an uncertain future might unfold. A plan, or at least the beginning of a plan, had begun to form in his mind. He would pursue it with deliberation. He tapped some codes into his monitor, identified himself as Henry Lucas, and asked to speak with Rolf Woodward. Woodward, Jarnell's Technical Director, came on the screen with a welcoming smile.

"Mr. Lucas! How is our favorite test pilot? Do I understand that Edgar Darby is no more?"

"You understand correctly," said Gersen. "My apologies for the damage to the Thribolt cannon control panel on Grabhorne, but that was the only means at hand."

"No problem there," said Woodward. "It has already been repaired. We have also initiated the training of several operators from the New Horizon community. They will be well protected from space pirates henceforth. But you did not call me about the Thribolt, I suppose?"

"You suppose correctly," said Gersen. "I have other business to discuss, specifically a development project that I think your technical staff will find both interesting and challenging."

"I am intrigued," said Woodward. "Tell me more."

"I would rather discuss the project in person, and at your facility so that we can bring others into the conversation as might be required."

There was a hesitation on Woodward's end. He was, Gersen imagined, mindful of the potential workload on his staff that might be caused by whatever hare-brained scheme Gersen had in mind. However, this is where Gersen's forty percent ownership would come into play. Woodward, along with other Jarnell senior managers, would be well aware of the transaction that had just occurred, and probably as well about the pending one.

"Why don't you join me for lunch in our cafeteria tomorrow, and I'll free up the rest of the afternoon."

"Excellent," said Gersen, "until tomorrow."

Gersen broke the connection, then called to arrange a hired Flitterwing to meet him at the hotel landing pad the next morning. Then he tapped in the code for Jehan Addels.

"Ready to discuss the Jarnell business so soon?" Addels began.

"Not yet. I called for another reason. Is Dwyddion still resident in Pontefract?"

Dwyddion, whose life Gersen had saved many years earlier, had been elevated to the rank of Triune — the most senior Fellow of the Institute. After rescuing him, Gersen had taken him to Pontefract, which also happened to be Addels' home base.

"I believe so," said Addels, "although it is hard to know for sure. At one time, he occupied a manse far to the northwest. However, as you know, he is notoriously reclusive."

"I need to speak with him on a matter of some urgency," said Gersen. "Can you find his contact information, or failing that, arrange to have a note delivered to his manse telling him that Kirth Gersen seeks to speak with him, and giving him my personal number?"

"I will see to the matter immediately," said Addels, and the connection broke off.

The next day, after an hour's flight on the hired Flitterwing and a brief but pleasant lunch with Woodward, Gersen found himself in a small conference room off Woodward's office. In attendance were Tibo Gatz and Hans Snell, Jarnell's 'Whiz Kids' on the subject of Intersplit technology. Gersen began to explain his project as follows:

"Imagine, if you will, a vessel that has broken down in deep space, light-years away from any base where it could be repaired. It is theoretically possible to rescue the crew. They could don air suits and come across by tether to a rescue vessel. But what about the spaceship itself? It cannot be towed or carried back to port.

"What I would like to see Jarnell develop, therefore, is a way to link the disabled vessel to a salvage vessel, and fly the two together back to port, using only the salvage vessel's power.

"What are your thoughts on that?"

Gatz, pink-faced and plump with a tangled mop of blond hair, whom

Gersen remembered well from his role in the Thribolt cannon affair, led off, "I don't see any particular problem linking the disabled vessel to a salvage vessel. It could be done with a handful of flange bolts. Since in deep space there would be no gravity or air resistance to overcome, the strength of the attachment would need only to be minimal. It would be helpful, of course, if the two vessels had a similar surface profile."

"What about propulsion?" Gersen asked. "Could the Intersplit of the rescue ship handle the mass of both vessels?"

"That question has two parts," said Gatz, sounding like a graduate student taking the oral exam for his PhD in engineering science. "Part One, every vessel powered by Intersplit is surrounded by a force field. This is necessary to protect against the shearing dynamics of faster-than-light speeds. It has never been tried, but it would seem theoretically possible to program the rescue vessel to generate a force field sufficient to protect both itself and the out-of-service ship.

"Part Two is where I see the real problem. Assuming both vessels had about the same mass, you will be asking the rescue vessel's Intersplit to take on double load. That could lead to over-heating, possibly catastrophic failure."

Not to be deterred, Gersen persisted. "What about fitting out the rescue vessel with an over-powered Intersplit?"

Now Snell chipped in, a fragile-looking young person with a bookish demeanor. "Interesting idea. What you are describing is very much like the propulsion system of the Intersplit LF. Still in the development stage, but looking promising."

"More than promising," said Gersen. "As you know, I've been flying the LF for almost a year now.

"Let me see if I can summarize what I've heard. Linking two vessels together, no problem, especially if they have similar hull profiles. Programming the rescue vessel to generate an extra force field, theoretically possible. Equip the rescue vessel with an LF power plant, and the package is complete. Do I have this right?"

Heads nodded around the table.

"Then here is what I would like to do. Pull a Pharaon Model III off the production line. Fit it out with an LF propulsion system and the software for expanding the force field. I'd like to have it ready within a month, at the most."

Gersen could see that Woodward was about to object, so he added, "Of course all costs will be for my account, and when I'm finished with the project I have in mind, I'll turn the vessel over to the technical department."

This addressed Woodward's departmental budget concerns, and the two tech folks were obviously elated at this new project. The meeting broke up with smiles and handshakes, and Gersen was on his way back to Avente by late afternoon.

The Flitterwing had traversed the grassy steppe that lay between Jarnell headquarters and the western outskirts of Avente, and the gleaming towers of the city were in view, with the vast expanse of the Thaumaturge spreading out beyond. Gersen's handset emitted the low tone advising that his confidential code was being used. He keyed the reply button and responded, "Lucas."

"Lucas? Who is Lucas?! I was advised this code would reach Kirth Gersen," came a voice like the rasping of dry sticks. *This must be Dwyddion*, Gersen thought.

"If you are responding to a message from Jehan Addels, you are Dwyddion. And I am indeed Kirth Gersen."

"Tell me about *Ctchm*, then." This was as good as a private code, as that name would be known only to Dwyddion and Gersen.

"Kim is well. Your recommendation was perceptive. He has proven both intelligent and capable, and above all trustworthy. I regret that I have never been able to pronounce his name properly, but he is amused rather than offended that I call him Kim."

"Your answer confirms your identity. I had my doubts, but Addels is a man of good repute. Now tell me what urgent business prompts you to unsettle my tranquility."

"I must give you a brief answer," said Gersen, "as I am presently hovering five thousand feet above Avente."

"Brevity requires one to be succinct," said Dwyddion.

"Very well. My urgent business is with the Star Kings, and I understand there is a Star King among the Institute's Fellows — of quite a high Phase, if my sources are correct."

There was a brief pause, as Dwyddion was likely wondering how Gersen had come into possession of this closely guarded secret.

"Suppose, just for the sake of discussion, that your sources are correct. What is the nature of this urgent business?"

"It involves Mongo Malagate. I would not care to say more on an open line. But if there is a Star King among the Institute's Fellows, and he concerns himself with the security of his people, he needs to hear me out."

There was a throat-clearing noise, then Dwyddion said, "You will hear from me when I have something to report," and the line went dead.

During the middle of the night, Gersen was extracted from a fitful sleep by the urgent tone of his communication screen.

"I suppose I have awakened you," came Dwyddion's gravelly voice, "but you insisted the matter was urgent. How soon can you be at my manse in Pontefract?"

Gersen did a quick calculation. Pontefract was on Aloysius, in the Vega system. "Four days," he said.

"Very well," said Dwyddion, "the party you wish to meet will be here then."

Four days later, *Quicksilver* put down at the Pontefract Spaceport, and Gersen departed in a slidecar that Addels had arranged, whose navigation system had been programmed with Dwyddion's domicile as its destination. The route led out of the Pontefract suburbs, skirting the exclusive Ballywood residential neighborhood, then into a deepening forest. With the vehicle mostly driving itself, Gersen was free to concentrate on his message to the Star Kings, although it had not changed much in the many dozens of times he had tried to refine it during the flight to Aloysius. In due course, the paved road became a hard-packed earth track in the forest floor, that finally gave forth upon the site of a rustic dwelling of modest size. The term 'manse,' Gersen noted, was perhaps a bit overdone, as the structure of rough-hewn timbers and slate roof, with three low-profile gables, was more like an oversized bungalow. Nevertheless, it was sufficient for a resident like Dwyddion, a person of spartan habits living alone.

Gersen parked in a space apparently provided for that purpose, proceeded along a flagstone path through a neatly tended garden, and knocked on the solid oak door. He was admitted by an elderly servant in a beige apron, and shown into a sitting room whose outstanding feature was that its wall space, except for a fireplace, two windows, and French doors leading to another garden, was entirely taken up by shelving full to bursting capacity with books. Dwyddion and another gentleman rose to greet him. Dwyddion's appearance had scarcely changed in the twenty-four years since Gersen had last seen him. His dome of a forehead with a high receding mat of now-graying hair, deep-socketed brooding eyes, gaunt cheeks, and pointed chin were all as Gersen remembered. His face still told of great intellectual force, with perhaps a note of sadness accumulated with the passage of time. His visitor's appearance, however, required Gersen to stifle a look of surprise, for he was a near copy of the person known to Gersen as Gyle Warweave, the alias adopted by Mongo Malagate. Like Warweave, this individual was tall, stately, and fit-looking.

"Welcome, Kirth Gersen," said Dwyddion, "the years have not treated you unkindly. Allow me to introduce my guest, Liam Harcour."

Harcour extended his hand. Evidently, Gersen had failed to sufficiently suppress his look of surprise because Harcour said, "Does my appearance startle you? Perhaps you think I am Malagate. But I can assure you, that is not the case. The one known as Malagate is derived from the same genetic sequence that created certain members of our race, including myself. All these matters I will explain, with your indulgence."

As he took Harcour's hand, Gersen noted some striking differences between this man and Warweave. First, Harcour's face and head were completely hairless. His head was covered by smooth skin, and he lacked all facial hair, including eyebrows. His expression, quite unlike the sinister glare of Warweave, was entirely benign.

"Please be seated, gentlemen," said Dwyddion. "Kirth Gersen, you said that your urgent business had to do with Malagate. We await your further explanation. But first, let me clarify that Liam is a Star King, although I should add that the term 'Star King' is a human mispronunciation of the name by which Liam's race identify themselves, which is *tschrkn*. The first humans to encounter the race incorrectly coined the term 'Star King,' and that appellation has persisted ever since. Liam is also a respected Fellow of the Institute, Phase 92." Dwyddion then picked up a small silver bell from the table next to his chair, and shook it softly. The aproned servant instantly appeared.

"Some tea and biscuits, Jeremiah, if you please," said Dwyddion. The servant nodded and disappeared; Dwyddion then turned to Gersen. "Your explanation is now appropriate."

Gersen proceeded, as succinctly as he could, to describe the history of his encounter with Malagate, how Malagate had raided the community of Willow Grove, how he had executed all who resisted or were deemed too old to work, and how he had enslaved the rest, some several thousand souls in all, on Grabhorne. He then described how the IPCC had raided Grabhorne, with minor assistance from Gersen, liberated the slaves, then how Malagate had escaped, kidnapping in the process a person who was dear to Gersen, how that person was now Malagate's captive on Ghnarumen, and finally, how Gersen was determined to rescue her.

"The kidnapping is reprehensible," said Dwyddion, "but do you expect the *tschrkn* to assist you, and if so, how?"

"All that I ask is permission to travel to Ghnarumen, there to communicate with Malagate, and persuade him to surrender the hostage."

Dwyddion made a thoughtful humming sound under his breath, then said, "Malagate is not known to be a conciliatory person. How do you expect to persuade him?"

"I have something that he wants, and I believe he wants it with as great a desire as I want the hostage freed."

"You said during our brief conversation earlier that this matter concerns the security of the *tschrkn*. What you have described so far is a matter between you and Malagate. How does the security of the *tschrkn* come into play?"

"Malagate, so I understand, is considered a renegade by the Star Kings. If so, it cannot be comfortable to have such a one living in their midst. My proposal to Malagate would remove him from Ghnarumen permanently."

"By violence?" interjected Liam.

"No. By his own free will," said Gersen.

"That is an important distinction," interjected Liam. "It is a cultural imperative among us that we cause no harm to another member of the race, even one we find objectionable such as Malagate."

The servant arrived with tea and biscuits, and after each had been served, Dwyddion resumed the conversation.

"Let me summarize what I have understood so far. You wish the *tschrkn* to waive their longstanding prohibition against human visitors, in the hope that you can persuade Malagate to leave the planet voluntarily. You say the *tschrkn* should accede to your request because Malagate is a renegade whose presence makes them uncomfortable. Is that the essence of your proposal?"

"Yes," said Gersen.

"With due respect, I must point out that discomfort is not the same as a threat to security."

"If that is insufficient," said Gersen, "there is more."

"We had best hear the rest, then," said Dwyddion, "because the argument so far leaves matters less than clear as to how the *tschrkn* will decide. Their reasons for restricting human presence are deep-rooted."

Gersen breathed deeply, and began. "There are strong interplanetary prohibitions against the crimes Malagate has committed — murder, extortion, and slavery being among the most serious. If a complaint were made by the survivors of the Willow Grove raid, or even by a third party acting on their behalf, an inquiry would be conducted. The investigators would discover that Malagate was on Ghnarumen; it would be presumed that he was being sequestered by the Star Kings. The Star Kings, therefore, would be deemed accomplices. Need I say more? Or can you see where Malagate's continued presence on Ghnarumen could lead?"

"Are you threatening the *tschrkn*?" asked Dwyddion.

"Not at all. A confrontation between humans and Star Kings would put Malagate's hostage at risk. It is the safety of that person that is my sole concern. However, it should be obvious that when thousands of innocent people are slaughtered or enslaved, there will be a demand for retribution, not just from the victims themselves but from many quarters of humanity. This is the risk of conflict that both I and the Star Kings share a desire to avoid."

"Very well," said Dwyddion, who now seemed to be acting the part of mediator. "You have made yourself clear. Now let us consider matters from the other side. If you were to visit Ghnarumen, you would learn things that the *tschrkn* do not want revealed. This is why human visitors are prohibited."

"I have no interest in learning any secrets. All I ask is a chance to communicate with Malagate. I believe he will respond favorably to what I have to say, with the result that he will be removed peacefully and permanently from Ghnarumen. Whatever I may learn by accident while engaged in this matter, I will give the strongest possible pledge never to reveal."

Dwyddion glanced over to where Harcour was sitting, and Gersen saw Harcour nod.

"I believe the three of us have taken this matter as far as we can go," said Dwyddion. "Liam will communicate with his ruling council, and they will make a decision. In the meanwhile, the hour grows late. Jeremiah has prepared a supper for the three of us, and made up beds in our spare rooms."

That evening found the three interlocutors siting around a yew-wood dining table, as Jeremiah ladled out portions of stew from a porcelain tureen.

"You may wonder," Dwyddion was addressing Gersen, "why the Institute has accepted one of the *tschrkn* race into its midst."

Gersen smiled. "That question has occurred to me."

"As you know," said Dwyddion, "one of the reasons for the Institute's existence is to anticipate and prevent the more perverse effects of technology on the human race. I do not need to dwell on this, because examples abound — nuclear weapons, engineered viruses, so-called artificial intelligence, and the like. The *tschrkn*, quite by accident, have managed to pass on acquired physical attributes from one generation to the next. Their methods are far from perfect, to be sure. But even this rudimentary ability in the hands of humans could produce either great good or great evil. Therefore, the Institute determined to maintain a constructive link with the *tschrkn*. Liam's membership is part of that plan."

Here Dwyddion regarded Harcour with an almost parental look of approval. "Liam has not disappointed us."

Gersen thought that this would be an opportune moment to raise a question that had been foremost in his mind since meeting Harcour. "Earlier today," he addressed Harcour, "you said you would explain the remarkable similarity of appearance between yourself and Malagate. Perhaps I could trouble you to do so now."

"Of course," said Harcour. "Let me begin by saying there are many misconceptions about the reproductive processes of our race. I've read the literature, and some of the ideas put forward by humans are amusingly inaccurate. As Dwyddion related earlier, the *tschrkn* do have ways of managing the transition of characteristics from one generation to the next, although I should add that there are limitations. Our reproductive mechanism involves combining the gametes of one specimen with those of another. There are many thousands of each, so that the number of possible combinations is enormous. In nature, only a few of these survive, and the survivors are largely a matter of chance. The *tschrkn*, instead of leaving things to chance, have ways of selecting the copy that best satisfies their criteria, then nurturing it to survival. I and some others like me are the result of that process. We are the copy that the *tschrkn* consider ideal. We are called *tchlan*, a word for which there is no exact human equivalent, but it means approximately, 'the ultimate.'"

"How many of you are there?" Gersen asked.

"Fewer than a thousand," said Harcour. "Trying to isolate the single desired combination out of the millions of possibilities is like looking for a needle in a haystack, to use one of your popular human expressions. The gamete combinations only survive for a few days, and if the ideal one is not found and nourished, it perishes."

Here Dwyddion interjected, "This is why humans have nothing to fear from the *tschrkn*. They have learned to copy the human form, but they will never be able to do so in great numbers. There are other survivors, of course, but they are inferior copies."

"It is widely understood that there are hundreds of Star Kings resident in human populations," said Gersen. "If so, that is a high percentage of all the human forms that exist."

"Another misconception," said Dwyddion. "There have never been more than six or eight *tschrkn* living among humans at any one time.

The belief that humanity is somehow infested by Star Kings is much like the belief in witches in the pre-Apocalyptic era — a peculiarity of human paranoia."

"What about Malagate, then," said Gersen. "How does he differ from yourself?"

"Alas," said Harcour, "our process does not rule out mutations. Malagate is identical to the ideal copy, but for one thing: he has a hyper-developed limbic system. That is the portion of the brain that gives rise to what human biologists colloquially refer to as the 'fight or flee' impetus. When hyper-developed, the limbic system subjects the individual to paroxysms of rage, envy, fear, greed, ruthlessness. The first copy with this aberration was Attel Malagate. Malagate then decided that he was the superior version of the *tschrkn* race. He managed to copy himself. That is Mongo Malagate. Attel's plan was to keep making copies, thereby creating a master race that would dominate first the *tschrkn* and ultimately humans. He died before he could carry out this plan, but Mongo undoubtedly has the same thing in mind."

"And yet the Star Kings refuse to destroy him?"

"It is an ironclad rule among the *tschrkn* — to do no harm to one another. This unalterable creed is what has allowed the race to survive, despite being weaker than many other species in our history."

"And this," Dwyddion added, "is the trait of the *tschrkn* that fascinates the Fellows of the Institute. Throughout our own history, the greatest enemy of humans has been other humans. We have much to learn from the *tschrkn*."

The conversation continued in this vein late into the evening, to the flickering light of candles, until weariness sent the parties to their sleeping quarters. Gersen's bed was comfortable, but sleep eluded him. Harcour would be communicating with his ruling council. What would their decision be?

CHAPTER XIV

An evil man will burn his own nation to the ground in order to rule over the ashes.
— Sun Tzu

Determinism is the doctrine that all events, including human actions, are ultimately determined by causes external to the will. Some philosophers have taken determinism to imply that individual human beings have no free will and cannot, therefore, be held morally responsible for their actions.
— William James

———

Gersen was awakened from a fitful sleep by the pre-dawn sound of bird-song filtering in through his open bedroom window. He pulled himself upright and launched into a program of stretching that he had practiced every morning of his life. Fully awake now, he left his chamber and felt his way down the stairs in Dwyddion's still dark house. He exited the front door and closed it quietly behind him. Looking out along the earthen track that he had used the previous day, the first flicker of rising Vega light was visible through the trees. He stretched his arms and legs once more, took a deep breath, and then began to walk. The track was smooth and there was just enough light to permit a steady pace. His mind sorted through the uncertainties that had kept him wakeful much of the preceding night. *Would Harcour present my case persuasively? Would the Star Kings agree to my requested visit? What would be my alternative if they refused?*

After a mile of walking, he turned and headed back. Arriving at Dwyddion's modest domicile, he did not enter, but sat upon the doorsteps gazing back into the forest. After a time, he heard the door unlatch; it opened and Dwyddion emerged. He started to rise to greet his host, but Dwyddion instead settled onto the steps beside him.

"You are an early riser, Kirth Gersen."

"I have a great deal on my mind," said Gersen.

"You may put your mind to rest on one point — the rulers of the *tschrkn* have granted you permission to visit. I was with Liam when he presented your case to them. I must say, he did so eloquently. This will be the first time in many centuries that Ghnarumen has hosted a human visitor."

"My thanks to Harcour, then," said Gersen. "I will try not to disappoint him."

"Nor me," said Dwyddion. "I spoke on your behalf."

"My thanks to you as well, then."

"After our brief communication a few days ago, I examined the Institute's files on you. You were a rising star, a person of noteworthy ability and perseverance. We had you marked as a possible future leader. But then you resigned. That was nearly four decades ago, and our files provide only one small hint of a reason."

"What was that?" asked Gersen, wondering what further information about him the Institute might have in their possession.

"Several years after your resignation," said Dwyddion, "you had an interaction with one of our senior colleagues — the late Duschane Audmar. As a result of his meeting with you, Audmar prevailed upon the Institute to advance you a considerable sum — a hundred million SVU. I don't need to tell you the rest, you know the story well, but the result was that you liberated Audmar's children from Interchange, in the process ruining that evil institution and becoming yourself extraordinarily wealthy. However, all of this is irrelevant to what I have to say this morning. Audmar filed a report that made some observations about you personally. He opined that you had withdrawn from the Institute because the level of detachment required of all senior Fellows was incompatible with your obsession about correcting certain wrongs that had been done to you. He also stated that you were, in his opinion, a person who honored his word. I shared that opinion with the rulers of the *tschrkn*, adding my own endorsement."

Gersen found himself observing Dwyddion closely while the latter was speaking. It was quite remarkable, he noted, how Dwyddion had changed since their first encounter. At that time, Dwyddion had been an irascible recluse, seemingly tired of the world and appearing at least a decade older than his then fifty years, with pursed lips and squinting eyes, and living on a storm-wracked mountainside. Today, however, Dwyddion must be in his middle seventies, but appeared no older than before. Perhaps the role of Triune, or supreme leader of the Institute, agreed with him. Whatever the cause, however, he seemed a person very much at peace with himself and with the world. Meanwhile, Dwyddion continued speaking.

"The quest that you are on today differs from the one to which Audmar referred. You are not seeking to right a wrong, which ultimately means to achieve revenge. Rather you wish to rescue a person dear to you. This I related to the *tschrkn* because, for reasons Liam explained, they do not want to be complicit in any injury to Malagate. I hope my assurance will not be mistaken."

"It will not be," said Gersen, "at least not due to anything I can control."

"This is where a problem lies," said Dwyddion. "You are a man of grim determination — some might say, obsession. In your single-minded pursuit of your goal, you might lose sight of your original intentions. The ancient Greeks had a word for people gripped by such resolve. The word was *zelos*, and those in the grip of that driving force were *zealots*. Many a time in history, zealots with the best of intentions have caused unintended injury to themselves or others. I only ask that you be mindful of this, and not allow your passion to overrule you."

"Wise counsel," said Gersen. "I will be mindful."

Dwyddion rose from the steps where he had been sitting. "I have said what I had to say. Now let us go inside and see what Jeremiah has prepared for breakfast."

After a brief, light breakfast, Gersen and Harcour were preparing to leave. Gersen was about to enter his slidecar to begin the return trip to Pontrefact Spaceport, when Dwyddion approached.

"A moment of your time, please," said Dwyddion. "I have a final matter to discuss."

Wondering what that might be, after all that had already been said, Gersen stood attentively and waited for Dwyddion to continue.

"We understand," said Dwyddion, "that a large block of Jarnell shares is soon to be offered for sale, and that Braemar Investments, in whom you have some influence, will be a likely bidder."

"You understand correctly," said Gersen.

"In that case, I would like to make a request on behalf of the Institute. For many years, we have debated at the highest level the possibility of acquiring an ownership position in Jarnell. This has to do with our interest in having some modest insight into the likely direction of space travel technology, which, like so many life-changing technologies of the past, has the potential to render humanity great good or, if not managed carefully, great evil.

"We further understand, however, that the single block of shares to be offered is substantial — forty-five percent, if our information is correct — and that it is not divisible, but must be sold to a single buyer. We seek, therefore, a dialogue with Braemar, the subject of which would be a partnership between Braemar and the Institute, whose goal would be the acquisition of the Jarnell block of shares."

"The person with whom to discuss this idea is Jehan Addels, the same individual who sent you the note with my contact information."

"I suspected as much," said Dwyddion. "This supports my inference that you have some small influence with Mr. Addels. Do I infer correctly?"

"Some small influence, yes," said Gersen.

"Would you be so good as to advise Mr. Addels to expect a call from one of our senior Fellows, and, if you are so disposed, to express a favorable opinion about the idea?"

Gersen tried to suppress the smile that was tugging at his lips. "I will give the matter full consideration. But, in the meanwhile, if I have as much influence over Braemar as you suppose, the Institute could be partnering with a Zealot."

Dwyddion smiled as well. "A keen observation," he said. "There will be much to think about on both sides. Thank you for advising Addels to expect to hear from us, and in the meanwhile, best wishes for the success of the venture upon which you are now embarking."

On the return trip to Pontefract, Gersen called Addels and explained that he would be contacted by a Fellow of the Institute. "Please consider any proposals courteously," he told Addels, "and we can discuss the details when I return, in approximately ten days' time."

Gersen and Harcour arrived at the Pontefract Spaceport to find that *Quicksilver* had been fully serviced and was ready for launch. Gersen invited Harcour to join him on the flight deck while he completed his pre-flight checklist, and keyed in the codes for Axel 13-274, the green-white star orbited by Ghnarumen. *Quicksilver* emitted the soft shudder that signified her thrusters were powering up, then lifted off. She accelerated through Aloysius' atmosphere, then out past Boniface and Cuthbert in their more distant orbits. As Vega itself became a diminishing speck, the Intersplit engaged and they were off on what would be a four-day voyage.

Gersen found Harcour, whom he soon came to address as Liam, to be a pleasant companion, a good conversationalist and a fiercely competitive chess player. Despite intensely concentrating on each move, Liam displayed little emotion at the outcome. That is, he did not react with pleasure at success or distress at failure. Instead, he seemed to be steadily learning from experience. This was one of the traits, Gersen imagined, that had allowed the race of Star Kings to survive despite, so it was said, competing with species who were stronger, more agile, and more savage than themselves.

Gersen intentionally avoided questions about life on Ghnarumen, as these were matters that the Star Kings might deem confidential. There was one substantive discussion, however, that followed from what Liam had earlier related about Malagate.

"You said that Attel Malagate had managed to copy himself," Gersen began, "and the result was Mongo Malagate. However, from what I understand, procreation among the Star Kings is a tightly controlled process. How did Attel Malagate accomplish that result?"

"You ask an uncomfortable question," said Liam. "It is a matter the *tschrkn* would prefer to forget. But if you are going to deal with

Mongo Malagate, you had best know the answer. In order to create a new *tchlan* — that is, the ultimate copy of our race — it is required that two existing copies share gametes. This, as you correctly understood, is done under closely controlled conditions. Attel Malagate took one of our *tchlan* prisoner and forced it to share gametes. This is a reprehensible act — the equivalent of what humans refer to as rape. In fact, it was this outrage that caused Attel Malagate to be pronounced a renegade and made him unwelcome among us."

"I am sorry to pursue what must be for you an unpleasant subject," said Gersen. "However, I need to clarify one point. If I understand what you are saying, Mongo Malagate would not be able to produce copies of himself without the cooperation of another *tchlan*. Is that correct?"

"Yes," said Liam, "and that would never happen except by force."

"Nor if Malagate were far removed from the Star Kings?"

"Yes, a situation much to be desired."

"And one that I plan to bring about."

On schedule, *Quicksilver* aproached the star Axel 13-274, the Intersplit disengaged, and Gersen guided the ship into an equatorial orbit around Ghnarumen. The image on the macrosreen filled Gersen with a sense of grim foreboding; he had never seen a planet so shrouded in dense fog. There was no way to distinguish ocean from dry land, or hilltops from flat plain. But somewhere down there was Malagate, and with him, Gabrielle. Liam had provided the frequency of a beacon placed at the outskirts of the Star Kings' major city, for the use of sporadic visiting freighters. *Quicksilver* was too imposing and suggestive of human presence to appear on Ghnarumen, so Gersen and Liam would descend on the auxiliary flyer.

Down they came through the roiling mists, with the autopilot homing in on the beacon, until finally at three hundred feet, they could see the ground, and the flyer touched down in an open field. In the distance were clusters of mostly squat and desultory buildings, with only a scattering of taller structures that were still no more than five stories by human standards. Liam gestured to one of the buildings at the border of the field.

"The ruling council will meet us there," he said.

They climbed out of the flyer and proceeded toward the building. The air was heavy, dank, and reeked of rotting vegetation. Arriving at the building, they found it empty.

"We must wait," said Liam.

After what seemed an interminable interval, the first Star King arrived, and then another, until in due course there were nine in all. Three were perfect copies of Liam, the others a motley collection of shapes and sizes, though none so tall as Liam and his fellow ultimates. They had in common Liam's smooth-skinned hairlessness, his distinctly human features, and his equanimity of expression. Liam spoke a few words of introduction in the local language. The ultimate at the center of the group and its evident leader replied in what Gersen took to be a questioning tone. Liam answered briefly, then waited. The leader glanced to his right, then left, then looked at Liam and nodded.

"We are free to go," said Liam. "You should nod respectfully and return to the flyer. I will join you shortly."

Gersen did as he was told, boarded the flyer, and sat thinking about what he had seen. The Star Kings seemed to come in all shapes and sizes; in their effort to breed a perfect human form, they still had some considerable distance to travel. Their tallest buildings were insignificant by human standards. They had no spaceport; occasional freighters were apparently their only connection with the inhabited worlds beyond. Indeed, Gersen wondered what business brought even the infrequent freighter to this uninviting place. Much of this was quite different from the common human understanding, including Gersen's own before this visit.

After a while, Liam returned. "What was that about?" said Gersen.

"The *tschrkn* wished to confirm for themselves what I had previously told them. As you might guess, in their efforts to find the perfect human form, they have spent much time studying human physiognomy."

"And what did they see in me?" asked Gersen.

"The face of an honest man."

"Malagate," Liam continued, "has established himself on the far side of the planet. The *tschrkn* have given me the coordinates; the distance is approximately 10,300 miles."

Gersen did a quick mental calculation. "About twenty-five hours," he said.

"We had best get started, then," said Liam.

The flyer rose and sped westward at altitude high enough to avoid unexpected obstacles. It was a tedious way to travel, however, with nothing but thick fog and the autopilot in control. Then the visibility cleared and Gersen descended to where he could get a better view of the terrain they were passing over. For a while, there was nothing below but dismal swamp, with only one living creature of note — a great, leathery flying reptile with a twelve-foot wingspan, a massive beak, and fierce talons. If this was typical of the fauna of Ghnarumen, Gersen thought, the Star Kings' survival was impressive. When the swamp turned to ocean, Gersen tried to catch some sleep, but abandoned that idea when he found his senses were too energized to relax.

Soon enough, the autopilot chimed, signaling that they were nearing their destination, and Liam pointed and exclaimed, "There it is."

Malagate had shaved the top of a low hill, creating an area of flat ground on which stood a single building, next to which was Malagate's Pharaon Model III. Gersen flew a wide circle around the compound, looking for defensive weapons but, seeing none, approached and landed next to the Pharaon. Gersen and Liam disembarked, and approached the building, an unimpressive single-story affair of riverstone and plaster. This was a significant come-down, Gersen thought, from Malagate's chateau on Grabhorne. At the entrance to the building, Liam called out in the Star Kings' language; they waited, but there was no response. Liam motioned Gersen to stand back while he strode to the entrance and pounded on the door. After a moment, the door opened and Malagate appeared. He had shed the hairpiece of tight black curls of Gyle Warweave, and Warweave's eyebrows were gone as well. Warweave's elegant dark blue suit and red sash had been replaced by a simple black cloak. To the casual observer, he and Liam would have been indistinguishable from one another. But to Gersen's now-experienced eye, their facial expressions could not have been more different. Malagate's features burned with malignant energy, while

Liam's remained serene and placid.

Malagate now noticed Gersen and fixed his dark, penetrating gaze on him.

"Darby!" he called out. "I should blast you to pieces where you stand!" Then he turned to Liam, "How could you allow a human on Ghnarumen? He will betray you the way he betrayed me."

"I made no pledge to you," said Gersen. "But if you shoot me down, you will lose what I came to offer you."

"Offer me? What could you possibly have to offer me?"

"Teehalt's Planet."

"Teehalt's Planet? What do you know about Teehalt's Planet?"

"I know where it is. In fact, I have been there. More than once."

"You have been there? Who are you?"

"I am Kirth Gersen."

"You deceived me, saying that you were Edgar Darby."

"And you deceived me, saying that you were Gyle Warweave. Now we are on equal ground, we each know who the other is. Do you want Teehalt's Planet or not?"

"Suppose that I do. What must I give you in return?"

"Gabrielle Richet."

"She makes pleasant music. I would prefer to keep her. Ask for something else. Money?"

"Not money. If you want Teehalt's Planet, you must give me Gabrielle Richet."

"Tell me the location of the planet. I will go there, and when I see it for myself, you may have the piano player."

"No chance, Malagate. Give me Gabrielle Richet, then I will tell you the location."

"Do you take me for a fool? If I give you the piano player, you will send me wandering aimlessly through the Beyond. I must see the planet first."

"Then we are at an impasse," said Gersen, "but I have a possible solution. I will return here with a salvage vessel. You will take your Pharaon into orbit; the two ships will be securely linked together; then I will fly both of us to Teehalt's Planet. We will land, and when your feet touch ground, you will release Gabrielle."

"Ha!" said Malagate. "When my feet touch ground, I will kill you. Then I will live on Teehalt's Planet and listen to beautiful music."

"Bad idea," said Gersen. "There will be an explosive device on my ship. If I do not return with Gabrielle, it will detonate and both ships will be destroyed."

"You are bluffing. Would you destroy the piano player as well?"

"If she cannot be free, that would be her preference."

Malagate stood not speaking for a long moment, still glaring at Gersen as if trying to read his thoughts.

"What is this salvage vessel?" he asked eventually. "Another of your tricks? I have not heard of such a thing."

"It is a new technology, developed by Jarnell," said Gersen. "It can attach itself to a disabled ship anywhere in space, and fly the two linked together to a port where the salvaged vessel can be repaired. I have access to a prototype that will enable me to accomplish exactly what I have proposed. You may keep the hostage in your possession until you set foot on Teehalt's Planet, and see it for yourself."

"Under those conditions, I accept," said Malagate. "But no tricks, or you will never see the piano player alive."

Gersen could scarcely conceal his elation. So far, his plan was working. But he admonished himself to maintain his focus; there was still a long way to go.

"I will travel to Alphanor, where the salvage vessel is waiting, then return here, let us say in two weeks' time. When I arrive and signal you, you will take your Pharaon into orbit. I will link the two vessels together and we will be on our way. Is Yatz still your pilot?"

"No, I will fly the Pharaon myself."

"What happened to Yatz?"

"I left him at Brinktown, to round up more companions."

"More companions? How will you pay them?"

"Do you think I was fool enough to leave all my money behind on Grabhorne? I have other sources equal to what I was forced to abandon."

"Your finances are not my business. I will leave now and return in two weeks' time. But first, I want to see Gabrielle Richet."

Malagate stared at Gersen, then displayed a hideous leer. "You will not see her until I see Teehalt's Planet."

"How will I know she is still alive and still your captive?"

"Captive? Not at all, she is my guest. Listen carefully and I will demonstrate her presence."

Malagate turned and retreated into the building, leaving the door wide open. Presently came the notes of a piano being played. This was the real thing, Gersen could tell; it could only be Gabrielle. Malagate reappeared in the doorway.

"There is your proof," he said. "I will await your return."

Malagate wheeled around, with his black robe flaring, and disappeared. Gersen stared at the closed door, then motioned to Liam; the two returned to the flyer and departed.

Gersen returned to Alphanor with a sense of grim determination. All the pieces of his plan had thus far fallen into place. He had extracted Malagate's location from Bruno Bolfo; he had discovered the presence of a Star King in the Institute, then secured agreement to visit Ghnarumen through the good offices of Dwyddion. He had then convinced Malagate to exchange Gabrielle for Teehalt's Planet. Now to implement the final portion of this plan — to liberate Gabrielle while marooning Malagate forever.

From his quarters at the Hotel Credenza, Gersen placed three calls.

"I have encountered Malagate, and learned something you should know," he told Miles Jaeger. "He says he left considerable cash on Grabhorne. If the folk of New Horizon have not already found it, they should initiate a thorough search. My good wishes to them all."

The second call was to Jehan Addels. "What news of the Institute and their interest in Jarnell?"

"I have had a most interesting discussion with a certain Julian Hartwell," said Addels. "He is an eighty-eight of the Institute, but also Chairman of Distis Corporation. He proposes that Braemar and the Institute share equally in a joint venture to acquire the Jarnell interest. The proposal interests me. Acquiring the full forty-five percent would tax even Braemar's substantial resources, so deploying only half the necessary cash has some appeal."

"You have my proxy," Gersen said. "I have other matters on my mind."

The third call was to Rolf Woodward. "Good timing," Woodward had reported. "We've pulled a Pharaon III off the line as you instructed, installed an Intersplit LF propulsion system, and made the other changes to fit it out as a salvage vessel."

Two days later, Gersen was at the Jarnell Technology Center in the company of Tibo Gatz and Hans Snell. Gatz handed Gersen a small aluminum case with a carrying handle. "Here are the bolts you will need to attach the disabled vessel to the rescue craft. The number of attachment points will depend on the surface profiles of the two vessels. If they match up well, five bolts should be sufficient."

"Both vessels will be Pharaon III's," said Gersen.

Gatz briefly looked surprised. How did Henry Lucas already know what type of vessel he would be rescuing? But he withheld any comment. Lucas's affairs were known to be mysterious and it was best not to ask too many questions. Instead, he said, "If you'd like, we can go out to the Pharaon III we've set up for you, and I'll show you where best to place the bolts."

"Good idea," said Gersen, and off they went.

Gersen's Pharaon III had been moved adjacent to the office building, and, fresh off the assembly line and coated in metallic silver, it was an impressive sight. As the threesome made the short walk to where the vessel stood, Snell explained that the force field generator had been re-programmed to detect anything of substance beyond its own ship's structure, and surround that with a protective shield as well.

"Of course, this has never been tried before," said Snell, "but technically, I see no reason why it won't work."

"What happens if it doesn't?" Gersen asked.

"Not a pretty picture, I'm afraid. With the Intersplit trying to pull matter though time, anything not protected will be utterly destroyed."

"Just the unprotected part?"

"Unfortunately, no. If there is any imperfection in the force field, everything inside will be subject to massive destructive forces — the disabled vessel, the rescue vessel, everything completely vaporized. We really should test the system before using it."

"How would we do that?" said Gersen, although he had already guessed the answer.

"Bolt the prototype to another vessel, take them into space, and activate the Intersplit."

"No time for that," said Gersen. "How confident are you that it will work?"

Snell hesitated, and looked a little pale. His lips pursed in concentration. "95 percent," he said.

"That will have to do," said Gersen.

They boarded the Pharaon, and Gatz went through the use of the bolts. These were 'umbrella bolts,' he explained. They would expand to hold the linked vessel tight, then retract to be withdrawn. This seemed simple enough to Gersen, and it was time to get to the main point of his visit.

"While the vessels are lashed together and in flight," he said, "I want to be able to disable the tethered vessel's Intersplit." Then he added, "Beyond repair."

There was a moment of shocked silence, then Snell said, "Beyond repair? The only way to do that is to remove the power supply."

"Then that is what I want to do. Show me how."

Snell began to stutter, "That is a job for a trained technician, in the maintenance shop. It's never been done under the conditions we're talking about."

"Don't worry about that," said Gersen. "Suppose it was a matter of life and death. How would I do it?"

"Well," said Snell, "you would need to remove the ttritium battery from its containment vessel, place it in a portable container, and take it off the ship." Snell had stopped stuttering now that he was focusing on the problem at hand.

"Tell me about the ttritium battery," said Gersen. "What is ttritium? How big is the battery, and how much does it weigh?"

"Ttritium is a top-secret material. Its discovery is what made Intersplit possible. It's not really a battery, that's just a term of convenience. It's actually a massively compressed energy source — the same amount of energy you'd get from a large nuclear plant."

"How big is it?"

"About the size of a grapefruit. And when compressed to that size, it resembles a large diamond. But don't be fooled, the force it can generate is massive."

"What about the containment vessel?"

"A titanium alloy, with a screw-on top. About the size of a paint can. But the material of the container is unimportant; it's the containment fluid that keeps the battery inert."

"And what is the containment fluid?"

"You won't believe me if I tell you."

"Tell me anyway."

"Palm oil."

"Palm oil?" Gersen uttered in disbelief.

"I know it sounds crazy, but we tried almost two hundred different formulas, and this was the only one that kept the energy ball from — well, blowing everything to kingdom come."

Gersen then instructed the two lab rats to walk him through the exact process of accessing the Intersplit propulsion chamber, opening the containment vessel, extracting the ttritium energy cell, placing it in a portable vessel, and removing it. He repeated the sequence several times until he was confident that he could accomplish it. He ordered the technicians to supply him with the necessary equipment — a set of tongs for handling the battery, and a portable container filled with palm oil. He was now as ready as he would ever be.

Four days later, at the time he had told Malagate to expect him, Gersen put the specially equipped Pharaon III into orbit around Ghnarumen, and signaled to Malagate that he was ready. Would Malagate link up with him as planned? Would Gabrielle be on board? For several of the most tension-filled hours of his life, Gersen waited, sending repeated signals every fifteen minutes, while staring at the fog-shrouded planet below. But then Malagate's ship came poking through the mist, rose to meet him, and floated alongside. Malagate was a competent pilot, Gersen was relieved to see. Then Malagate's sonorous baritone came over the intercom, "Are you ready? Teehalt's Planet for the woman. That was the agreement."

"Let me hear her first," said Gersen. There was a momentary pause, then to Gersen's great elation came Gabrielle's voice, "Kirth? I've missed you!"

Malagate cut in, "That's all you'll see or hear of her until Teehalt's Planet. Stop wasting time and get on with it."

"Hold your position steady, and give me time to bolt the ships together. Then we'll be on our way," Gersen replied. As soon as he was finished attaching five bolts as Gatz had prescribed, Gersen came back on the intercom and said, "That job is finished. Now shut down your ion power, and I will take us both to Teehalt's Planet."

Malagate did as he was told; Gersen powered up his own ion drive and steered the harnessed vessels out of Ghnarumen's orbit, then beyond the Axel 13-274 system. Here is where he would engage the Intersplit LF and put the force field generator to the test. Snell had guessed a 95% chance that it would work. But if it failed, both ships and their passengers would be vaporized. What would Gabrielle want him to do? Would she opt for a permanent future as Malagate's captive, or would she choose the chance, however risky, at freedom? He gritted his teeth in determination, and pulled the lever that would activate the Intersplit. There was the now-familiar sense of otherworldliness as space and time collided, but the Intersplit engaged and the force field held. Gersen checked his instruments. The LF system was powering both vessels comfortably, and they were hurtling through space toward Teehalt's Planet. So far, so good, thought Gersen, with no small measure of relief. After a few hours to make sure everything continued to run smoothly, it would be time to implement the final stage of his plan.

The Pharaon III had two removable panels, one on either side of the ship, that opened into a narrow crawl space that led to the Intersplit propulsion chamber. Normally, service would be performed by a trained technician while the ship was parked on dry land. As Snell had cautioned him, work on the Intersplit had never been attempted in deep space.

"Well," Gersen told himself, "There's a first time for everything."

Since both ships were encased in the force field, there should be no problem removing the panels, as atmospheres would quickly normalize. Gersen unclamped the interior latches and opened the panel on his ship. There was the slight hissing sound of air pressures equilibrating, but that was all. Then he opened the panel on Malagate's ship, again with no adverse result. Gersen now crawled through the service tunnel, pushing the set of tongs and the portable containment vessel in front of him. Gersen had never felt comfortable in confined spaces, and he began to feel that not-so-irrational fear building in his gut. But this was no time to give in to it. He kept crawling forward until at last the space opened up and he was in the Intersplit propulsion chamber, and there before him was the container that held the ttritium energy cell.

Now for the main event, he thought. He removed the lid from his portable container, then did the same for the vessel that held the energy cell. And there it was, just as Snell had described, a grapefruit-sized object, glowing like a perfect diamond. With both hands on the handles of the tongs, he reached in, grasped the cell, and gently, carefully, lifted it out. *Whatever you do, don't drop it,* Snell had cautioned. Finally, he placed it in his portable container and re-fastened the top. Then he backed out of the access tunnel and replaced the panels on both ships. The task was finished. Malagate was now deprived of Intersplit propulsion.

Two days later, still piloting the two ships bound together, Gersen sighted the glorious golden-white star of Teehalt's Planet. He disengaged the Intersplit and coasted into orbit around the planet itself. Through his macroscreen, he studied the sparkling green, blue, and white textures of the surface. If he could see this, so could Malagate. He called Malagate on the intercom.

"We have arrived," he said. "Turn on your macroscreen and see it for yourself. I have fulfilled my part of the bargain. Now you must fulfill yours."

He found the spot where he had landed with Attel Malagate on board many years earlier, and brought the two ships gently down. As soon as he touched the ground, he removed four of the five bolts holding the ships together. As far as Malagate would know, the bolts were still in place, and he could not try to leave without tearing his ship to pieces. Then Gersen activated his boarding platform and lowered himself to solid ground. He saw that Malagate was descending likewise, and had donned his ceremonial rich blue outfit, with crimson sash running from shoulder to hip. And in his company was Gabrielle.

The two figures confronted one another, with Malagate looking something not quite human with his Star King's hairlessness and his malevolent black-eyed stare.

"Remember," Gersen cautioned Malagate, "I have armed an explosive device that will destroy both ships if I do not return forthwith."

"You are a fool," said Malagate. "You have given away this magnificent planet, and exchanged it for a paltry human."

With that, he made a sweeping gesture in Gersen's direction so that Gabrielle could pass. She did so, and came to Gersen's side.

"This will be my kingdom," Malagate declared, "and I will be its king. I will create a new race of Star Kings, just as Attel had planned. In time they will dominate the world of men."

Gersen handed Malagate a piece of paper, folded over, then activated his ramp and began to rise. By the time Malagate had finished reading, he and Gabrielle were at the Pharaon's entry portal. Gersen took a last look down before entering and closing the door behind him. Malagate stood staring upward, with the paper in his hand. His malignant glare had changed, so it seemed to Gersen, to something like bewilderment.

Gersen entered the ship, removed the final bolt, and powered up the ion drive. He took one final look at Malagate through the viewscreen as the ship lifted off. Within a moment, Malagate was nothing but a speck, lost in the surrounding vegetation, then he was gone altogether.

Gersen extracted from his pocket a copy of the note he had handed Malagate, and read it:

Dear Malagate,

Enjoy your stay on Teehalt's Planet. It promises to be a long one, I'm afraid. If you try to leave, you will discover that your ship's Intersplit has been disabled. Of course, you can fall back on ion propulsion, but at its maximum speed of 100,000 miles per hour, it will take you over 700 years to reach the nearest habitable planet.

Farewell,
Kirth Gersen

Gersen finished reading and turned toward Gabrielle. She threw her arms around him, and spoke softly to his ear, "I knew that you would come for me."

EPILOGUE

lthough summers on the Atlantic coast were mostly warm and pleasant, only a few days — perhaps one in twenty — could be deemed 'perfect sailing days.' That is, enough breeze to move a sailboat briskly, but not so much as to demand intense concentration and physical exertion. It was on such a day that Kirth Gersen returned to his dwelling on White Island, after an outing on his newly commissioned forty-footer that he had named *Zealot*.

Zealot was unlike contemporary foil boats that could skim across the water at breath-taking speeds under perfect conditions, but were dangerous in rough water and useless in light air. Instead, hers was a traditional hull, sleek and beautifully balanced, and easily managed by a single-handed sailor, allowing Gersen to enjoy the wind and water by himself.

He rounded up into the wind and coasted to the mooring in White Island's sheltered cove. The end of another perfect sailing day, he told himself. These moments always filled him with a sense of bitter-sweetness because he could not help wondering how many such days were left to him. He furled the sails, coiled the lines, checked that all else was ship-shape, then clambered into his small dinghy to row ashore.

As he approached the dock, Gersen saw that Kim was occupied with cleaning fish. Another bitter-sweet moment for Gersen, as this would be Kim's last summer as his steward. He had passed his pilot's exam with flying colors, and would soon be joining his cousin Kwan in IPCC's newly established Galactic Freight business. In addition, in recognition of Kim's loyal service, Gersen had presented him with a fully reconditioned Model 9B. He would now be free to roam the highways and byways of interstellar space. Kim looked up and smiled as Gersen passed him on the dock. Gersen nodded and proceeded up the granite steps that led to his island lodge.

As he neared the door, it opened, and Gabrielle emerged. Even from a distance of ten paces, her blue eyes were dazzling. She waved, and her welcoming smile, as it always did these days, filled Gersen with a happiness unlike anything he had ever known.

Colophon

This book was printed using 11,5 pt Adobe Arno Pro as the primary text font, with NeutraFace used for titles.

Special thanks to Steve Sherman.

Book composition & Typesetting: Zeno ter Brughe
Typographic design: Joel Anderson
Jacket blurb: John Merrill
Management: John Vance, Koen Vyverman